Fireflies in a Jar

A Novel

by

Beka Wueste

Fox Island Press

Copyright

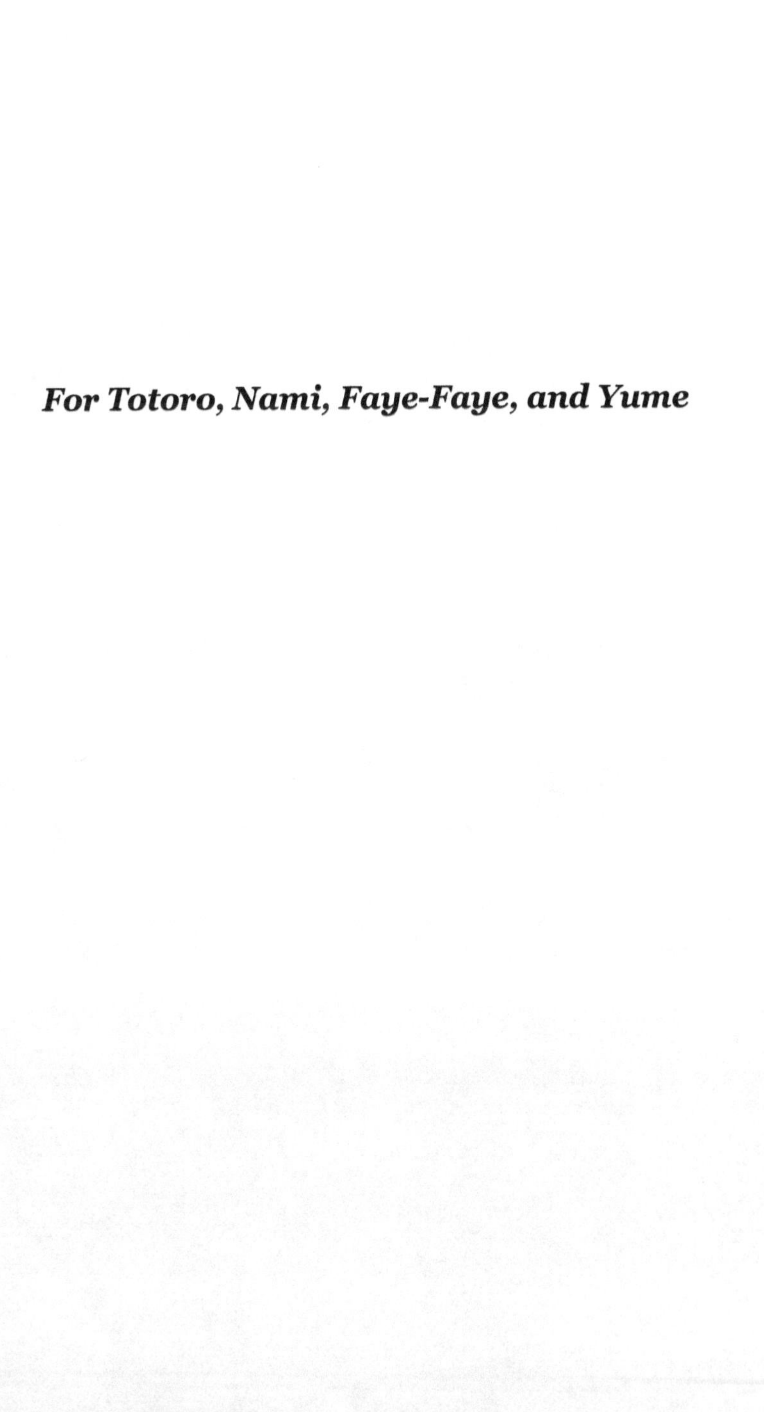

For Totoro, Nami, Faye-Faye, and Yume

"If happy little bluebirds fly
beyond the rainbow,
why oh why can't I?"

-Dorothy Gale

"If you can't love yourself, how in the hell
you gonna love somebody else?"

-RuPaul

Chapter 1: Fireflies in a Jar

NOVEMBER 1, 2019
(THE INAUGURAL GUY FAWKES DAY OBSERVATION BONFIRE AND
S'MORES FEST)

Sam never meant to become indiscreet, but as her recent outburst at Molly's apartment revealed, her unrequited crush now had a life of its own. It turned out that years spent placing all of her romantic hopes on Tali—a woman she barely knew, with whom had only a superficial relationship—was not actually a solid life choice.

Sam lost sight of who Tali truly was, allowing the imagined version of Tali to take hold of her. She acted more familiar with Tali than she should, not because it was inappropriate, but because it was unearned. It shouldn't have surprised her that Em finally noticed.

The confrontation occurred during the Guy Fawkes Day observance party. The November 5 holiday fell on a Tuesday, so Johanna and Eddie decided to host the backyard fire fest in advance on Friday, November 1. As Sam arrived, she appreciated how endearing it was that her friends, Johanna and Eddie celebrated anything—even a British holiday that had no relevance to them—as long as it gave them a reason to see friends.

Many of the attendees had seen each other on the previous Saturday, October 26, for Halloween festivities in DC. Sam, however, had never liked that particular holiday, and had passed on the invites to join. The idea of an all-day bar crawl though Dupont Circle followed by a late night of watching her friends dancing during the Graveyard Jam at a local pub held no appeal for Sam. Listening quietly to people telling stories about their costumed adventures, she was reassured that she'd made the right decision in skipping out. Here in the yard with people she knew was much more her speed.

Sam was socially lubricated thanks to the whiskey toddies being served, and soon found herself next to Tali, standing around the fire pit as they chugged their libations. Tali, as ever, greeted Sam with absolute welcome, as if Sam was the only person in the world she'd expected or hoped to see. They immediately fell into conversation, Sam letting Tali lead her once again through a conversational hopscotch.

"Is there anything that matches the magnificence of Angkor Wat? Why don't people understand that pecans are better than walnuts—they are the superior tree nut! Do they still make those orange circus peanuts? Have you ever read *Portrait of the Artist as a Young Man*? I think I'm a reincarnated armadillo. Maybe a pangolin."

Tali was a whirlwind by whom Sam was happy to be whisked away. Sam acted as if they were the only two people at the party, for a moment genuinely forgetting anyone else was there.

Reality came roaring back abruptly when Molly walked up to them. Shit. Sam's cover was blown. As a coping mechanism to recover from the humiliation of their previous encounter, Sam convinced herself that Molly was a non-entity in her life. She was so successful in blocking Molly out of her mind that she didn't even allow the possibility of seeing her again so soon. Fear washed over Sam, anxious of what Molly would say after their brief yet embarrassing post-wedding make out session.

"Hi, I'm Tali!" Tali threw out her hand and grabbed Molly's, giving a genuinely enthusiastic squeeze and shining her most winning smile.

"I'm Molly."

"Hi Molly! This is Sam." She placed her hands on Sam's shoulders as she said this. Sam was at a loss for words.

"We've met." Molly eyed Tali for a moment, then followed with, "You must be the lucky lady."

"Lucky in life, lucky in love!" Tali confirmed, having no clue what Molly meant, but nonetheless happy to be identified as a lucky person.

Molly's eyes strained not to roll in her head. She looked at Sam. "Cute. Well, have fun you two." She said this last remark with neither sincerity nor conviction as she briskly departed.

Sam watched her recede, relieved it hadn't gone worse. Sam's pulse still raced from the fright she felt that Molly might spill the details on their ill-fated encounter. She told Tali she'd be right back, and went to get another round of drinks.

Sam wanted to return to the sanctuary of her private conversation with Tali, but another voice pulled her attention. "Molly is very attractive."

Tali's wife, Em, looked at Sam as she stated this fact. Sam didn't expect this encounter, and Em caught her off guard with an intensely focused gaze.

"Yeah, she's pretty. Pretty girl. Pretty." Sam lost the ability to speak normal human sentences.

"You guys hook up or something?"

Thoughts raced through Sam's head. Did Em know? Did Em know Sam liked women? No, how could she? She knew nothing. She certainly didn't know that Sam and Molly had... well, done whatever they had done. No, Em had no idea, and it was a good thing because if she did she might suspect that Sam liked Tali, and then...

"It's just, she acted a little like you had some history. Bad history." Em brought Sam back to the present conversation.

Sam didn't know how to reply, then the words rushed out of her mouth. "We sort of kind of hooked up at her place after Toshi's wedding in May, but I guess I messed up and she's still got hurt feelings."

Em stared. She wasn't giving Sam any help.

"I guess, I was kind of a jerk and she's right to be annoyed with me. I'm annoyed with me," Sam confessed, with a sad little chuckle. She didn't know how to get out of this situation.

After years of worrying how to come out to her friends, this was how it happened: confessing to her would-be paramour's wife that she was inadequate and blew her chance with the undeniably amazing Molly.

Sam wanted to reach into the air, grab the words, and stuff them back into her face, to un-speak them.

"You were a jerk?" Em was dubious. "I've known you for what, fifteen years? I've never thought of you as a jerk. Never heard anyone else say anything like that about you, either. So suddenly you decided to be a jerk to, of all people, Molly? To one of the nicest, most wholesome people on this planet?"

Sam wasn't sure if it was a question or a statement.

"What happened, Sam?"

Sam refused to respond, hoping T-Rex rules would apply, that if she just stayed still Em would lose track of her and walk away.

"You seemed like you were having fun that night. You looked like you had fun when you were dancing with Tali."

Sam wanted to disappear. Was this actually happening?

"You looked like you were having fun when Tali was telling you all kinds of stories. Like you were watching a fireworks show, couldn't take your eyes off her or stop grinning."

She spoke with neither accusation nor anger in her voice. Em was correct that they'd known each other for fifteen years, and just as no one could say Sam was a jerk, no one could say Em was anything other than cool. She was calm personified. When other people got worked up or angry, she was the one to defuse the tension.

When people got amped up on drugs and wanted to make stupid decisions, Em was the voice of reason who had the power to make people reconsider. When people were sad or anxious, she was the one who logically walked them through to seeing a light at the end of the runnel, not with false hope, but with her collected, assured presence.

Em was a good person. In an instant, Sam's trance was broken. She had not just developed and nurtured an inappropriate infatuation, but had done so at the disregard of a friend. Not a close friend, true, an acquaintance really, but nevertheless a person who didn't deserve such treatment. A friend who would never do that to anyone else.

In that moment, Sam hated herself, and tried to think of how to adequately express her apologies, how to beg Em's forgiveness. She was prepared to throw herself on a pyre, to prostrate herself, whatever was necessary.

Seeing the turmoil play across Sam's face, Em spoke up. "You're not the only one."

"What?" Only one what, Sam wondered.

"It's not like you're the only person who has ever fallen in love with her."

"Em, I'm so sorry. I didn't realize you knew how I felt. I don't know what I was thinking. I did not mean to disrespect you, or Tali, or your marriage. I'm sorry if I made you feel like your relationship was in danger."

Em let out the loudest guffaw Sam had ever heard. "In danger? Damn, Sam. Who knew you had that kind of ego? No, you can't threaten what we have. No one can. No army of people can."

"Hell," Em continued laconically, "you're not the first person at this party to fall in love with her. You think of all our friends we've known since college you're the only one to become smitten? She's charming as hell, of course you want her. Everyone does.

"Strangers she meets for two seconds on the street fall under whatever spell she casts with her little *bruja* energy. Sure, every now and then she encounters, say, a Molly. Those people are immune to that Tali magic, and frankly confused and annoyed that everyone else is so enamored with her. But, on the whole, she just has that vibe, and people respond to it. You'd frankly be weird not to."

Sam was in shock. She'd never imagined this moment, but if she hadn't she certainly wouldn't have seen it going this way. But of course Em wasn't mad. She was Em. Nothing shook her.

"You know why I don't feel threatened?" Em asked, a little smirk on the side of her mouth.

Sam shook her head, blurting out, "Because you're the coolest person anyone has ever met and I'm homely and shy and awkward and not special in any way and until I guess I came out in Molly's apartment by making out with her I'd been deeply entrenched in my closet while you've been your authentic self for ages?"

Em laughed again. "Shit. I knew you were gay. Everyone knew, Sam. Well, actually Clarissa thought you were asexual, like a nun or something. But that 'closet' you thought you were in was as see-trough as freshly Windex-ed glass, my friend."

"The reason," Em elaborated, "I never feel threatened is because I know Tali. In her whole life I'm the only person who has gotten remotely close to knowing the real her, or as much as she'll let anyone truly know her. You think she's this carefree sprite because she flirts with every man or woman in her vicinity, and you think because she gives you attention you know her.

"You made the mistake everyone else does. You see 'Party Tali' or 'Wedding Tali' or 'Beach House Tali' or even 'Guy Fawkes Bonfire Tali' as the real Tali. But that's just what she wants you all to see. It's the version of herself she projects, and wants people to find irresistible. That alter-ego she has curated and developed over her adult life is a façade, as confident, radiant, and easy going as she wishes she could be. That is who you, and everyone else, falls in love with. Not me."

"You don't love her?"

"I love the real Tali. Plain old Natalia."

"You don't get annoyed though, at her for encouraging it, or, or, or at people wanting to be with her? She's your wife."

"She's not 'my' anything. She's a firefly in a jar, man. People just aren't with her long enough to see it."

"Firefly in a jar?"

"Look, when I was a kid, we lived in a big city, and not in a safe part. It wasn't ok to play outside even in the daylight, let alone after dusk. I was the youngest of four girls, and my parents finally decided they didn't want us growing up that way. So we moved, across the country, to the boring little suburb of their dreams.

"For my sisters and me, it was like a different planet. There were so many trees to climb and streams to splash in and places to explore. We couldn't get enough of being outside. We rode our bikes everywhere, we were out all day until it got dark and we had to go home for dinner.

"Everyday we came home covered in grass stains, begging our mom to let us keep whatever turtle or frog or newt we'd found that day. She'd say no, that wild animals weren't toys for our entertainment. She'd make us take the creatures back where we found them so they wouldn't be scared and could be with their families.

"One night we were walking home past this bridge and saw what felt like a million fireflies. Lightning bugs, you know? We'd never seen one before. It was like all the fireflies in the world in one place. We saw kids catching them, so we tried, too. We were a little nervous letting them crawl in our hands, but seeing them light up for us was like some kind of fairy tale.

"So the next day, we took some mason jars from our house. We decorated the jars so each one of us had one with our name on it. At dusk, we sped over to the bridge, and between the four of us we caught what felt like hundreds of them. The whole way home we walked with them and it was like 'we were holding lanterns, they were so bright.

"We knew mom wouldn't let us keep them, so we decided they would be our secret and hid them. My oldest sister said we should punch some holes in the lids so the fireflies could still breathe, and she helped each of us with our jars.

"Later I was worried the holes weren't big enough, so I took a mallet and a big Phillips head screwdriver and pounded huge holes into the lids. Feeling proud I'd helped my little friends, I went to bed.

"A few hours later, my sisters and I woke up to my parents yelling our names. We ran down to the basement and found them there, furiously chasing the fireflies. Turned out I made the holes a little too big. My parents were maaaad. We tried to deny having any part in this, but there were the jars, labeled with our names, with some of the bugs still hanging out inside.

"My parents were so annoyed, and said no one was going to bed until every last 'ugly bug' was captured and set back outside. I argued they weren't ugly, but I was alone. My sisters agreed that in the jars on the way home they glowed so lovely, but on the walls and furniture, they were just plain bugs, an infestation. None of them got it. Sure they looked like ordinary bugs, but they were still beautiful to me, even if they weren't glowing.

"Anyway, when we captured them all, Dad made us walk him to the spot near the bridge. He set down the jars, took off the lid, and told us we should go home and leave them to exit the jars at their own pace. As we walked back, he told us we had no right to take them from their home in the first place.

"'Wild things don't belong to us. They aren't glowing for you, they light up for themselves, because it's what they are born to do,' he explained. I realized we'd been wrong to capture them and expect them to shine for us continuously, as if they existed just for us.

"Tali's like a firefly. She captivates people with her glow, but that's all they see, and they think that's how she always is. Then they want to scoop her up in a jar and keep her all for themselves. What you all don't see is after the short time she glows, when she goes back to being herself. And who she is, is an insecure woman with a raging inferiority complex, who will never believe that anyone really likes her."

"But everyone likes her!" Sam protested.

"No, she understands you all like the version of her that dazzles you with jazz hands and fun stories, the life of the party who brightens everyone's experience with her presence. She's convinced, though, that if people saw the true her, the boring old bug, they would reject her. So, she hides who she really is and when we go out, she fucking shines, man.

But at the end of each party, each wedding, the same thing happens. She's exhausted from putting on the show, and falls into the passenger seat with barely enough energy to buckle herself up. Before I even start the car, like clockwork, she's asking the same old questions:

Did everyone have fun?

Did everyone like her?
Did this one particular person like her?
Did she overstay her welcome?
Did she talk too much?
Did she say something stupid?
Were they all just humoring her?
Do they secretly hate her?
Will they never want to see her again?
Will she ever be invited anywhere again?
Was I embarrassed by her?
Did she look ok?
Did I have a good time?
Do I still love her?

"Every. Single. Time. She doesn't give herself a moment to enjoy the fun she had before she unravels it all, and examines it to find some made-up flaw about herself or some faux pas she thinks she committed. She goes to bed miserable and anxious. Then the next time we get an invite, she is vibrant and can't wait to go."

Sam was silent. She wasn't sure what she'd done to earn this openness from Em, or if she was complicit in some betrayal of Tali by even listening. She also felt strangely sympathetic to Em. "It sounds tiring for you, to always have to cheer her up?"

"Nah, other people might be turned off by that, but I love her for the bug she is. She's my favorite person in this whole messed up universe. You can't get mad at a firefly for glowing, can you? It's what they do. I can't get upset at her for lighting up at a party and turning it back off when we leave. It's how she's wired.

"As much as I wish she could love herself the way I love her, and to see in herself the amazing woman I see, I can't make that change happen in her head for her. But I will never stop trying.

"And she loves me for the weird bug I am. She picks me up when I'm down, and puts up with my moods. Like, I'm not always easy to deal with… I know because she tells me. I get in my head, I don't reveal what I'm thinking or feeling, and then she has to draw me out…

"Which is exactly what you need, my little lesbian grasshopper."

"Excuse me?"

"Get out of your head, Sam. Stop hiding. Be you, whoever that is, and find someone who loves you for exactly who you are. All those things you said earlier, is that really how you think of yourself?"

"It's not how I think I am. It's true. There is absolutely nothing special about me. No one is ever going to love me like a shiny insect or whatever. There's nothing there to love. My sister has spent her whole life making sure I understand that I'm boring, I'm beige,

I'm 'human oatmeal,' that I'm 'an anthropomorphic pair of khakis'."

Em choked on her beer at that last one.

"First of all, your sister sounds like a total asshole. I hope I never meet her. But out of morbid curiosity, I kind of want to. And for what it's worth, I don't think you are qualified to assess how you come across to people. For crying out loud, Sam, you thought, that we all thought, that you were straight.

"Second, and more important, you're a good person. You are the only you there is, you just need to embrace that, and let people get to know you. Like, what are your interests? You don't open up to people at all. I've known you for almost fifteen years and if a gun was to my head all I could really say is you have good hygiene, you're polite, and you love nature. And of course the more recent discovery that you are an amazingly confident dancer for a person of limited skills in that area."

"Ouch."

"No seriously Sam, who are you?"

"You know what, I don't really want to talk about this, and it looks like they are done setting up the s'mores table so..."

"Don't you 's'mores' me, missy. You're not getting out of this so easy. You walked around with little cartoon lovebirds circling your head and hit on

Tali, in front of the whole world, and me, repeatedly. I think the least you could do is hear me out: I want to help."

"What?"

"If there's one thing Tali and I agree on, it's helping others. I think we can help you. She loves a project, I love a challenge, and for better or for worse we both love you. As a friend. You need to shed your khaki chrysalis and burst forth confidently, make the world see who you are. And then, we can help you find a woman to share the world with. We both remember what it was like at the beginning of our romantic lives. It's overwhelming, but you don't have to face it alone."

"I don't think we need to involve Tali..."

"You're the one who involved her. You wanted her, now you get us both in your life. Sure, not in the capacity you'd like, but I think this is an upgrade to you crushing on her like Ralph Wiggum mooning over Lisa Simpson on Valentine's Day. Honestly, it will be good for you, it'll help you get over her.

"Consider it, I don't know, 'exposure therapy.' I assure you, the more time spent with Tali in the wild, rather than these social events, the more you'll learn to let go of the imaginary woman you've been crushing on. Then you can concentrate on finding an adult, reciprocal relationship with someone you are actually attracted to.

"So you agree? I take your silence as a yes. Tali! Tali! Come here!"

"Coming, lover!" Tali called across the yard, arms full of plates.

"Please don't call her over here." Sam regretted showing up at all this evening.

"Why not? You like spending time with her. Besides, she's bringing us s'mores. You wanted s'mores, remember?"

Sam groaned as Tali glided toward them, balancing a plate in each of her hands, triumphantly announcing, "S'mor-ays for *mis amores!*" She flashed Sam that disarming grin she always gave her, though Sam saw it differently now. "What are you two over here conspiring about?"

"Nothing," Sam denied.

"Actually, we were plotting, but realized we need your help." Em replied as she stuffed her mouth full of s'more. "Mmm... man, why don't we have s'mores more often," is what she meant to ask next, but it came out more like "Mmm, mmm mmmm mmm mmmmph mmmm mmmmmm mmmphmmmph?"

Draining the rest of her beer bottle, Em smacked her mouth and slapped Sam on the back, leaning in to whisper to Tali, "Sam needs our help. She wants us to give her a makeover."

"EEEEEE I love a makeover!!" Tali squealed with too much delight for Sam's comfort.

"Not just clothes, though. She needs a personality makeover. We're going to help Sam be the most... Sam she can be. And then she needs to find a lady."

"Yay!" Tali could barely contain her delight as she clapped her hands. "This is going to be so much fun! How about this Sunday? We're free!" Bowing to Sam with absolute sincerity, Tali said, "It is an honor that you entrust us with this mission."

"No, really, you don't have to do anything, I'm fine."

"Oh really?" Countered Em. "Maybe we should ask Molly what she thinks."

"Molly?!" Gasped Tali. "Ooooooh, I thought there was something going on. Did you and her? Eh? Ehhhh?" She was apparently totally unaware that her mouth was covered in melted chocolate and that she had bits of marshmallow on her chin. This, combined with her goofy expression and awkward, insinuating dance suddenly made both Sam and Em dissolve into laughter.

"Fine, you win. Just do two things for me?" Sam bargained. "One: please wipe your face, you've got candy all over, and I think there's even some graham cracker in your hair? How did that happen? And, two:

please, please, as a personal favor to me, never dance like that again."

Sam's request of course caused Tali to dance even more aggressively and unattractively. None of them could stop laughing. Finally, Tali cleaned the s'mores from her face. For the rest of the party, the three huddled close together, making plans for Sam's future.

At the end of the night, Sam helped Em walk an exhausted Tali back to their car. As Em settled Tali into the passenger seat, Sam heard a drowsy voice ask, "Did everyone have fun?"

Chapter 2: The Extraordinarily, Ordinary, Invisible Girl

NOVEMBER 1, 2019

"No seriously Sam, who are you?" Em's question played on a loop in Sam's head the whole way home from the Guy Fawkes Fest, and continued as she got ready for sleep. She didn't know who she was, or maybe she did, and she just didn't like who she was. A lifetime of being disregarded and excluded in all facets of her life coupled with intentional attempts to make herself palatable to anyone had made herself unmemorable to everyone. Em wasn't being harsh when she said Sam

made it hard to get to know her, she was being accurate.

Em's query forced Sam to face the hard truth: in short, as a single woman in her mid-thirties with no strong relationships—and no idea how to change that—Sam was a passenger along for the ride in everyone else's life. Sam felt like a perpetual plus-one, and had since her early childhood, which her family reinforced by consistently mistreating her.

Although Sam evolved into the forgotten child, she hadn't always been. In fact, when she was still the youngest child Sam functioned as her parents' little sidekick and enjoyed their attention

Her dad, Ray, often took Sam to the movies, followed by a meal where they'd discuss what they liked about it. He didn't seem to realize that they had completely different tastes and half of the time Sam didn't even care for the action movies, horror films, or crime thrillers they'd seen, but she was so eager to please her dad that she'd find at least a few positive things to share. Her favorite was when he'd take her to the burger place with the upside down ice cream cone sundae that was decorated to look like a clown. Sometimes he'd take her to their favorite Chinese restaurant, and if they were in no rush to get home, they'd wander into the bookstore that was next door to it.

"All right Sam, you can get as many as three books," he offered, and she always took him up on it. If he was in a really good mood, she got a new bookmark, too. She devoured the books, and couldn't wait to talk about them with father and with her older brother, Brad, who was also an avid reader.

Sam's mom, Beverly, didn't take her on such fun outings, but Sam didn't care, she just liked being together. So, when Bev ran errands at the grocery store or watched one of Brad's sporting events, Sam loved being her mom's mini-me. She always tried to make sure her outfits matched Bev's, and felt like they were friends or sisters.

When Bev became pregnant, four-year-old Sam even accompanied her to medical appointments. Bev would call out, "Let's go big sister, we've got to see how your little brother or sister is doing!"

Witnessing the process of cold gel squeezed over her mother's increasing mound of a stomach followed by an instrument pressed on her mother's flesh made Sam visibly queasy.

"It's fine sweetie, it doesn't hurt," Bev reassured her.

Sam liked being close to her mother, feeling like she was an integral part of the family unit. At the time, it didn't seem strange to her that Ray never showed up for any of these check-ups. Sam just thought it was special girl time, and couldn't wait to meet the little baby for whom she'd been helping the family prepare.

She'd been so anxious for her new sibling to arrive that Sam never considered it might not be a good thing. Unfortunately, her world changed for the worse with the arrival of Kimberly-Anne, who later demanded to be called Kimmy. She was an agent of chaos who turned the household upside down, finding cause for conflict wherever she could—most often with Brad. With Ray and Bev's time divided between their high-achieving oldest child and their troubled youngest child, there was none leftover for Sam.

When Kimmy started school, her teachers noticed issues immediately, which monopolized her parents' attention. At back-to-school nights, Bev began to skip going to Sam's classes entirely, focusing only on her youngest daughter's performance.

After an early assessment showed that Kimmy exhibited anxiety, caused by low self-esteem and being in the shadow of her siblings, Bev and Ray sent her to a behavior camp for a few weeks.

"She gets to go to camp?!" Brad couldn't believe it. "She's a brat and you reward her with a fun retreat? If I break this lamp will you send me to an amusement park?!"

Bev tried to calm him, asserting: "Camp is not a reward, it's a necessity. It's supposed to help her feel like she matters, and learn tactics to maintain her confidence."

Unfortunately, Kimmy overcorrected, and came back not just more self-assured, but as a certified bully. Her favorite past-times included insulting Sam and infuriating Brad.

Kimmy and Brad fought so much that they took all of her parents' energy, leaving Sam to raise herself. Bev and Ray remained constantly on guard, stepping in to stop their conflicts and trying everything to keep the peace. Most often this resulted in Ray and Bev taking Brad and Kimmy to dinner or a movie just to get them out of the house and break the tension.

Sam often came home to find her family had gone out without her. When her family got home, she'd mention she, too, would have enjoyed a meal out or a trip to the movies, but her parents were too exhausted to deal with her.

"Sam, don't be petty," Bev dismissed her. "We take you to movies and restaurants plenty. Not everyone can do everything all the time."

Ray had no sympathy, either. "You're a big girl, perfectly capable of feeding and entertaining yourself." Her father would then completely flip it on her. "Why didn't you eat with your friends, or watch a movie with them at their houses?"

"Because she doesn't have friends," gloated Kimmy. "Sam's jealous!"

"Enough!" Ray hit his limit on being around children for the night, disappearing to his study until bedtime.

"I'm sorry Sam. We didn't mean to forget you. It's just hard to get Kimmy to calm down, and we get caught up in the moment. You understand, right?" She adored Brad, but even this reassurance provided little comfort.

No matter how many times Sam mentioned she had an upcoming school trip, needed permission slips signed, or required supplies for a specific class project, it was as if her parents had selective hearing loss where she was concerned. This led to a number of instances where Sam's teachers or counselors intervened by directly contacting her parents, which only aggravated Beverly and Ray.

"Really Samantha, you're supposed to be the easy one. The last thing we need is you causing trouble, too."

She felt she was becoming an invisible child. Ray and Bev even overlooked mandatory school events, begrudgingly dropping Sam at her band concerts as an afterthought, uninterested in staying beyond securing Sam a ride home with someone else. (When they even bothered to do that.) They so frequently forgot to pick her up that other kids' parents got used to assuming she'd need a ride. Sam tried to play down her embarrassment, but no one wants to be the kid whose parents clearly didn't care.

Ray didn't completely ignore her, though—a fact which Sam clung to in order to not feel like a complete outcast in her own family. From time to time, Sam got attention all to herself when her father, tired of dealing with their other family members, took Sam to Pizza Hut to redeem one of her many Book-It program coupons.

Each time a student read a certain number of books, they got a certificate for a free personal pizza. As Sam was a voracious reader, preferring the company of books to the cruelty of people, she earned many free pizzas. Eventually Ray's interest in this activity waned, though, and her unused pizza coupons stacked up on her dresser, a symbol of her parent's disinterest.

Sam was hurt and frustrated. In her youngest days, she and her family were so close. She felt like an equal member of a team, and she always knew she could count on them. Her parents both needed breaks though, so even the errands on which she used to reliably accompany her mother came to a halt. Beverly instead left Sam to babysit Kimmy, despite Sam begging not to be put in that position.

Kimmy not only disobeyed Sam, but fully terrorized her, especially when emboldened by friends. Her brother Brad always used cute nicknames for her, like "Sam-I-Am," "Samwise," or "Yosemite Sam." Kimmy, however, landed on calling her "Samanth-*duh,*" with great emphasis on the last syllable. Kimmy's friends joined in the teasing and took to calling Sam this mean-spirited moniker.

Naively, Sam gave her little sister multiple second chances at being kind, but nothing improved their relationship. If Sam made a mistake, Kimmy was there to pounce, not only ridiculing Sam but also making sure everyone knew about it. When Sam tried to do something new and didn't immediately excel, Kimmy was ready.

"Why don't you just give up, Samanth-duh? You're never going to be good at anything."

There was nothing Kimmy couldn't make fun of: Sam's appearance, her clothes, her voice, her taste in books, music, or TV; Sam could do no right in Kimmy's eyes. When Sam struggled to keep friendships at school, Kimmy reveled in reinforcing Sam's feelings of being unwanted and unlikeable. Sam hoped by the time she went to college Kimmy would outgrow her mean girl behavior, but it continued into their adult lives.

Kimmy's constant taunting became the voice of Sam's inner saboteur, an anti-Jiminy Cricket. Every time Sam considered taking a risk, she stopped, overrun by doubts, heard in Kimmy's distinct delivery. When she made a mistake, even with no one to witness it, Kimmy's past criticisms resurfaced, reinforcing the error and making it an even bigger deal to Sam than it should have had been.

Sam's entrenched belief in her own inherent inadequacy made it difficult to make the effort to form relationships with people. Her fear of rejection led her to keep to herself, and by the time she was in her mid-thirties it seemed that all of Kimmy's negative projections for Sam's failed life had come true.

Who was Sam? Sam was alone.

Chapter 3: She Leads a Lonely Life

2008 - 2019
(POST-COLLEGE)

Sam had not intended to be alone. Despite her many missteps and misadventures, it never occurred to her that she might wind up here in her mid-thirties, closeted, living by herself with no close friends and no dating life of any kind. If she'd imagined her current state was actually possible, perhaps she could have taken steps to avoid it.

Although she had savored quiet moments during her childhood, when she was overwhelmed by family fights or friends asserting their personalities too intensely, Sam still craved companionship, but she'd never found it. She envied Em and Tali, she wanted what they had, what Johanna and Eddie, Brad and his wife, her grandparents, seemingly everyone else in her life had. And with every year that passed, the likelihood of finding it felt increasingly impossible. She was terrified that a lonely future was unavoidable.

Sam had tried to shake up her life before her Guy Fawkes fireside chat with Em. During her late twenties she'd half-heartedly thrown herself into volunteering, but each time quickly realized the connections she made were superficial. Searching for meaning, Sam tried a variety of causes, such as food distribution, rebuilding a house, or reading to kids, but she couldn't connect with the other volunteers. They seemed to have existing, insular communities she couldn't fit into. With her history of being excluded, she struggled to assert herself, eventually abandoning each new cause and beating herself up for failing.

By the time she turned thirty, she'd run out of energy to keep trying to break into new places, accepting her solitude. In fairness to herself, Sam tried to focus on the good, convincing herself she didn't have such a bad life after all. She cared deeply about the environment, and found a career that let her contribute to saving it. She worked at a conservation organization focused on preserving her beloved Chesapeake Bay, which gave her a sense of fulfillment. As a Virginia native, Sam loved everything about the Bay. (Except of course, the Bay Bridge. She would never *not* be afraid of driving over either span.) She was good at her job, rarely experiencing workplace drama.

Sam worked on the land stewardship team, which let her combine her meticulous planning and tracking skills with her love for being outdoors. Sam was particularly talented at taking large objectives and breaking them into small tasks, organizing schedules and allocating resources.

She helped create project plans for short-term efforts of three to five years aimed at achieving specific outcomes. Her role let her feel like she was making a difference on campaigns she really cared about, such as protecting endangered nesting sites for birds, getting public participation in waterway clean up days, and raising awareness about the blue crab population.

Sam liked that her job required her to go out on site visits and join in hands-on activities to make the environment even a little bit better. She tracked progress and created reports which she handed off to members of other teams—fundraising and donor relations, lobbying, communications and public relations, commercial partnerships, marketing and social media—whose staffers were confident engaging the public in their more visible roles.

Her colleagues were kind and during her first few years invited her to happy hours or parties, but she was always too anxious about making a bad impression so she never went. She even struggled with small talk at the office, getting flustered if she felt put on the spot to share opinions. Members of the marketing team would often walk around the office to test out campaign slogans or taglines, prompting Sam to hide herself rather than weigh in on whether she thought, "She sells sea shells but she never sells she-crabs... throw them back," would be effective marketing copy.

Still, her job enabled her to afford a nice place in a safe neighborhood. Sam lived alone in a small, tidy apartment. It was about as vibrant and interesting as you'd expect from someone with nearly no personality to call her own. Its overall vibe was "polite." Most people she knew had roommates due to the high cost of living, but Sam had never had anyone she could ask to split with.

Sam sometimes went for days at a time without experiencing a physical touch from or conversation with another living being. Occasionally, Sam considered getting a pet, which only brought up unpleasant memories from her childhood. Bev forbade any discussion on the topic because Brad and Kimmy fought so much they couldn't agree on a dog or a cat. Now intimidated by the responsibility of caring for one as an inexperienced adult, Sam talked herself out of any animal companions, and continued her life of solitude.

It wasn't as though Sam didn't like aspects of her solitude. After living much of her life with strong personalities who dictated her circumstances or exerted control, she appreciated independence. She liked being able to decide what went where in her home. She liked that she could buy herself special snacks and they wouldn't be gone before she got to take a single bite. (She hid hers from Kimmy growing up, but her sister always found them.) She liked that there was order. Order meant calm. Sam treasured calm.

One of her favorite hobbies was going to the movies at odd hours, which didn't feel lonely to her, since in her mind no one was supposed to talk during a movie anyway. She didn't really care much for loud action movies, and gravitated toward independent films and international cinema, especially light-hearted romances. She liked the movies with simple, predictable plot lines in which people change their lives and end up in a better place than they started, especially if it was happily ever after with a declaration of love or a wedding. Sometimes she'd get carried away and imagine herself as one of the protagonists, even though she didn't believe it was actually possible for her in real life.

Her favorite spot was an old movie theatre that hadn't changed on the outside in decades, and that somehow stood the test of time when other stores in that area shut down and remained empty. The theatre had not only survived, but had thrived, keeping its intimate charm while updating to digital screens and luxury seating. They mostly showed indie movies, anchored by at least one blockbuster. On Sundays, they dedicated one screen to rerunning classic cinema, and Sam happily treated herself to seeing the musicals she'd already seen countless times before.

She had a routine at this theatre. She greeted the ticket checker at the stanchion, and headed immediately to the concessions.

"I'll take a small popcorn, medium diet soda, and Goobers, please. Thanks so much!" (On some weekends, this became the only time she spoke out loud to another human.)

She'd stop at the butter station to drizzle a little on top, then grab a straw and a generous handful of napkins. Upon settling into her seat, she'd eat a small handful of the popcorn from the top of the container, just enough to make some room to empty the Goobers into it, something Ray taught her.

"Can't beat salty-sweet, Sam! The trick is, you have to shake it around, distribute the candies juuuust right in the popcorn."

Fondly remembering these moments with her dad, she took an inaugural sip from her soda, and stared at the screen, ready to be transported.

Some people don't like going to movies alone, but Sam had never really gone with anyone other than Ray, anyway. When she started going with friends in college, she missed being able to fully focus on the film. Going solo meant no one leaning over and interrupting her in what they thought was a hushed tone, but was still loud enough to annoy the other patrons. Sam liked to lose herself in the experience, and that was easier on her own.

She especially liked that this theatre attracted an older crowd, which she found often meant a quieter experience. It also reminded her of summertime movie marathons with her grandparents, and she liked to think they would have fun coming to this theatre with her. She enjoyed the early morning shows, when she was, more often than not, the only patron. It felt like the whole movie was running just for her, which made her feel special. So few things in life were just for Sam. She left the theatre feeling like she'd been treated to an immersive getaway from real life.

Still, all the satisfying calm did nothing to help her feel engaged in life. She found herself talking to her plants. She was often unnerved by the involuntary quiet, and resorted to leaving the TV or music on nearly round the clock. For a girl who frequently sought solace on her own terms, the forced silence was too much to bear. She wanted someone to talk to at the end of the day, to say good morning to before heading off to work. She wanted a partner.

Chapter 4: The Moon Belongs to Everyone

1991 - 2003
(CHILDHOOD SUMMERS)

Sadly, the only company she found was in the ever-present memories she could not avoid. Sam admired her friends who, from her vantage, constantly moved forward in life, unplagued by the past. Sam lived in the past constantly. She hated herself for it. She felt sometimes as if she was drowning in inescapable sludge of every bad thing that had ever happened in her life. She tried everything to forget, but her memory could not be deterred. Worst, her recollections weren't just precise, they were so realistic and detailed that they felt interactive, leaving her mentally, emotionally, and physically drained.

When bad memories popped up, Sam's first course of action was to—unsuccessfully—try directing her mind to happy memories, most of them being with her grandparents, Bev's mother Jeannie and father Tony. Bev seemed somewhat indifferent to her parents, but they were among Sam's favorite people in her life. They were the only ones around whom she'd ever felt truly comfortable being herself. Even with Brad she had to keep a small guard up because she needed his approval, and because she saw how he was toward their sister he didn't like.

Grandma Jeannie and Grandpa Tony were incredibly kind to Sam, and treated her like she mattered. She spent nearly every summer with them at their Illinois home, sometimes with her siblings or cousins, but often by herself.

Her visits were the only time in her childhood she felt listened to, and that she was a priority. From the moment she stepped off the plane she felt like she was at home, and ran from the jet bridge straight into her grandparents' arms. Even before she reached them, she could always hear Grandma Jeannie calling out, "Sammy! My Sammy-Girl!" They were genuinely glad she was there, and unlike Sam's parents or sister,

Grandma Jeannie and Grandpa Tony actually wanted her company.

As an adult, Sam knew intellectually that she'd had countless fulfilling experiences with them, but she was unable to recall them with any specificity, and when she tried to force one to the forefront of her mind, she didn't relive them the same way she did her more upsetting recollections. In her negative memories, she was reliving them in real time from her first-person perspective. But the positive memories she actually wanted to re-experience were less immersive, and she saw them more as an observer watching out-of-context snippets.

All those tiny moments meant so much to her but she couldn't control her memories and focus on just one at a time. Sam wished she had photos or videos of the little moments, the moments she never would have thought to document, some way to recall single memories instead of clumps and montages of hikes and board games and cooking lessons.

She wanted to dive deep into the memories of Grandma Jeannie teaching her to cook and bake. Bev never let Sam or her siblings help out in the kitchen, so it was a treat to be Grandma Jeannie's sous chef. If she tried to think of something specific they'd made, Sam could only see glimpses flashing by too quickly, stirring brownie batter or tasting a sauce, sharing little preview bites before declaring the food ready to eat.

She tried to think of all the time they spent outdoors. Her grandparents adored sunshine and fresh air. Sam helped them in their garden, where they grew flowers, fruits, and vegetables, many of which made their way onto the dining table. They also frequently took her hiking or on nature walks, teaching her about local plants and animals. Her grandparents always held each other's hands while they strolled.

Sam wanted that for herself; she wanted to know what it was like to feel the touch of someone who genuinely loved her. During these outdoor excursions they'd talk to Sam about her life, asking about her hopes and dreams, her likes and dislikes, and offering their encouragement. Sam knew they'd had so many valuable conversations during this time but couldn't recall a single one.

On rainy days, they'd stay inside playing board games for hours on end. Sam was content to play with them, even games she didn't really like, because she appreciated their attention. She also liked that they never treated like a kid or took it easy on her, but actually challenged her and taught her how to improve her skills in each game.

Sam also appreciated their recommendations on books and movies. Grandpa Tony and Grandma

Jeannie took Sam to the library once a week to pick out a new stack to read, and she would happily chat with them about what she liked in each book.

They also watched just about every classic movie, regardless of how good it was or how age-appropriate the plot points might be. After visiting the library, they'd take Sam to the local Blockbuster and let her pick out movies for the coming week. Sam could remember the movies and books in great detail, but not their conversations about them. She tried and tried, to no avail.

Shifting focus, she'd sometimes try to think of all the celebrations they'd enjoyed together, all the parties and receptions. Her extended family often gathered for birthdays, weddings, and anniversaries, which Sam got excited for because she loved to dance, even if she knew she wasn't particularly coordinated. Dancing was one of the only activities during which Sam could get out of her own head and be present in the moment. She didn't always have anyone to dance with, but she always joined in the group dances when everyone flooded the floor, to "We Are Family" or "Celebration."

At every event, Grandpa Tony made a point of dancing with his daughters and granddaughters. Kimmy always refused, but Sam cherished the opportunity. He had a special song he'd request for each of the important ladies in his life. Sam's was the June Allyson and Peter Lawford version of "The Best Things in Life are Free." If Sam often tried to recall a specific instance of the dance, they all melded together.

She couldn't summon the smell of the specific cologne Grandpa Tony wore—perhaps it was just his deodorant or aftershave—but knew it had always comforted her. So too had the scent of cigars he'd smoke on special occasions. Some cozy combination of nutmeg and vanilla. She knew Grandpa Tony always sang along with June and Peter, but from the distance of years his voice was muted.

Sam wondered why she could become involuntarily stuck in negative memories and view every detail of every person she wanted to forget, but for the people who mattered, like her grandparents, the memories faded, their voices became less specific, and their facial features softened out of focus as if blurred.

After Brad graduated high school, Sam had felt outnumbered and alone in her house. Her only respite became summers spent at her grandparents', several states away from Kimmy, and away from bullies her own age, too. A total escape. Each year, on the day after school ended, Sam was shipped off by herself on a plane to stay all summer, flying home the Friday before school began. Her grandparents understood that Sam was often forgotten and left out at home, so they made a point to buy her extra-special school supplies before sending her back home, which made Kimmy jealous.

During the year, they sent little gifts just for Sam, causing Kimmy to throw such a fit that eventually Bev asked her parents to stop sending Sam presents. Still, they called Sam on a regular basis. She looked forward to the calls, which made her feel safe and loved to know that even from a distance her grandparents were looking out for her.

If Sam had her choice she'd happily be stuck forever in any one of the moments with her grandparents, but to her frustration, with each passing year the moments slipped away and became vague for her. They stopped feeling like her personal memories as they diminished to echos and shades.

Sometimes in trying to seize an individual moment of joy from the archives in her mind, Sam instead landed on one of disappointment, becoming locked into the memory until it finished replaying.

[2003]

Grandma Jeannie had recently passed, leaving Grandpa Tony alone in an assisted living facility. He started to slow down and disengage from conversations, and on each visit Sam noticed he responded less to direct stimulus. When Sam visited him, she usually found him in the TV room where he took in daily propaganda from a conservative news channel that remained on 24 hours a day. Sam noticed a change in his attitude on certain topics, upset that his demeanor had been influenced so quickly.

One day, the channel showed live video from a Pride parade. Sam marveled at the people in the crowd, and got carried away with the feelings of joy they exuded. The self-confidence, the camaraderie, the bright colors... Sam wanted to be part of it! How exciting it must feel to be among a crowd of people so sure of who they are, and so unashamed. They were brave. Sam wanted to be brave.

Her admiration was quickly disrupted as one of the residents, a man Sam hadn't met yet, snarled at the TV, "Why can't these people keep anything to themselves?"

Another resident, on elderly woman, concurred, "They don't want equality, they want attention. They always have to make a scene. Look how they're dressed! I can't tell which ones are men, or women, or... or both!!"

The first resident nodded his head. "And to be out like that, forcing kids to see… I just want to mind my own business but they won't let me!"

"Exactly! I'm not afraid of them, and I don't hate them, I just wish they'd be less loud about it."

Sam felt that they were judging her, specifically. Her cheeks were on fire and she stared at the screen trying not to make eye contact. She quickly glanced at her grandfather, hoping he would stand up for her, and for all those people on screen. But he wasn't alert enough to realize what was happening, and even if he was, he didn't know how Sam felt or that Sam identified with the parade participants. Sam didn't even fully understand how much she identified with them.

* * *

Although she'd avoided looking too long at the two judgmental residents who rained on her Pride parade, decades later she could still see the ugly expressions they wore. It wasn't fair. Her own grandparents' faces became less specific each time she tried to summon them, but these strangers she only knew that one afternoon were crystal clear. Every wrinkle on their faces, the spots on their skin, their thick nails, and their worn, drab clothing. She could even hear, with great fidelity, each of their voices.

The only other memory associated with her grandparents that actually did replay vividly for her was actually a memory of Kimmy.

[2004]

Grandpa Tony passed within just under a year of losing his wife. Weighed down with grief, Sam absorbed every detail of Tony's funeral, from the compressed texture of the carpet, showing the wheel lines from the rolling casket, to the smell of the overwrought floral arrangements, and the exceptionally cold bathroom filled with an impressive volume of tissue boxes.

Brad was deployed at the time and couldn't come home for the service, leaving Sam on her own. She was inconsolable and wept openly until her face was red and raw from all the tissues she used on her eyes and nose. As she prepared to get into the family car to go home, Kimmy stepped in front of her.

"Oh no, now you really don't have anyone who likes you, huh?" Kimmy mocked Sam for mourning so deeply. "Such a drama queen. Way to make this all about you!"

Sam was closer with her grandparents than either Brad or Kimmy had been, but even taking that into consideration, she couldn't understand how Kimmy could find glee in their deaths.

As her parents drove them home from the reception, Sam tried to drown out her sister's jeers, closing her eyes and humming to herself:

The moon belongs to everyone
The best things in life are free
The stars belong to everyone
They gleam there for you and me
The flowers in spring
the robins that sing
The sunbeams that shine
They're yours! They're mine!
And love can come to everyone,
The best things in life are free

* * *

Chapter 5: Light as a Feather, Stiff as a Board

2016
(THREE YEARS BEFORE GUY FAWKES FEST)

It seemed cruel to Sam that her awkward, uncomfortable, embarrassing, or even traumatic memories could trap her in a total paralysis, while the precious memories she actually wanted to recall were reduced to vague digests.

When Sam had an upsetting flashback, she didn't just recall the key events or outlines. In her mind she relived them, reenacting them in full, excruciating detail as if she was physically there. As a result, she also re-experienced the visceral emotions of the moment. Shame, grief, guilt, whatever it was, she had to endure it again and again. It was like some kind of cosmic torture, but Sam couldn't quite understand what she'd ever done in life to deserve this punishment.

Sometimes at night she'd flop into her bed, ready for sleep, when a parade of unpleasant moments suddenly surged through her brain. In the latest hours in the darkness of her bedroom, her face burned crimson at these intrusions, as they enveloped her. A few memories in particular occurred over and over, like a punishment. The worst was Gretchen's slumber party. She'd try to brush it away, but as soon as it popped into her head, she was at the mercy of her memory.

[1993]

Sam was in elementary school, preparing for her first-ever sleepover, which was being held at her classmate Gretchen's house. She knew it must be a significant occasion, because Bev took time away from Kimmy to give Sam a special shopping trip for a new sleeping bag and a gift for the birthday girl.

At the store, Sam felt absolutely spoiled as Bev told her, "Sam, pick out any bag you like! Whichever one is your favorite, it's yours! Your first sleepover!"

Sam picked the one with characters from her favorite video game, and as they walked over to the toy section, Sam found the perfect present for Gretchen. It was the most coveted item in her grade: a Japanese school supply holder, with little drawers that swing open, a dispenser filled with sparkly tape, and secret compartments that popped out when you pressed a button.

Back at home, Sam could barely stand the anticipation as she helped her mom wrap Gretchen's gift in iridescent mermaid paper and pack an overnight bag. She changed into her party outfit, ready for the biggest night of her life.

The party was held at Chuck E. Cheese, and everyone in her second-grade class was invited. Sam tried to memorize everything about the night and how special it was: the noise, the smells, the sounds, the sticky floors that gave the impression of snow-shoeing across greased fly paper.

With all of the stimulus, Sam was overwhelmed trying to keep track of her classmates. She saw the two boys from her class banished from the ball pit for being too rough, before her friend Joey waved her over to sit with her and share some pizza.

"Ugh, it doesn't taste like much!" Sam was disappointed by how bland it was, and by the gummy texture of the crust.

Joey showed her a trick. "If you cover it in enough sprinkle cheese and pepper flakes, it's not bad! Here, try." With a heavy hand, Joey poured generously from each shaker until he covered the surface of the entire slice. He was right: it was much better when you couldn't taste the actual pizza!

After thanking Joey, Sam tried to overcome her unease with groups in social situations, and forced herself to join in conversation with some of the girls. She felt awkward, especially when she realized Katie was making fun of Gretchen's grandmother, who was also at the party. Katie was holding court, all eyes on her as she performed impressions of the elderly woman. Sam didn't cackle along with the other girls, and instead tried to slip away, unnoticed.

Moments later, the unpleasant conversation was gone from her head, replaced by a feeling of total triumph when Gretchen screamed in delight upon opening Sam's gift. Gretchen jumped up and ran around the long table, past all the other kids from class, just to thank Sam with a big hug. Gretchen then made a show of letting each girl look at her sparkly, fancy pencil box. It was clearly one of her favorite gifts, and Sam liked that the other girls complimented her on having excellent taste. (The boys, meanwhile, seemed confused at their fuss over a pencil box.)

Before leaving Chuck E. Cheese, Sam felt a buzz of excitement at the prize counter, with glass cases full of loot, where she got to redeem some tickets she won at skee-ball. She felt an unusual sense of power in getting to choose her rewards: stickers, a ruler, a bouncy ball, a clacky-toy, and a little rubber finger puppet.

After the pizza party, Sam and the other girls from class went to Gretchen's for the sleepover. Sam hadn't really spent much time outside of school with the girls individually, so she thought it was fun to be with all of them at once. It was a great time of bonding over eating candy and watching movies. When it came time to pick, Sam was too timid to suggest one of the many she liked, instead listening to the other girls decide which was the most daring selection. "I'm not allowed to watch PG-13 at home!" exclaimed Shana, as if she was an outlaw.

Sam had the growing feeling she was part of the in-crowd. She'd always been shy, feeling like she was on the periphery, riding her popular brother's coattails. Now, she was finally making a good impression on her own merit. Gretchen still hadn't set down the pencil case since they got to her house. She insisted Sam sit next to her, letting her share some of her sour gummy worms.

At bedtime, the girls arranged their sleeping bags in little clusters around the furniture in the living room, although they felt too excited to sleep.

Gretchen's mom reminded them, "Girls, don't stay up talking all night," as she turned out the lights and went upstairs.

"We'll go to sleep real soon, Mrs. Ferris!" she heard her classmates falsely promise, accompanied with conspiratorial snickering. Sam joined in their giggles, but despite their efforts to stay up all night, the room grew quiet as they began drifting off to sleep.

Drowsy and full of junk food, Sam felt proud of herself. Before the party, Bev warned Sam that at every sleepover there is always one girl who gets homesick or anxious and calls her parents, begging to be picked up in the middle of the night. She urged Sam to be brave.

"Don't be 'that girl' at the sleepover, Sam, no matter how much you might want to come home. If you leave, all the other girls will make fun of you the moment you walk out the door."

Sam had no desire to go home, because she was having the best time ever. She had made it through her first slumber party like a pro, like a video game in which she unlocked an achievement to reach the next level.

Then, as she closed her eyes to fall asleep, snuggled in her new sleeping bag, she experienced the feeling of total disaster. She heard Katie (four sleeping bags away from her) whisper quietly to Gretchen (five sleeping bags away).

"You know, Sam was being really mean about your grandma earlier." Sam froze, unable to think or breathe.

"What?!" Gretchen whispered back, alarmed.

"Yeah, she was making fun of her a lot, and she made fun of you, too, for having her at your party."

Sam wanted to yell, to defend herself, to tell Gretchen that it was all a lie, that Katie had been the one telling jokes. But something stopped her. Despite how upset she was, she couldn't physically force herself to move. She felt like her mouth was locked shut and her body held in place by some powerful gravity that only affected her.

"Thanks for letting me know... what a jerk!" Gretchen sounded angry in a way Sam had not previously heard her speak.

"You're welcome, I just thought you should know," simpered Katie. The two went on to criticize Sam's sleeping bag, her pajamas, anything they could. It was a real bonding moment for the two, all at young Sam's expense.

The next morning, Sam, who hadn't been able to sleep, was the first girl packed up to go. She snuck into the study and called her mom, asking Bev to pick her up a little earlier than expected, making up a lie about the family being tired of hosting all the girls.

"Sam, are you ready for pancakes with the other girls?" Gretchen's mom called as Sam walked past the kitchen.

"Um, actually, my mom is on the way, she needs to get me early for some errands."

"Oh that's a shame. Gretchen! Say goodbye to Sam, and thank her again for bringing such a thoughtful present." Mrs. Ferris had no idea.

"Thanks." Gretchen complied tersely, then pointedly resumed conversation with the other girls.

Destroyed, Sam gently refused a party favor bag held out to her by Gretchen's dad. "No thanks, Mr. Ferris, I have to go. I told my mom I'd wait out front."

Avoiding eye contact with the other girls, Sam treaded slowly down the hall to the front door. She heard laughter from the kitchen behind her, and knew it was at her expense. Just like her mom had warned her, even though she tried to do everything right, Sam had become 'that girl.'

The following week at school, many of the girls in Sam's class froze her out completely. Suddenly, she became the victim of fierce bullying. While Sam previously enjoyed the protection of her cool, well-loved older brother, Brad had moved up to middle school that fall. Sam was on her own, and people were prepared to hurt her both emotionally and physically. During gym class, when they played dodgeball, Sam pretended she was sick and went to the nurse, rather than be a target for intentional pelting by her former friends.

The girls were merciless in their daily attacks. They told Sam she was ugly, that she looked like a boy, that she sounded like a boy, that she was stupid, that her clothes were unfashionable. She wasn't allowed to sit at certain seats during lunch or use now off-limits parts of the playground at recess.

"Mom please, please don't make me go to school, please! Everyone hates me." Sam tried repeatedly to engage her mother, to seek advice, and even to beg for help. Unfortunately, Beverly was too taken up with working full time while also managing Kimmy's struggles, and by this point Ray was too preoccupied trying to bask in the reflected glow of Brad's athletic achievements.

Left on her own to navigate the increasingly hostile environment, she started taking solo walks around the perimeter of the playground during recess, which was only met with calls that she was a "weirdo." She even asked the teacher to let her spend lunch in the library.

"Sam, don't you think it would be better for you to make an effort? Just try, you'll see. You can't make friendships if you don't even try."

Sam started bringing a book to recess, sitting as close as possible to the door that led back into school, trying to lose herself in the pages until her daily nightmare was over.

When Sam's birthday arrived, Bev ignored every cry for help Sam made regarding her scholastic suffering, and invited the whole class.

The girls teased Sam for her lack of social awareness and her hubris in expecting any of them to attend. Only the boys showed up. Learning her lesson, the next year, in third grade, Sam invited only the boys, which of course made the girls in class verbally accost her for excluding them, even though Sam knew they would have declined, anyway.

By fourth grade, birthday parties grew smaller across the board, and most students, boys and girls alike, invited only a handful of close friends to sleep over at their house. Sam couldn't have the boys sleep over, but she tested the waters to see if she could make something else work. She brought up her birthday in advance with some of her classmates, but their non-committal responses filled her with the fear of throwing a party to which no one might show.

Deflated, Sam asked her family if she could just go out somewhere to dinner with them, which led to a round of mocking from her sister. (Which, as always, led to a fight when Brad stepped in to defend her.) By the time she was ten years old, Sam resolved to never celebrate her birthday again, because it simply wasn't worth the disappointment and dread. Her family respected her wishes and from then on ignored her birthday as well.

* * *

Staring at the bedroom ceiling in her apartment, Sam wished she could go back in time and skip Gretchen's party, or at least stand up for herself when blatant lies were told about her. How many times had she imagined calling out Katie? But it was too late, the damage was done and played out over and over each day for the rest of elementary school. She remembered the desperation she felt each time she asked her parents to let her switch schools, and the devastation when they denied her requests because it would be complicating for Kimmy.

No matter how much she tried to forget this memory, she couldn't prevent it taking her mind hostage. Sam could remember every insult as if it was being hurled at her all over again in real time. She could physically feel the pain and shame. Sam knew it was the reason for many of her issues that shaped her life: her inability to trust other people, difficulty in making friends, and fear of participating in social activities.

Sam despaired that it had so much power over her. She hated that neither Gretchen nor Katie probably had the slightest memory of what they did to her, nor that she even existed. That Sam's tormentors could forget her but she couldn't forget them added insult to injury. Even more, she hated having to relive it as if she was time traveling back into her younger self each time. The pain never lessened.

The memory ran its course, for now. Sam adjusted her pillow, pulled her covers more tightly, and tried to think of better memories to help her fall asleep. That didn't work, so she attempted to exhaust her mind. She recited the states alphabetically, forward and reverse. She named all of the state capitals. Then she listed, in alphabetical order, every country in the world she could think of. But this just caused her to be annoyed when she reached the letter "K" (Kenya) and realized she had forgotten a country that started with a "B." (Bhutan)

When it became clear geography was unsuccessful, she tried to wear herself out by recalling, in chronological order, each President of the United States, along with their respective Vice Presidents. Just when she started to feel her eyelids get heavy around James Garfield, she suddenly remembered a dreadful presentation she once gave in her American history class. The humiliation shot through her body, and she was once again wide awake.

Chapter 6: King of the Hill

2018
(ONE YEAR BEFORE GUY FAWKES FEST)

One morning, after a long night of reliving a cavalcade of her deepest regrets, Sam groggily wiped at her eyes as she reached for her glasses. Slowly she remembered what caused her anxiety the night before: she was scheduled to go to her parents' house for a family brunch. She wasn't ready to face the day, and like an automaton went through the motions of showering and getting dressed.

She didn't feel like seeing her family, but there wasn't really a way to get out of it at this point without causing trouble. It was about a year before the Guy

Fawkes party, and she'd been feeling especially stuck in a rut. Returning to her childhood home would not improve her feelings of having made no progress in her life. Going home only made her feel more panicked that she still hadn't hit any of what she considered to be average adult achievements in her life. Every time she stepped through the front door she imagined how much her younger self would be disheartened to learn that, no, things did not get better.

Sam couldn't recall many happy gatherings with her immediate family. Mostly she thought of ruined holidays, from New Year's to Christmas and everything in between, as well as milestone events like Sam's graduation. There was no occasion her sister couldn't hijack and make about herself, causing grief for the entire family. Events usually ended with Kimmy attacking Sam, Brad attacking Kimmy to defend Sam, her dad disappearing, and her mother splitting up her siblings before sending them to their bedrooms to cool off.

As a child, while the others fought, Sam slipped out of the house and rode her bicycle to the creek as an escape. Nature always welcomed her, which perhaps was why she had pursued both a degree and a career in environmental conservation. At night, to avoid family drama, Sam crawled out on the roof of the garage, accessed from an upstairs window, where she could be alone with her thoughts. She felt guilty, but sometimes she found herself wishing on the stars for her family to be like it was before Kimmy was born.

Even into adulthood, going home to family events filled her with dread because she knew that if Kimmy was there, she'd be ready to judge her life with a fresh load of humiliating barbs. Sam was surprised how much interest Kimmy seemed to take in her life, when Sam knew so little about her sister's.

As adults, Sam and Kimmy had no direct contact outside of occasional family gatherings. No emails, texts, calls; they weren't even connected on social media. Half of the time Sam wasn't even sure where her sister lived, as she bounced from city to city, frequently changing jobs not long after starting them. Bev tried to downplay Kimmy's trouble in keeping a job, and treated each move like the fresh start where Kimmy would finally find success and settle down. Sam knew Kimmy had lived in Pittsburgh, Buffalo, Toledo, Fort Wayne, and Evansville... and maybe somewhere in Michigan, too, but she wasn't certain.

She recalled Kimmy always being popular and having many boyfriends in high school. Although she dated a lot in college, she'd never brought any of the guys home with her. From what Sam could pull together from conversations with Bev, who was in regular communications with her youngest daughter,

Kimmy had an active dating life as an adult, and had once even moved to a new city to follow one of the men she was seeing. It didn't work out, but Bev believed that Kimmy would find "the right one," eventually.

Sam tried to avoid seeing Kimmy as much as she could when her sister was in town, which got easier as they grew older. Kimmy came home less frequently as she moved around, although sometimes she'd make surprise appearances. Whenever Kimmy did show up at family gatherings, skewering Sam was high on her list of must-do items. Kimmy's favorite topic was Sam's lack of a romantic life, emphasizing how very lonely Sam must be. Sam was used to it, and had learned long ago to stop fighting back. Nothing she said would change Kimmy's mind or bring her roasts to an end.

Their parents weren't much help in encouraging Kimmy to be a better person—Bev would make a small protest to leave Sam alone, but give up as soon as Kimmy pressed on. Ray would often excuse himself from the table and disappear into his study for the rest of the visit. Brad always stood up for Sam when he was present, but it didn't change the fact that Kimmy's judgements hurt, especially because Sam truly did feel alone.

She was always glad to see Brad though, who Sam, without hyperbole, considered her hero throughout her life. Even before he joined the Air

Force, before his multiple deployments, before he earned citations and medals for his exemplary actions, he was the bravest person she'd ever known.

Sam's high opinion of Brad was not one she'd reached on her own, but had been cemented in her mind, along with the minds of every kid in their neighborhood, when Sam and Brad were children. As she got ready for brunch, Sam's mind drifted to the moment she knew Brad was not like other people. She could see all of it clearly.

[1991]

Sam was in kindergarten and Brad was in fifth grade, and they had just moved to the neighborhood. Sam struggled to work up the nerve to introduce herself to the other kids. During her first week of school, she had practically no one to interact with, except her deskmates during assigned class activities.

Everyone already seemed to know each other from preschool or church or sports. While she could push herself to say "hello" to her peers one-on-one, she was daunted by pairs and groups, and couldn't propel herself forward to speak with them. Each day she was relieved at any opportunities she had to sight her brother around the school, even if only to wave to him, because she knew she wasn't completely alone.

Brad was both charismatic and naturally outgoing, and assimilated easily into his new environment. He quickly made many friends in the neighborhood and had no shortage of people to sit with during lunch at school, but a few older kids remained reticent in casting their approval on him. He knew he needed to earn their respect, and learned that the fastest way to do this was on their turf. In this case, their turf came with a particular challenge that only the boldest could conquer.

While it was neither large nor significant enough to merit a real name on a map, to all the kids in the area it was known as "Suicide Hill." Hidden through a small bit of woods with a few houses spread out nearby, it was perilously steep, difficult even to walk down. The hill led to a creek at the bottom, just before the deeper woods with no houses began.

The rite of passage took two separate forms, depending on the time of year. In the winter, volunteers were tasked with sledding downhill headfirst, with the goal of hopping the creek before falling into the icy water running over frozen rocks, and landing safely on the other side.

In warmer weather, a bicycle was the vehicle of choice. At this time, helmets and knee pads were unheard of, so the challenge was not without real danger. However, anyone who attempted it earned respect to go along with their bruises. If you could successfully get down the hill, pull a wheelie over the creek, and pump the brakes before smashing into a tree, you become an instant legend.

Year after year, older kids judged the efforts of younger kids and any new arrivals in town to see who deserved to hang out with them, receiving head nods and high fives in school. No one could remember how this tradition started, nor how long it had been going on. It was simply one of those things that was taken for granted.

It was mid-September, so Brad knew what he needed to do. Sam spied him trying furtively to creep out from their house, undetected. Why wouldn't he want anyone to know he was going out? She decided to follow him, just to keep an eye on him. Sam wasn't as outgoing as Brad, but even she had heard of Suicide Hill, and wanted to avoid the area at all costs. So when Sam saw him walking his bike in the direction of the woods, she realized that was exactly where Brad was headed.

Her stomach dropped, and she ran as fast as her feet could carry her to catch up, gasping and breathless beyond ability to form complete sentences.

Brad set down his bike, concerned something was wrong with her. "Sam? Are you ok?" He knelt to look directly into her eyes, placing a hand on her shoulder.

"No suicide!" She exclaimed in an exhale. "Not safe!" She wheezed.

A smirk broke over his face. "Is that what you're worried about? Samwise, I'll be fine." He saw that she was unconvinced, and still looked terrified. "But if you don't want to watch, that's ok. It won't hurt my feelings. How about this? You stay here, and when I'm done, we'll walk to 7-11 and I'll get you a Slurpee. And a Butterfinger too, if you want. Sound good?"

Sam burst into tears. "The kids at school said people die in that creek, Brad. They DIE!"

Brad looked around for a moment and let out a deep sigh. "That's just because they want to sound tough. You think if anyone really died people could still go there? No way. It'd be gated off or something. They probably just want to impress you since you're the new kid."

Looking both anxious and resolute, he added, "I gotta go, I heard they get there early, and I want to make sure I get a chance to show 'em what I can do. Don't worry Sam. I'll be back soon."

"I'll go home and... I'll... I'll tell Mom!" The threat was the last resort, indeed in Sam's mind it was the nuclear option guaranteed to stop her brother. She could think of no worse warning.

"Sam, I gotta do this. Look, you can go tell Mom, but by the time you get back with her and Kimberly-Anne, I'll already be done, and she'll be annoyed you interrupted her. Don't make her worry for nothing, Sam. All that will happen is people will know who I am, so they'll be nicer to me, and when they find out you're my sister, they'll be nicer to you, too."

With a confident, loving smile, he pulled her face up to look at him and brushed away the tears rolling down her cheeks, adding, "Be brave, little hobbit."

With that, he picked up his bike and walked toward the peak of Suicide Hill, leaving Sam beside herself with panic and dread. She stayed behind for a moment, trying to make herself brave like Brad wanted her to be. Her brother could die, a notion she couldn't bear, but she understood there was no stopping him, and that maybe her being there and cheering him on would even make him successful. Wiping her face, Sam followed her brother, her only friend in the world, feeling like she was watching him go to his execution.

Brad was deep in conversation with a group of fifth and sixth graders when she arrived, hovering just outside their circle. One of the older boys gestured, explaining the rules by which a run down Suicide Hill could be deemed successful.

Sam didn't think she could stand it, but then to her relief saw some of her classmates gathered in a clump with the other spectators. She sidled over to them with feigned calm, giving her best attempt to hide her absolute terror over her brother's impending doom.

"Sam, is that your brother?" asked Renee, a fierce girl from her class whose shiny, bobbed hair always perfectly framed her face.

"Yeah." She was afraid to say more, lest they notice that she'd been crying.

"He's going for it, huh? Think he'll make it? Like, how good is he?"

"Never mind how good he is," a third grader interjected. "How good are his brakes?" He dissolved into a fit of cackles, obviously amused at himself.

"Shut up, Kevin!" fired Renee, looking ready to tackle him into submission.

Jenny, a sweet girl with long brown hair, forever dressed in floral turtlenecks, velveteen pants, and a big, plastic heart locket, reached out and grabbed Sam's hand.

"Ignore him Sam, he's never even tried it, and when his older sister did, she wussed out and cried like a baby. Remember?" Jenny looked to Renee for reinforcement, which she provided.

"Yeah, she slammed her brakes two feet down the hill and wiped out. It was, like, really embarrassing. She was in sixth grade, and couldn't even make it halfway down the hill before crying. She ran home and hasn't come back out here ever again. She left so quick she didn't even take her bike with her! As long as your brother doesn't do anything like Kevin's sister, he'll be fine!"

Sam did not feel reassured. What kind of people were these, judging each other for the natural reaction of not wanting to kill or maim yourself for the amusement of others? Would she be expected to do this some day, too? She didn't want to.

If that's what it took to make these people like you, then they weren't worth it, and she needed to let her brother know she thought so, that it wasn't too late for common sense to prevail, that if they left now they could spend the rest of the afternoon playing Super Mario Bros. on the NES.

A sudden chorus of "Here we go, here we go!" sharply drew her attention.

The crowd quieted and lined up to watch the main event. All eyes were on Brad, except from Sam, who squeezed hers shut and seemed to stop breathing. She was grateful for Jenny's hand wrapped around hers, for Renee's shoulder bracing her. In an instant, she heard the sounds all jumbled together, the chanting of "3...2...1," the crowd screaming "GO," and then the splash, combined with the horrific sound of metal scraping against rock.

Brad made it down the hill alright, but unable to clear the creek, he fell short, tumbling into the water, landing on some rocks in the bed. From the top of the hill, Sam could see the blood, and froze. She wanted to run to him, sobbing and screaming, but something told her that would only serve to upset him and make the other kids mock both siblings. She couldn't do that to him, not as his first impression on so many of these people they'd have to face every day for the rest of their lives. She simply took a huge breath in, as Jenny, Renee, and all the other kids clapped for him. They didn't care that he hadn't made it. He'd tried, and in their books that made him one of them.

Renee and Jenny tried to cheer Sam that her brother was cool, that it didn't look like so much blood, and at least nothing was broken. She was confused at their calm, and annoyed at the realization that some of her brother's cool now reflected on to her. She didn't care if these wild people liked her, she just wanted to know if Brad was going to live. Renee especially made a point to let everyone know that the kid who just made it down the hill was Sam's brother. Sam felt faint, and channeled all of her energy into meek head nods and smiles in acknowledgement of the congratulations she received.

As her brother reached the summit once again, she saw his bike was fine, but his leg was not. There was a huge gash on his left shin, cleaving it from the calf. Sam tried not to vomit, steadying herself, placing one deliberate foot in front of the other, attempting to create a distance between the crowd and herself to reach her brother. She made it about three whole steps when she heard gasps, and took in the latest development.

Not satisfied at simply making the effort and surviving, her brother geared up to go again. What madness had taken hold of him? The kids around Brad looked nervous, patted him on the back, and reassured him, "You're good, it was cool, you don't have to go again, no one ever goes a second time in a row, and maybe you should get your leg cleaned up."

One of the older girls emphasized, "Look, I'm not sure where you lived before, but I can tell you that the creek water here is the last thing you want in an open wound. You need to get cleaned up before it gets infected."

Head nods from the spectators affirmed her wisdom, but Brad didn't listen. He didn't hear or see anyone, he was completely focused on his objective. Sam had never seen that look on his face, locked in only on what he perceived as his mission. She wanted to stop him, but like everyone else she was struck silent by his bravado.

He took off. Down he went, gliding like a Tour de France champion, effortlessly sailing down Suicide Hill, as the creek water and blood on his leg flew behind him like a comet's tail. Sam couldn't close her eyes this time. She felt that if he died, she should at the very least be able to tell their parents in grisly detail how it happened.

Brad was in the air. The whole crowd collectively held their breath in anticipation, and then he landed, safely on the other side. Turning his handles and applying the brakes, he stopped just short of crashing face first into a giant poplar. Facing the crowd, he flared a huge, triumphant grin at them. The kids cried out in disbelief and amazement, as if his safe landing was their own.

Brad crossed back through the creek, and as he brought his bike up the hill, found himself surrounded by a throng of people wanting to give him high fives, help him carry his bike, and introduce themselves. The older kids warmly welcomed him back to the top, and, knowing exactly how to play the moment, he deferentially thanked them for letting him give it another try. They approved of his humility, and after downplaying their own excitement for a moment, joined in the merriment of the other children.

Todd, a fourth-grader perpetually dressed in a Cub Scout uniform, walked up with a field bag on his hip, and an air of authority.

"All right everyone, give us some room and let me take a look at that leg." He gestured for Brad to sit on a near-by stump, and Brad, too bewildered by this little boy's confidence to ask questions, obliged.

Todd lived with his grandparents and had seen every episode of M*A*S*H, so he was the closest they had to a medic. He routinely stole first aid supplies from the full, floor-to-ceiling hallway closet his grandparents kept stocked with such items. The crowd obeyed, moving back, while their resident field surgeon assessed the damage.

"I've seen worse," he offered Brad. Then, speaking to the crowd, "Remember when Kerry broke her ankle and her wrist, or when Chuck bashed his face and nearly lost an eye on his handlebar?"

Brad chuckled in relief, looking at his sister, "See Sam, it could have been much worse, I could have wound up like Kerry or Chuck."

The crowd agreed, they had seen worse and Brian, a second-grader oddly obsessed with Monty Python, called out, "It's just a flesh wound," which elicited a mixture of groans and chortles from kids who'd heard him shout that too many times.

"Well, let me just clean this up for you," Todd set to work. From his bag he retrieved bottles of alcohol and iodine, a roll of gauze, scissors, and some medical tape. Looking at Sam he asked, "You're the sister?" She nodded in affirmation.

"Good. Now when you get home, you'll want to take your mom's tweezers and make sure you get all these little bits of rock out." To Brad he added "It will probably sting when you shower, but you need to make sure you get it really clean."

Todd deftly cleansed the leg, rinsing first with alcohol and dabbing with iodine, before applying gauze and securing it with tape. Although blood seeped through, Todd confidently proclaimed, "You'll live." Todd's prognosis caused additional celebration from the onlookers. Todd used the alcohol to rinse his own hands, then gingerly placed the items back into his makeshift med kit.

Sam finally managed to form words, whispering thanks to Todd for his attentiveness, and inquiring, "Will he have a scar?"

"If he does," Greg, one of the sixth graders pronounced, "it will be AWESOME!"

More elation filled the hill. Someone handed Brad a bright blue beverage in a tiny, opaque, barrel-shaped plastic bottle, which he chugged gratefully. Sam took it from him as he stood back up and accepted his bike from, of all people, Kevin.

It felt like ages before they were done saying goodbye to everyone. They headed back to the house, hoping to sneak in and hide the bike until Brad could clean it. Beverly was outside, Kimmy in her arms, looking for them. When Brad tumbled into the creek, his watch stopped working, and with all the post-jump elation they'd lost track of the time.

Sensing the shifting circumstances, Sam stepped in front of her brother, trying unsuccessfully to block their mother's view. Bev immediately had all three kids in the mini-van, racing toward urgent care. After a brief wait, a doctor saw Brad and gave him no small number of stitches for his still-bleeding leg.

When asked how it happened, Sam opened her mouth to brag that he'd beaten Suicide Hill, but one look from Brad stopped her. She looked away and busied herself with her baby sister, trying to tune out her mother and brother who were loudly arguing in front of the doctor. Brad finally stood by his story that it had been a simple accident, that he just wasn't used to the area yet, and he promised in the future he'd be more careful.

The doctor was no fool, speaking over Brad's promises directly to their mother. "I know you're new here, so word of advice. Don't let your kids near Suicide Hill again. You wouldn't believe the stitches, casts, and crutches I've had to administer over the years thanks to that stupid creek. Not that they'd ever admit that's where it happens, but

I'm no stranger to the Hill myself, and well, kids never learn, do they?"

Beverly looked confused but thanked him. She loaded herself up with a diaper bag, purse, and Kimmy in her car seat, before angrily snapping at Brad and Sam that it was time to leave. As they exited the room, Brad and his mother continued to snipe, while the doctor whispered to Sam, "Did he make it across?" Sam looked at the doctor with a conspiratorial smile, nodded her head yes, and followed her family to the car.

Ray was home by then, asleep in the living room, sprawled on the armchair with an open book. Somehow, he'd missed the fact that the house was completely empty, his entire family unaccounted for. This only increased Bev's indignation at the entire day. Livid, she woke him and explained her best interpretation of the incident. Ray, clearly wanting to shut the whole thing down, sighed, and yelled at Brad not to do anything so stupid again. "Can't you see how upset your mother is?"

Sam felt confused by the emotions fighting within her. She was mad at her brother for risking his life, exhilarated at his victory, overwhelmed by the children who rushed up to her, scared of how angry her parents had been, but most of all, she was inspired. She wanted to be brave like Brad. At school on Monday, Sam found her adoration for Brad reinforced by the sudden fame her brother had achieved, which earned her the benefit of second-hand admiration from many of her classmates.

Walking in to school, Brad received a hero's welcome, and Sam was suddenly imbued with being cool by association with the man of the hour. People oohed and ahhed over Brad's extensive stitches, crying "Gnarly!" less with repulsion than appreciation. He was dubbed a local Evel Knievel, and everyone wanted to see him and be seen with him.

People who had been at Suicide Hill wanted to relive the triumph as if it was their own. As they excitedly retold the story with increasing hyperbole and extreme exaggeration, they invited Sam into the conversations, even if only for the purpose of backing up their version of events.

"Then he went up ten feet in the air, then did a wheelie!" a fifth-grader recounted, with her younger sister happily embellishing, "And took his hands off too, and crossed them over his chest like this, because it was so easy for him! Right Sam?" She asked, pulling Sam into their circle to verify her brother's heroics.

For the kids who had, unfortunately, missed the bike trick of the century, they couldn't get enough detail, trying to live it vicariously through the retelling. All week long, they asked Sam for her take on things. Although she was unused to the attention, she didn't mind that Brad's death-defying stunt had broken the ice with, seemingly, the entire school in one moment. She was one of them, now, sharing a common bond.

Suddenly, it didn't matter that Sam was shy. Brad fixed it and arranged for her to be known by the whole school as his sister. Still, she felt a nagging sensation that people didn't actually like her for herself, only for her affiliation with her brother. She felt that she couldn't trust their interest as a real desire for friendship, rather than wanting to be part of the big story. For the rest of her life, part of her always carried this self-doubt. It held her back from jumping in to make deep connections, never sure if people actually liked her for who she was, rather than for who she knew.

Brad's trip down Suicide Hill became a formative moment for a girl who was not naturally bold. When she found herself in situations requiring courage, she thought back to how her brother looked before his second run down Suicide Hill. Sadly, it also meant sometimes placing herself in precarious positions simply because it's what she thought would impress him, even when he wasn't there to witness it.

During the few years after his triumph, desperate to earn companionship on her own merits, she accidentally injured herself more than a few times, trying not to embarrass herself in front of potential friends by channeling Brad. These memories left her feeling stupid, embarrassed, and also a little afraid. Thinking of trying to perform stunts with her bicycle like her friends or jump into a pond with her cousins that was realistically too shallow for safe diving, she would flash back to these moments and feel the literal fear again, amazed she'd allowed herself to be goaded into potential harm just to show she was as brave as Brad.

Brad's triumph at Suicide Hill was the first time Sam saw her brother so intent on completing a mission that he didn't care about the expense to his own safety or well-being. While this attitude served him well, and earned him distinction during his deployments, it was also the first moment in his lifelong disregard for his own safety in service of putting on a brave face.

* * *

Realizing she'd spent far too long lost in her flashback, Sam got into her car, mentally on auto-pilot until a notification on her phone caught her attention.

"You on your way?" The text read. "She isn't coming, btw." Brad anticipated Sam's concern.

Relieved to avoid Kimmy's latest performative interrogation about her life, Sam continued driving to her childhood home. She replied to Brad that she was en route, which was met with a thumbs up. Along her drive, Sam anticipated the usual order of events: Sam would arrive, and her parents would be underwhelmed, giving her a tepid greeting. Ray would shuffle off somewhere until food was ready to serve. Bev would excuse herself to the kitchen. Sam would offer to help her mother cook, but Bev would wave Sam out of the kitchen explaining she'd only be in the way and that everything was under control.

Sam couldn't begrudge her father making himself scarce so often when Bev clearly didn't want to deal with any of them. When the food was ready, they'd all gather at the dining room table to engage in surface-level conversation on neutral topics. If there was an important sports event airing, they might stay for a while to watch TV with Ray, and then everyone would go home.

Every time she went home, she wished she had someone to bring to these awful things, to help her get through them. Sam didn't understand why everyone kept going through the motions and forcing these brunches to happen when no one seemed to enjoy them. At least she'd get to see Brad and his wife, Stacey, whom she adored more than almost anyone else. While Kimmy's arrival in Sam's life brought darkness, Stacey was a radiant light of love and warmth.

Brad and Stacey met as cadets at the Air Force Academy. Stacey was two years older than Brad, and by all accounts didn't give him the time of day at first, but he quickly established himself as a standout, not just for his skills but for his fearlessness.

Although Brad intrigued Stacey, he had an uphill battle winning her affection, because a relationship was the last thing on her mind. Stacey's home life had made Brad's look idyllic. She never talked about it, but from visible markings, including the thick, jagged scar across her clavicle, combined with the few comments made by Brad over the years, Sam pieced together the kind of violent upbringing Stacey had survived before starting over at the Academy.

With persistent kindness and reliability, Brad eventually earned Stacey's trust. They married not long after his graduation. The only relatives of Stacey's in attendance were a great aunt and uncle with whom she lived with for a time when she'd run away from home as a child. From what Brad explained, they hadn't been legally allowed to keep her. Stacey's parents restricted contact between them, but they had persisted in being there for her anyway. They were the only people who had attended Stacey's high school graduation, and sent her care packages throughout her time at the Academy and in the Air Force.

After completing her five years of active duty, Stacey moved into the reserves while Brad moved up the ranks, frequently volunteering for dangerous missions. Sam didn't know all of the details, but he got injured several times, with one situation being a particularly close call.

No matter what challenges they faced, though, Stacey was there to support him. When family gatherings went badly, as they often did, Sam marveled at how Stacey consoled Brad, wishing she had that kind of support. Brad and Stacey had a baby they'd named after Ray, affectionately called Ray-Ray, who became the center of their world.

Stacey not only brought out the best in Brad, she was also the sister Sam always wanted, and more than that, a friend. Stacey showed great sensitivity toward Sam, making her feel seen, even when Sam's parents forgot about her. Stacey honored Sam's wish to keep her birthday low-key, but still made sure to send her a card and text each year to mark the occasion. When Kimmy got out of line, Stacey was the only person able to wrangle her, keeping her from escalating her verbal attacks on Sam. When Stacey asked Sam to be Ray-Ray's godmother, it was the first time in ages Sam could remember feeling wanted.

Focusing on the opportunity to see Brad, Stacey, and Ray-Ray, Sam summoned up the courage to face her parents as part of the deal. The brunch was easy enough, and without Kimmy serving the role of Grand Inquisitor, Sam avoided discussing her personal life. She focused on work, which both Brad and Stacey spoke of positively. She also spent time playing with Ray-Ray, experiencing a longing to have a child of her own some day. It seemed a far off possibility, which prompted her to remember just how single she was, which then led her to think about the one woman in particular for whom she'd developed serious feelings.

Tali was the only person in her life with whom she actually found herself imagining a future together. Sam felt that with Tali, she could have what Brad and Stacey had. The only problem was that the attraction took place entirely within Sam's head, where it had been planted years ago, encouraged each time Sam saw her again.

Chapter 7: The Object of Sam's Affection

2005 - 2019
(COLLEGE - GUY FAWKES FEST)

Fourteen years was too long to pine for someone, and yet, for nearly a decade and a half, Sam harbored a slow-growing, unrequited affection. She mistook it as love, but anyone who has been in love clearly would recognize it more accurately as infatuation. The affection was not only one-way, but the object of it, a married woman, remained keenly unaware that such serious feelings were growing in her direction.

They attended the same college together, but even Sam would admit they hadn't been friends. In fact, they only passively circled in each other's orbits, in that particular way which happens at small schools. If Sam really thought about it, she'd realize they'd never even been directly introduced.

During sophomore year, some of Sam's friends lived with Em, a tall, lean woman, nearly devoid of physical features that would have tilted her in either the masculine or feminine direction. To say she was physically attractive was not entirely accurate. Em was by no means ugly, but what really made an impression was her presence. Despite her slim frame, Em was an imposing figure who effortlessly caught the attentions of everyone around her. Em never walked; she strolled with the confident swagger of a Hollywood cowboy.

Sam's mental image of Em nearly always included an amused, closed-mouth smirk tilted on her face, with a bottle of what passed for "nicer" beer in their less well-funded days firmly in one hand, and a beautiful girl beside her. Their friends teased that she had a seemingly magical ability to "turn" every woman she spoke to just a little bit gay. Em argued that these ladies had actually always harbored latent homosexual feelings, but simply never before acted on them. Still, by junior year, she'd dated so many formerly-thought-to-be-straight women that her friends jokingly called her the "queer alchemist."

Em, however, was not Sam's quiet crush of half a lifetime. That person was Em's final partner in college, now her wife, Tali. A wee thing, barely five feet tall, with big, dark curls and mischievous, onyx eyes. Sam knew a little of Tali's story, but it was so similar to Em's previous gaggle of girlfriends that by now it was almost a cliche.

Tali came from a strict, southern evangelical upbringing, and her family grew increasingly dismayed by her life choices. First, she cared about high school to the exclusion of a romantic life. They couldn't recall ever seeing her give any of those poor, "nice" boys from their church the time of day, no matter how overt their attention.

Then, despite her parents' desire for her to attend an evangelical university, she decided to go out of state to... a liberal arts college. To study humanities. (The horror!) This was, in fact, her parents' nightmare. That is, it was as bad as Tali's parents could have feared, before she discovered her sexuality and, after a month of dating Em boldly, defiantly, came out.

If Sam was honest with herself, she'd admit that she never really noticed Tali too much during college. Firmly entrenched in her closet (save for one covert kiss in high school), Sam was more impressed by Em's personality. Only later did Sam become aware of her feelings for Tali.

For the first four or five years after college, Sam tried not to mind being alone in life. However, that most insidious force—comparison—crept into her mind. Over the next few years through her late twenties, it took hold, defining her life not by what Sam had, but what her friends had that she lacked.

As her former college classmates began to put down roots, get married, buy homes, and have kids, Sam found herself stuck in neutral. Everyone else seemed to have been given some kind of life charter and were following it to admirable results, while she was rudderless. She was unsure of how to jump start her adult life.

More than just companionship, Sam wanted love. This was a bigger challenge, as Sam didn't know the first thing about getting into a relationship with another woman. She had kept her feelings so tight to herself during high school and college that she'd missed the natural opportunities to make low-stakes dating efforts.

She tried visiting gay bars on her own, but they only made her feel more out of place. Other people arrived in packs, scrutinizing each other's prospects. Sam still didn't have a wing woman to guide her. She often wound up standing awkwardly for a few hours, nursing the same beer or cocktail all night, giving timid, hopeful glances, until, feeling discouraged, she slunk out and went home.

Sam's most satisfying moments of human interaction in adult life were the fairly frequent parties when she saw her old college friends, especially Eddie and Johanna, who threw parties for seemingly any reason or holiday. Arbor Day, Flag Day, Groundhog Day—they threw parties for them all, fully committing to the themes. While Sam never took for granted that she would be included in each subsequent gathering, she kept finding herself on the invite list, and always accepted.

She knew she was not anyone's best friend, but nor would she consider many of them her close friends. After all, they did not even know she was hiding part of her identity from them, and had been for years. Afraid to tell them the truth or ask for their help navigating the dating scene, Sam never felt completely at ease opening up to them. Still, these college friends were the primary source of socialization for Sam.

For their part, it seemed to her friends that Sam's preference was to be alone so she could live life on her own terms. None of them really knew what Sam did, nor how she filled her days. They were always warm and welcoming, though, asking her easy questions about her work or books she'd read lately or shows she watched.

However, the conversation usually trickled off when Sam ran out of contributions to share. Outside of consuming culture, she had no shared experiences with them—relationships, travel, creative endeavors—which she could draw on to keep conversations going.

Over time, some people recognized her recurring lack of input, and anticipating it, switched the conversation as soon as they covered the basics. She understood that her friends were trying to spare her from feeling put on the spot when she had nothing to say, but nevertheless Sam often felt inadequate, and a little humiliated. The only people who never made Sam feel this way at parties were Em and Tali.

Initially after graduation, Sam had given neither Em nor Tali much thought. They weren't people she sought out specifically, having never achieved the instant messaging or texting level of friendship with them during school. Yet, without intending to remain in their lives, she saw them regularly throughout their post-college lives. She ran into them at mutual friends' birthday parties, engagement parties, bridal and baby showers. She never saw them outside of a festive setting, but at a succession of post-college social events she began to gravitate toward them to pick up where they had left off.

They were nearly always in a larger group of people, usually completely enchanted by Tali's storytelling. Em, who no longer gave off that strong vibe that had drawn so many women to her in college, was content to stand to the side, helping Tali tell her stories by occasionally providing more details.

As a pair, they were captivating, and Sam liked that she didn't have to provide much to the conversation when she was in a group with them. She could enjoy the party without the pressure of being "on." They never seemed to get tired of her, and instead, made Sam feel like she belonged. Tali had an infectious energy that Sam caught more deeply the longer they spent time together.

Sam knew that as long as Em and Tali were at a party, she wouldn't have a hard time finding her way into a conversation. With each event, Sam grew more eager to see them, especially Tali, who always gave Sam a huge smile that gave the impression Tali was genuinely delighted to see her.

Sometimes, when they were in a big circle talking, Tali put her arm around Sam's shoulder, pulling her into the crowd and making Sam feel like she wasn't just a courtesy invite, but a vital part of the party. She liked the way being in proximity to Tali made her feel, how she could ride Tali's conversational momentum and be a more engaging, interesting person by being near her.

Unexpectedly, Sam found herself growing resentful of Em and Tali, of their partnership. It made no sense to her, the way they were so wildly different, yet complemented each other just so. One night, when she realized they'd left a party without specifically saying goodbye to her, she felt grumpy and disenfranchised, which caught her by surprise.

Examining her feelings once she got home, Sam understood that her resentment wasn't just for what those two had together, but was specifically related to Tali. She wasn't sure the exact moment it happened, but somewhere along the way, Sam had developed feelings for her. It was more than just having guaranteed conversation partners; it was being close to Tali, to her energy, to her light. Sam thought it must be love. She didn't know when she'd see Tali again, but she hoped it would be soon.

Chapter 8: Now, Voyager

2018
(ONE YEAR BEFORE GUY FAWKES FEST)

As Sam and her college cohort entered their mid-thirties, invitations for formal events arrived less frequently. People tend not to have too many repeat weddings, and there are only so many baby showers a person is willing to have, so it's natural for fewer such events to occur.

More than simply being disappointed she had no set date to see Tali again, Sam realized she hadn't fully appreciated how much she relied on these milestone celebrations to help her feel moored to life and connected to other humans. She worried that her entire existence needed a serious change—a disruption to get her out of her rut—but she didn't know where to look.

Having watched *Now, Voyager* and *Summertime* perhaps too many times with her Grandma Jeannie, Sam looked to those movies as inspirations on how to fix everything she felt was wrong with her life. On a whim, she decided to go abroad. No more waiting to live, no longer content to be a spectator in someone else's life, she planned to fill her life with a series of adventures. Then, she would have something to share with her college friends. They wouldn't avoid asking her what was new in her life, because this time she would actually have something to say.

She talked herself into the belief that since many people travel alone, intentionally and successfully, she could, too. Reading blogs and books, she learned the advantages of solo travel—namely, that she didn't have to care if other people were interested or entertained. She would be master of her own schedule and budget.

Sam became convinced that, just like Bette Davis in *Now, Voyager*, she was going to get an automatic personality makeover simply by being in proximity to worldly travelers and ancient places. She'd come back a changed woman, confident and glamorous, ready to find her partner.

Sam had never traveled internationally before, but she was committed. It was time for Sam to see the world. She was methodical and relied on lists, so she created one to decide where to go. She chose a few places to consider, evaluating time and cost, language proficiency needed, and alignment with her interests, particularly the environment.

With so many places she wanted to see, Sam decided to look into a cruise. She wasn't sure how she'd be on the open sea, though, having never been on a large ship. In addition to her fear of becoming sea-sick, she also worried about being stuck on a floating hotel filled with rowdy children.

One night, Sam saw an ad for a guided river cruise of Northern Europe. In conducting research, she compared the demographics, and decided to go with this more low-key crowd. The idea of being on a ship full of people who reminded her of her grandparents was comforting. She wouldn't need to worry about impressing everyone or being able to keep up with their pace. She booked a single cabin on a July river cruise which would take her to six countries in one vacation.

During the lead-up to her trip, Sam prepared studiously. Learning Japanese in high school and Spanish in college suddenly struck her as silly, since neither would help her at all on this journey.

"Oh well," she thought, "I can always visit Japan or a Spanish-speaking country next time."

She learned at least basic phrases in German, French, Norwegian, and Danish, hoping to use this skill any time they'd disembark. As always, she had a great capacity for memorization, even if her pronunciation would never help her pass for a native speaker. It would at least show the locals and her fellow passengers that she had put in the effort.

As the day of departure approached, she imagined all the new memories she'd make and the stories she'd come home with. So many of her friends were well-traveled, and she'd finally be able to share in their conversations about sites they visited, foods they tried, art they saw, and people they met. On her flight, Sam couldn't seem to get tired enough to sleep. She was too giddy to see whatever the world had to offer her.

Upon arriving at the ship, however, her bubble burst. She immediately discovered that while she was at peace with a solo adventure, other passengers had clearly missed the articles and publications she'd read to build her confidence. The sad looks from fellow trip-goers, betraying their pity for her being alone, became unnerving. For someone who was used to flying under the radar thanks to being unremarkable, she wasn't prepared for how traveling solo had inadvertently cast a spotlight on her.

She was easily two or three decades younger than everyone else on her ship, which caused them to assume a parental attitude toward her. They treated Sam a little like a mascot of sorts, a stand-in for the younger adults in their lives. Many of these well-meaning older travelers took it upon themselves to involve her in their plans, no matter how much she protested.

"Are you sure you won't join us dear? That won't be any fun by yourself. Sit with us, there's room!"

Sam couldn't take these invitations at face value, assuming there was an ulterior motive, or that they thought they were doing a good deed by including her. Quietly offended, Sam told herself she didn't need their pity inclusion.

At the same time, she also didn't like how difficult it was to be alone, especially at meal times. She hadn't considered that at each group meal she would have to find someone to sit with. It was her public school cafeteria nightmare come back to life. Multiple times each day she had to brace herself to find an open seat with someone who wouldn't mind her joining them. She hated having to initiate the seating arrangements.

During the first conversations she had with people, she realized she didn't have much to discuss with them. They were all at very different stages in their lives from Sam, so she didn't have shared reference points. Many of them had also been traveling for decades, and swapped casual references to vacations she could only dream of.

Her nostalgia for how easy it was to be herself with her grandparents had clouded her expectations of how easy it would be to fit in, and it didn't take long for Sam to realize that, like every other situation in her life, she didn't belong. Her tour guide was much closer to her age than the rest of the passengers, so Sam tried to find a way to make a positive impression on him. He seemed nice, and everyone else was easily able to joke and laugh with him, but Sam's lifelong insecurities held her back, making her feel like she must be an imposition. He interacted with her in the same welcoming, professional manner he showed each guest, but she couldn't ignore the sense that he was only humoring her.

Sam also felt foolish at how she'd packed. It had been a gap in her research, a rookie international travel mistake. She didn't know that people would have so many types of outfits, and nicer clothing for dinners. She thought they'd be exploring and walking, so she had mostly brought hiking clothes and boots. No matter what they did, she felt as if she was dressed inappropriately for the occasion. Not that it was any different at home, where she'd never known what to wear at any point during her life.

Overwhelmed by her constant faux pas and slip ups, she took to hiding in her cabin until meal times in an effort to limit small talk, which was invariably peppered with questions ranging from mild curiosity to blunt interrogation about her lack of companionship.

"Tell us about yourself. Is there anyone special in your life? Why are you traveling alone? Do you want to be single? Would you be interested in meeting my grandson?"

Although Sam had intentionally chosen a trip with an older demographic, she hadn't counted on just how slow some of the passengers would be. Their itinerary seemed reasonable to Sam, but in reality it was too ambitious for many of her shipmates. The group often fell behind schedule during just the first stop of the day, so they frequently had to adjust the agenda and cancel activities that had been planned for later in the afternoon. Sam resented not being able to see sites she had built up in her mind. At the end of each day, she looked at her printed schedule of what they were supposed to have done, and with a pen scratched out all the things they missed.

Of course, could have made up for this during some of their free, unstructured time, but she skipped out on several excursions that she realized were more geared toward couples and groups. There were some options for individuals, but Sam realized that no matter how much she assumed she'd be fine, she did not feel as confident on her own as she'd hoped. A woman traveling alone must always have her guard up, which is tiring. Still, she couldn't overcome her natural discomfort with new relationships enough to accept overtures of friendship from other cruisers. She heard the other passengers return from their outings, full of life and enthusiasm, and felt more isolated than ever.

Even Sam's linguistic preparation for the trip failed her. She had left home feeling confident in the local languages. After a rough start at making friends on board, she thought perhaps showing people her competence in communications would impress them and make it easier to connect. But the first time they disembarked in Strasbourg, Sam tried to place an order at a cafe. She could remember the French vocabulary, but it all stumbled out of her mouth in an incomprehensible stream.

The cashier patronizingly blinked her eyes, and in slow, loud English, asked Sam what she wanted. Sam felt like the worst stereotype, the ugly American she'd studied so hard not to be. From then on she was too afraid to open her mouth to any wait staff, so she allowed other people to order for her throughout the rest of the trip.

On the final morning of the cruise, Sam heard a loud buzz of activity as she walked into the dining room. She watched her shipmates compare notes on what they wrote in their thank you cards to their tour guide. Feeling foolish, Sam chided herself for not knowing thank you notes were something people did on guided tours—not that she had anything specific to say to their guide, anyway.

She tried to make herself a plate at the buffet, but watching everyone exchange contact information and hug goodbye, promising to stay in touch back in the States, was too much for Sam. She slipped back to her cabin to check once more that everything was packed for her flight home. Confirming it was all accounted for, she sat on the edge of her bed and sighed heavily, trying not to cry.

Overall, the trip disappointed. She'd missed out on many of the landmarks and events she'd most looked forward to experiencing. She hadn't accumulated new memories to carry her through the next time she saw her friends.

She also didn't make any meaningful connections with people even though she'd spent two weeks with them, more time than she'd spent with any group of people since college. Sam accepted that could travel the world, but no matter where she went, she would always be stuck with herself.

Devastated, Sam knew that when she got home and people asked her about the trip, instead of wowing them with her tales of adventure, she would instead want to quickly change the subject. On the flight home, she replayed all the awkward moments from the trip, admonishing herself for the time and money she'd wasted.

Chapter 9: Hazed and Confused

2018
(ONE YEAR BEFORE GUY FAWKES FEST)

Sam felt annoyed with herself for ever believing a single vacation was enough to change her life. It shouldn't have been a surprise that her planned instant personality makeover hadn't worked, and she hadn't suddenly become an interesting and fulfilled person. She knew better. She knew a makeover of any kind wasn't possible, not for someone like her.

On the flight back from her European expedition, she had the displeasure of reliving one of the most recurring intrusive memories: a hazing ritual in her high school marching band.

[2 0 0 0]

Sam didn't want to participate in most of the traditions and social activities that came along with being in the marching band. She still carried suspicion toward too many of the kids she'd come up with from elementary school who had made her life miserable. Unfortunately, certain activities were difficult to avoid, especially when her own family didn't have the energy to look out for her.

The most dreaded was when seniors "kidnapped" freshmen—with each family's consent and cooperation—showing up at their homes early one Friday morning while the unsuspecting ninth-graders were still asleep. The freshmen girls weren't allowed to shower or change into school clothes. (Except in the case of one girl who, as it turned out to even her own family's surprise, slept in the nude.)

The only prep activity allowed was a brief toothbrushing and quick application of deodorant, all under supervision to ensure no one tried to improve their ambushed state. As they were ushered out of their homes, the parents handed the girls their backpacks and sleeping bags, before the girls piled into a van for a day of activities which culminated in a sleepover at the team captain's house.

It was obvious that some of the girls had parents who warned them. Sam was not among them. The day was a disaster from start to finish. She hated being pranked, and while she wasn't surprised that her family didn't warn her, the betrayal was no less hurtful. She didn't have a cute set of matching pajamas like so many of the other girls. She didn't even get to throw on an adorable robe, like the clarinetist who had been sleeping in a lingerie top that would get her sent home from school.

Sam was braless in an oversized t-shirt of a band she didn't even like, a hand-me-down from Brad. This was complemented by some too-baggy mesh athletic shorts that were frayed and had stretched out elastic in the waist, bright fluffy cartoon character socks that clashed with her ensemble, and finished with bulky black athletic slide sandals. Her hair was wound up in a wrap she only used at bedtime, and would never intentionally wear in public.

Their first stop was a team breakfast at a restaurant, where no one really talked to Sam. She was too shy to interrupt her fellow freshmen, and too intimidated to talk to any of the seniors. She was terrified at having to go to school, and wished she had slept in a sweatshirt, flannel pants, anything other that what she had on. Her stomach hurt, and she could barely eat anything. Sam wasn't a morning person in the first place, requiring slow quiet time to get going, so the cacophonous dining experience wore her out quickly.

At school, the other students teased the freshmen as much as you'd expect. The annual kidnapping tradition extended beyond the band to include the dance team, most sports teams, and even the yearbook staff, resulting in a sad army of dazed and confused freshmen from across extracurriculars. The whole school seemed to support and enjoy this routine violation and humiliation, making an event of mocking the victims.

Even the teachers took turns critiquing the outfits, except for the few who treated the freshmen as hostile offenders for disrupting their class with disgraceful appearances. Sam was annoyed she didn't have gym class that day, which would have given her a chance to shower and put on a sports bra.

She was humiliated to be seen in this way by anyone, let alone members of the band. Sam had so wanted to belong, and had a hard time feeling accepted by her bandmates so far. Sam preferred to always blend in as much as possible, and now in her tragic bedtime ensemble she stuck out in the worst way. It didn't help that some of the other girls looked put together, and it certainly didn't help that Sam noticed how cute some of them were.

Feelings of attraction toward other girls were still surprising and confusing to Sam, especially since the last thing she needed was something to make her stand out even more from everyone else, to give people something else to make fun of her about. She tried to force herself to have the same feelings for guys at school, but it didn't work, so she did her best to ignore having feelings for anyone at all. If she didn't dwell on who she liked, she didn't have to accept it about herself, and wouldn't have to worry about how people would react if they knew.

After school, the sophomores and juniors joined in, and the entire team went out to dinner. More public humiliation. Sam felt gross and embarrassed, and several times considered just leaving, but she didn't want to put a target on herself. She remembered what her mom had told her all those years ago about not being "that girl" who leaves, because then it gives bullies material to work with. Bev had been right then; no need to bring that on herself again.

Surviving dinner, Sam only had to make it through the sleepover portion. She hadn't been to a sleepover since Gretchen's. Sam steeled herself and tried to go into it with her head held high. Unfortunately, a key aspect of the sleepover was a makeup tutorial. Each senior was assigned a freshman to makeover, with prizes going to the teams judged best by the captain.

With Sam's usual makeup routine consisting of spot cream to reduce acne, concealer, and flavored chapstick, she was wildly unprepared for this. The senior to whom she was assigned, Cara, a flautist, did little to hide her disappointment at not getting one of the more bubbly, exuberant girls. Sam tried to make small talk, but Cara wouldn't engage on any topic. Glaring at Sam's freckles, Cara pointedly explained that she didn't think any of her makeup would work with someone of Sam's color or complexion.

Sam felt horrified that Cara was annoyed at how plain Sam was. There'd be no chance to win a prize with such an obviously unattractive girl. Sam's horror compounded when Cara recoiled at Sam's unwrapped hair. She never had good self-esteem, but there, in that basement, Sam truly hated her own face, her hair, her skin, and every part of her physical being.

She looked around and saw the other pairs clicking, helping each other with makeup, getting to know each other, and having fun. Some of the sophomores and juniors joined the pairs, while others sat in small groups of their own. Sam realized it didn't matter who she'd been paired with—she never could have felt at ease with anyone. Between her weak conversational skills, her lack of anything interesting to talk about, and her discomfort over feelings of attraction she'd experienced for some of the girls, she was doomed to fail at socializing.

After a few minutes of half-hearted attempts, Cara gave up and turned to some of the other upperclassmen to chat. Left to her own devices, Sam observed the other girls using gel product and their fingers to scrunch up their hair into beachy waves. Every girl started to blend into one another. Sam reached for a bottle and tried to scrunch her own hair, feeling like a failure when it was clear that her hair texture did not support the attempts. Deflated, she sat in silence looking at the other girls until it was time for judging.

One by one the captain, Eileen, evaluated each freshman, complimenting her on aspects of natural beauty: "You have such great cheekbones, I'd kill for your lips, your skin is flawless."

She'd also praise the senior beauticians, with comments such as, "I love what you did with the eyeliner, you chose such a good color for her shadow, her hair looks amazing."

When she reached Sam, with her mussed hair and aborted makeup, there was an awkward moment as Eileen searched for anything nice to say, eliciting a nervous smile from Sam.

"You have really...symmetrical ears. Are you wearing any makeup though?" Eileen looked at Cara with confusion.

Cara helpfully explained, loudly and with contempt, "She just doesn't really have a face for makeup, and I didn't know how to work with her skin or her hair. There wasn't much I could do."

Sam wanted the floor to open up and swallow her whole. She could feel the collective judgment of every girl in that basement, agreeing that she was helplessly homely.

Sam longed for a distraction, anything to take the attention off her, when thankfully one arrived. A transom window popped open and several of her bandmate's' boyfriends slipped in. Each boy was armed with a pack of cheap beer or malted fruit beverages.

Many of the girls feigned being scandalized, but were clearly excited at the rebellious turn the night had taken. Sam recognized one of the boys from a few days before, when she'd seen him near the bleachers making out with the freshman xylophonist, Leslie. She noticed Leslie's face light up, and immediately go dark when the boy disregarded her in favor of a junior bassoonist.

In the chaos, Sam was able to slip away to the bathroom and remove the little makeup Cara had applied. She couldn't look herself in the face, she wished she didn't have to use the mirror to ensure she'd effectively cleared off the cosmetics. Walking out, she saw Leslie stealing into a room filled with large packs of household goods and holiday decorations.

Leslie was crying, and although she didn't know her well, Sam instinctively went in to reassure her.

"Are you ok?" she asked, placing a gentle hand on one shoulder.

Leslie looked up at her with complete hostility and snapped, "Leave me alone, you fugly freak. What are you, some kind of lesbian? Well I'm not into you, so get the fuck out!"

No one had ever alluded to Sam's sexuality before, and while she was sure Leslie was just saying it for effect, it still caused her confusion and panic. Had she been found out? How could anyone know, when she herself wasn't even sure? Shocked, Sam scuttled back into the main area of the basement, which was increasingly loud.

Anyone should have seen that they were going to get busted, which they quickly did. In the chaos of Eileen's angry parents descending into the basement—while the boys tried to escape and the girls attempted to hide the alcohol—Sam decided to cut her losses. Who cared if they talked about her for leaving? They already hated her. At least if she left she wouldn't get in trouble with anyone's parents.

She quietly snatched her belongings, glad she hadn't unpacked, and set out for the nearest shopping center. Wandering through the 7-11, Sam slowly contemplated the unnatural colors of sugary snacks. Settling on some shocking-pink frosted sugar cookies she knew she wouldn't enjoy, paired with a tropical Slurpee for which she had no real desire, she started the long walk back to her house.

It took her nearly an hour to make it home, and while she knew it wasn't safe, she couldn't bring herself to call her parents for help. Besides, the cool night air felt refreshing after the surreal day she'd experienced. She was overwhelmed by everything that had happened since her rude awakening that morning, and as she rambled along she tried to process the series of tragic moments.

Thankful that she always kept her house key in her back pack, she was able to let herself in through the side door without waking her family. She dreaded seeing them in the morning, having to lie about how and when she got home.

Of course, her family didn't really pay attention to her anyway, and no one thought to check in on her for most of the weekend—especially not with Kimmy in fine form, demanding to be taken to the mall for even more expensive clothing than she'd gotten the month prior during back-to-school shopping. In the end, Sam had no explaining to do, and could keep her shame and hurt feelings to herself.

On Monday at band practice, the other girls were all bonded. The shared experience of being caught with boys and booze had made them all fast friends, conspirators, comrades. Sam wasn't sure if they resented her for leaving, or had simply forgotten she'd been there in the first place, but the increased isolation was noticeable. For a moment she feared that perhaps the lesbian accusation had picked up steam as a rumor, but that was too terrifying to consider, so she dismissed it.

She noticed many of the freshmen were wearing makeup and scrunched hair like they'd been taught during the sleepover. They all looked like they belonged, marching row after row. Sam felt herself stick out even more. Everything about her always felt wrong. She knew that in terms of social acceptance and physical appearance, she was beyond help, and could never be normal like other people.

* * *

Chapter 10: Back to Life, Back to Reality, Back to Wedding Season

2018
(ONE YEAR BEFORE GUY FAWKES FEST)

Dispirited from her two-week journey that had failed to instantly improve her life, Sam returned home. Sorting through her mail she found yet another invite for another wedding, this one scheduled over a long weekend in October to celebrate her friend Jolan, whom she knew from college.

Every past wedding she'd ever been to consolidated into a single memory that swirled unpleasantly in her head. Why should she go to another wedding? It wouldn't be any different. Sam wasn't sure she could muster the strength to RSVP without a plus one, again.

To arrive alone, again.

To sit awkwardly at a ceremony, trying not to take up space a family or a couple needed.

To silently plead for assigned seating, guaranteeing her a table with at least one person she knew, saving her from small talk with strangers.

To sip a responsible volume of wine while everyone around her got drunk and danced the night away.

To leave early, before the dance floor inevitably winnowed away to the long-haul couples tipsily slow dancing in various states of undress. (How did other women always know when it was socially acceptable to take off their high heels?)

To get home and peel off another uncomfortable outfit, which she hated anyway.

To promise herself that next time, she'd RSVP, "No."

Still, she knew invitations wouldn't keep arriving forever, and they were a good chance to provide her friends a proof of life on her. Besides, Jolan was a deeply sensitive person and Sam didn't want to hurt his feelings by declining without a valid reason. So, she dutifully RSVP'd (she chose the chicken over the beef or salmon), tossed the card in the mail, and gave it no thought until months later. She had more than enough time to decide which unflattering dress to wear, and to become anxious that the whole thing would be unbearable.

Jolan's wedding was outdoors at a family farm. It was a sunny day and, gratefully, a brief ceremony. Out of the corner of her eye, Sam saw Em, in her typical slim cut vest and slacks combo. To her disappointment, she didn't see Tali anywhere. She craned her neck in an effort to locate Em's petite partner, but at that moment a family asked Sam to slide over a few chairs and make room for them to sit together.

Instead of round tables typical of an indoor reception, the guests sat at a series of long tables, dressed with simple linens with wildflower centerpieces. Sam noticed Em again, and this time, to her great relief, set eyes on Tali. She was here after all! Catching Tali's eye, Sam gave a poor excuse for a wave, keeping the palm of her hand on the table and wriggling just her fingers. Em noticed, and gave a "what's up" head nod of acknowledgment.

Someone seated nearer to them caught Em and Tali's attention, and Sam watched them react to the guest's story. As the conversation went on, both women doubled over. Em howled, wiping away tears, and Tali tossed her head back to let out a loud peal. Sam noticed how, after Tali finished laughing, her eyes looked like they were still giggling, and a smile lingered near her dimple. Sam's mouth went dry, prompting her to drink too much wine.

After the obligatory spotlight dances, attendees filed onto the floor. Sam, full of extreme wine confidence that was foreign to her body and her brain, stumbled toward the edge, slowly swaying. She saw Tali prancing with two flower girls. The smaller of the two took off her flower crown to place on Tali's head, which she accepted with an exaggerated curtsy. The music picked up tempo, and everyone filled up the dance floor, twisting and shouting and waiting a minute.

Sam was totally out of her element, wincing at the repeated, "Shout shout shout shout!" Regretting all of the wine, she wished the floor would stand still long enough for her to depart. Attempting in vain to cross through the mob and make her exit, Sam felt a hand on hers. It was Tali, grabbing her, twirling Sam around. Sam could not remember ever dancing with anyone before, except of course for Grandpa Tony or other elderly relatives at her family parties. This was very different.

Those moments on the dance floor were unlike anything she had ever experienced. She felt alive. Tali grinned at her, and Sam became aware their friends were watching them. Her instinct was to feel awkward, to assume they were judging her, but...they were clapping. For her.

Tali, emboldened by their claps, dragged Sam into the middle of a circle that formed. Despite her small stature, Tali was strong, and led Sam around like a doll, spinning, dipping, and pulling. Sam, inebriated out of her mind, tried not to be sick so that she could enjoy the moment.

"Just focus, just on one thing," she urged herself. She closed her eyes and inhaled. "Just focus on one sense. Focus on smell. Mmm, lavender. Tali smells like lavender, or maybe it's just the flower crown."

As quickly as Sam ascended, she came crashing back down. The DJ called for all couples to come to the floor. Em ambled toward them and swept Tali away. It was over. Sam stood along the edge of the dance floor, waiting and hoping for another dance that never happened.

Em and Tali danced every slow dance, whispering and nuzzling, oblivious that a world existed beyond them. Sam, beginning to sober up, felt like an idiot. Her turn on the dance floor garnered positive attention from other guests, but, ignoring their invites to an after party, she grabbed her shawl and left.

Over the next several weeks, Sam tried to forget about her turn on the dance floor, but in quiet, unexpected moments the memory flooded back in front of her eyes, causing her cheeks to flush. She tried not to dwell on it, but it insisted upon itself, interrupting her, and leaving her feeling unsettled and even more alone than ever. Next time, she wouldn't be so easily discouraged, she'd find a way to make herself stay, maybe even accept an after party invite, and have a chance for the evening to turn into something more.

In the spring of 2019 Sam attended one wedding after another. Jolan's invitation turned out to be the first of many in a new wave of nuptials. Friends Sam had thought were also long-time bachelors like herself were now getting married. Some of her fellow late bloomer friends found love in their mid-thirties, and the wedding invites started picking back up.

Heartened by her last experience, she was grateful she'd responded yes to all. Each time she saw the save-the-date magnets on her fridge, she couldn't help herself. She'd smile, and start whirling around the kitchen by herself, trying to remember exactly how it felt to be Tali's partner.

She was so preoccupied planning her dance moves for the next wedding that it hadn't occurred to her that Tali might not be there.

Sam tried not to be mad at herself. "Of course she isn't here! We hadn't seen each other for some time before Jolan's wedding, so why would we suddenly see each other at every consecutive event?"

Wallowing in her disappointment, Sam convinced herself that Tali probably didn't even remember dancing together. After all, while it had been exhilarating, they hadn't spoken during, and Sam knew if Tali thought of any dancing, it was likely the intimate swaying she and Em engaged in for the rest of that night.

"So we danced. People dance all the time at weddings, it doesn't mean anything!"
Trying to console herself, Sam opened herself up to the possibility that there was nothing special about Tali, nor their experience, at all.

Sam settled in by the dance floor, wearing her best attempt at an expression that said "ready to party." She waited for someone to emerge from the crowd, grab her by the hand, and rescue her evening. No one did.

Sam saw a woman standing alone, and decided to swallow her nerves and make a move to talk with her...only to be immediately intercepted by the very drunk bride demanding that Sam join a group photo. Sam wasn't usually involved in the wedding party, as she had never even been a flower girl nor a bridesmaid.

As Sam exchanged quick "hellos" with the other photo subjects, the groom made a fond pronouncement to the crowd that Sam was a serious dancer, and had put her impressive moves on display at a recent wedding. This elated Sam. She wasn't the only one who remembered. It was real! It wasn't something that had made an impression only on her. This wedding hadn't been a total loss, after all.

During a May 2019 wedding the DJ relied heavily on the tried and true hits, prompting people to mob the dance floor not as couples, but in clusters, which proved perfect for Sam, who bravely joined one of the mobile blobs. Sam lost herself in the moment when suddenly she saw her. Tali was gamboling with a covey of tipsy relatives of the bride.

Faced with the reality of seeing the woman about whom she'd been fantasizing, Sam tried to catch her breath and look away, avoiding eye contact, but Tali saw her, already waving Sam over to her. Sam couldn't refuse, and maneuvered her way toward Tali, narrowly escaping the overenthusiastic embraces of the groom's very inebriated aunts, who were convinced that every stranger was a best friend waiting to happen.

Sam lost track of how long they danced. She struggled to remain present, too busy wondering if this was actually, finally happening. When the DJ relented to pressure and spun a slow song, Sam immediately slumped off toward the tables, only to find Tali walking with her.

"Where's Em?" Sam had never actually had a direct one-on-one conversation alone with Tali. She tried not to let that intimidate her.

"The groomsmen absconded with her! They're out sneaking premium liquor from a car trunk since this wine bar wasn't up to their standards."

"They happen to have a trunk full of top-shelf booze?"

"Always be prepared!"

Sam considered recommending they return for the slow jam, but didn't want to seem forward. She couldn't dismiss the concern over what other people might think. As excited as she was to be in Tali's presence, that didn't lessen the dread of facing her friends as her true self. Instead, she and Tali stood at the bar, tipping back one glass of sparkling wine after another.

As usual, Tali leapt swiftly from one subject to the next, sweeping Sam up in her conversational drift. Tali made no segues, no pivot between topics, just whatever popped into her head. She was a tidal wave of non-sequiturs, and Sam didn't mind.

Happy just to hear her talk, Sam occasionally responded, but mostly drained her beverage. Before too long, Sam felt the carbonated effects converge with the excitement from Tali, surprised by how relaxed she felt. She inadvertently stayed for the whole event, even the last dance.

After the wedding, a group of guests organized an impromptu outing for pancakes and grilled cheese sandwiches at a nearby diner. Sam ignored her every instinct to call it a night, make an excuse, and run away. Buzzed from too much prosecco, Sam was scarcely aware of climbing into a car. She rolled down the window to let the warm evening breeze hit her face. It was bliss.

Only when Sam got to the restaurant did she register Tali was not with them. She asked someone, a stranger, where Tali had gone. The person, unhelpfully, replied she had no idea who Tali even was.

She continued asking, until finally someone informed her that Em escorted a tired and tipsy Tali to their car back at the venue. Sam envisioned it in her head, the only thing she could see clearly as the wine continued to play with her senses. She decided to make the best of it, and settled into a booth next to a very cute woman named Molly.

They hit it off. Throughout their conversation, Molly moved closer to Sam, giving her undivided attention, staring intently into Sam's eyes with an encouraging smile, softly touching Sam's elbow, her shoulder, her knee. With the check settled (Sam had no idea what she owed, she just threw all the cash from her wallet on a pile in the middle of the table) Molly strolled with Sam to the door.

"It's nice out; want to walk?" Sam had nowhere else to be, so she agreed, and found Molly's arm linked in her own. Soon, they were in front of Molly's apartment, and Sam heard herself agreeing to go inside.

By this time Sam started sobering up, and worried about what Molly would think of her. Panic set in. Not only had Sam never had sex with another woman, she still hadn't come out to anyone. Would Molly tell? Sam never met Molly before, but somehow they were mutually connected. Would Molly gossip to everyone, until word spread to the entire guest list that Sam was not only gay, and also terrible in bed?

Molly kissed Sam, and together, without pulling their mouths apart, they moved on to the couch, making out slowly until Sam began to relax and even enjoy herself. She let her hands move over Molly's body, pulling her as Molly also moved closer to Sam.

She began to lose herself in the moment when she heard Molly ask, "Do you want to go to the bedroom?" Molly beamed at Sam hopefully, but Sam didn't know how to respond.

No, she didn't want to go to the bedroom, she didn't want to be in that apartment, she didn't even want Molly to know she existed. The whole thing was a mistake, and Sam wished she had an eject button to hurl herself out of Molly's apartment toward her own. Refusing to look Molly in the eye, Sam awkwardly said it was nice meeting her, and followed on with a series of incoherent, inaudible remarks, prompting a confused Molly to become both hurt and humiliated.

Visibly crestfallen, Molly asked Sam, "Did I do something wrong?"

Unable to bear making someone else feel bad, especially someone who seemed so kind, Sam said the only thing she could think of.

"No, you didn't do anything wrong! It's just that I'm in love with someone. She's the love of my life and I'm still hoping it will work out with her, so I don't think it's fair to you for me to be here tonight. I'm so sorry, I just don't want to be an asshole who leads you on. You're beautiful and sweet, and you deserve someone who isn't still stuck trying to get back the one who got away. I'm just not ready to be with someone else. I thought I was, but I'm not. I'm really, really sorry. Really."

Sam had no idea where any of this came from, but knowing her actions had wounded Molly made her feel terrible. She could see that it wasn't going to help Molly recover completely from her embarrassment, but

Molly seemed a little reassured, and at the very least, equally ready for the night to be over.

Clearing her throat, Molly uttered a series of monotone sentences. "Thank you for being honest. It was nice to meet you. I hope it works out with your dream girl. I'm going to sleep now. Get home safe."

Sam was dismissed. Walking toward the door, she timidly wished Molly a good night. The door shutting in her face was the only response Sam received.

The next morning was not kind to Sam. She'd collapsed into her bed the moment she got home, and now Sam lived to regret neither taking off her wedding clothes, nor washing her face nor brushing her teeth. She smelled like a diner, with a hint of Molly's perfume. She tasted a foul mixture of alcohol and late-night, greasy spoon-fueled indigestion, exacerbated by the pain of realizing, in the light of day, what a disaster the previous night had been. She finally met someone who liked her, and then she ruined it all. The raw pain of the memory churned her stomach.

To distract herself, she focused more on the happy moments of the evening, the time she spent with Tali. Yes, she got to be even closer with Tali, who lit up Sam's life and dazzled with her radiance. Sam focused so keenly that, at least for a while, she buried the memory of her catastrophic near-hook-up while embellishing the joy Tali brought her.

As for the threat of being outed by Molly, she decided not to worry about it, embracing denial that Molly would ever be a factor in her life again. If thoughts of Molly intruded, she closed her eyes and concentrated on how expressive Tali's face was, as she spun her stories for Sam. Just for Sam. She couldn't wait to see her again. But first, Sam needed something to talk about the next time she saw her. She needed some hobbies.

Chapter 11: Anything You Can Do, Sam Can Do Competently

MAY 2019
(SIX MONTHS BEFORE GUY FAWKES)

Taking another run at giving herself a late-in-life personality was a daunting prospect to Sam. It wasn't just her failures at filling her life with volunteering in her twenties or reinventing herself through international travel the year before that gave her pause. No, what held Sam back was how thinking of what new interests to pursue caused an avalanche of miserable memories to seize her, highlighting her mediocrity at everything she'd tried.

[1991–2004]

Sam had lived a second chair life. She achieved, but never excelled. She was remarkably unremarkable. In every aspect, she was exactly competent. While Sam's teachers appreciated that she could be relied on to complete her assignments and answer correctly when called on, she never impressed them. Always a good student, she never rose to the top of any class. She routinely came in third or fourth in spelling or geography bees.

Her teachers pushed her to take initiative or offer a unique perspective, but she was unable to capture the spark that distinguishes an exceptional student. Sam didn't like being average, but didn't see any way to change who she was. She tried diligently, sure that her efforts would pay off, but to no avail. Teachers eventually gave up, nodding at her with a brief, "that's correct," before moving on to someone with more potential. She coveted the "Well done!" and "Very good!" bestowed upon her more brilliant classmates.

In music class, Sam followed directions to a tee. She liked the recorder because it was simple and required rote playing. She could hit each note exactly as instructed. When other students improvised and made up their own songs, Sam remained quiet, humbled by their abilities.

Her elementary school required each student to decide between studying choir, band, or orchestra. Sam chose band, assuming the oboe was close enough to a recorder for her comfort. Once again she performed with reliability, but not the kind of virtuosity that would secure first chair.

During the few parent-teacher nights in which her family actually participated, her mother had to pull out a picture from her wallet to prompt puzzled teachers to remember which student belonged to Bev. Finally, with the dawn of recognition, her teachers confirmed that yes, she was a student and was exceptionally adequate.

Several teachers, once they recalled her, remarked something to the effect of "Oh yes, she's polite. She helps clean up from activities and stack chairs. A reliable, good girl." Then the teachers quickly moved on to chat with the parents of a more exciting pupil.

This continued throughout high school. Sam's teachers commended her ability to retain information and recall it for tests, but observed that she neither challenged her classmates nor elevated the level of discourse. She wrote essays full of fact, but with no point of view. She was non-controversial to the point of being a non-entity. Exasperated, Sam wavered between wanting approval and not wanting to draw any attention to herself.

During senior year when Sam needed recommendations for college applications, she struggled to secure them because her teachers didn't have much to say on her behalf. Not that they had any criticisms, but because, if pressed, they'd admit that they hardly knew her at all. She wasn't bad, she simply didn't make an impression. She accumulated the humiliations of each teacher's confused or off-putting response:

"Are you sure you wouldn't rather have a teacher you're close with write one?"

"I don't know, I have so many I'm already committed to, and I'm not sure I'd be able to give yours the attention it needs."

"Well, this is a surprise... could you tell me a little about yourself?"

"Remind me how many classes of mine you've taken?"

"Sure Sam, if you write one for me, I'd be happy to sign it."

"Do you... do you have any activities you're involved in that I could mention?"
Sam knew she didn't have much for her teachers to work with, as she'd never had luck with extracurricular activities. She had her freshman stint with marching band, but that wasn't exactly impressive. She didn't have experience volunteering, as that would have required her parents to take her places, which also limited her ability to join after-school clubs. (Not that she wanted to explain her parents' disinterest in her to her teachers.)

When it came to athletics, she'd had a brief elementary school career during which her soccer teammates routinely outshone her. She kept up with her team as they moved forward and back on the field, but never scored a single goal, never made an effective defensive play, never did anything that directly changed the outcome of a game.

At the end of each game, her coach assigned superlatives, which ended awkwardly. "Nadia, great hustle, you set the pace today! Olivia, you were unstoppable! Teresa, way to follow through and stick with the ball! Erica, those footwork exercises are paying off! Alexis, you are, without a doubt, the best defender in this league!"

Her teammates emphasized each compliment with high fives and pats on backs. Until he got to Sam. "Sam... you... were on the field... at the start of the game... and... you were still on it... at the end."

Silence from her teammates. This was usually the point her coach dismissed the team. Sometimes, she worried that she could disappear from the field without anyone noticing. Sometimes, she wished it would happen. She hated these memories, she hated the feeling of being so unnecessary to other people, so inconsequential.

* * *

Now an adult, weekends gave Sam too much time on her own, making her susceptible to memory paralysis. After a particularly excruciating Saturday afternoon of reliving her childhood failures to find a hobby—and through those hobbies find friends—Sam brought herself back to the present moment. If she didn't want to end up alone forever, she needed to get going, and gave herself a pep talk. "Lots of people try new things at

141

my age. I'm not even forty yet, I have plenty of time to cultivate a new me if I just go for it. I just need to figure out what 'it' is."

As a side effect of hero-worshipping her brother, friendships with narcissists in public school, and constantly dodging criticism or attention throughout her life, Sam never developed a strong sense of who she was, or what she wanted. In attempting to shrink herself out of view, she inadvertently shrunk her entire personality. If asked her interests, she could rattle off a list of things she felt she *ought* to like, but if pressed, would not have been able to explain what it was she enjoyed about any of them.

So she decided to try out a broad range of hobbies. As was her habit, Sam began with a project manager's approach, pulling out her graph paper notepad which always helped her feel capable of transforming chaos into order. First, she documented potential forms of recreation she thought she wanted to try. Then, she researched the time commitment and cost to try them out. Finally, she ranked the level of effort to try an activity once, and prioritized them in order of how easy and inexpensive each was to explore.

Reflecting on the pastimes she previously enjoyed but missed, Sam thought first of music. She couldn't justify purchasing an oboe when she wasn't entirely confident she remembered how to play. Instead, she bought a recorder. The moment she put it to her lips, it instantly came back to her. Before long, she strolled around her apartment serenading herself with "Hot Cross Buns," "Three Blind Mice," and "Kookaburra."

She also decided to invest in a new bicycle. As a child, she was passionate about bike riding. It got her out of her house, away from family fights, and also didn't require any friends to participate. It was the perfect solo activity for an ostracized little girl. She remembered how the rush of the wind on her cheeks filled her with confidence and excitement. Sam couldn't figure out why she ever stopped riding, but there was no time like the present to get back to it.

Her biking interest finally gave her something she could discuss with her teammates at work. Her supportive colleagues helpfully recommended a local shop where she got fitted for a bike and bought the accompanying helmet, basket for groceries, and repair kit. Next to the river cruise, it was the single biggest amount of money Sam ever spent at one time on herself, but she knew after years of saving she could afford it.

Straddling the bike and pushing off, slowly, cautiously, soon she tore full-speed down the trail near her apartment. She knew remembering how to ride a bike was a cliche, but she was pleased at how quickly she felt fully in control. She began to bike a little every day, and felt the differences in her body and mind. At work, she showed her colleagues photos of her new bike, which made it easier to transition into casual conversations.

She challenged herself to start initiating friendly conversations around the office, realizing that if she asked questions, people were happy to talk about their weekends, their hobbies, or their families. She even allowed herself to participate in a brainstorming session with the marketing team for a new campaign aimed at getting local restaurants to return shucked oyster shells to the region's dwindling oyster beds. She couldn't believe her own ears when she heard herself offer up the tagline, "Keep our bay bOysterous." She cringed at first when everyone in the room laughed, until she realized the laughter was a positive response because they liked it. "All this because I bought a bike," thought Sam, marveling at the big ripples that could result from small actions.

Playing the recorder and biking were solitary pursuits, though, and Sam wanted to get out into society to meet people. She hoped to form new friendships, practice small talk, and build up the belief in herself that she was an interesting person with whom others might enjoy spending time. She tried a number of activities, including paint nights, horseback rides, and cooking classes.

Each time she signed up for something, she felt so nervous on the day leading up to it that she tried to talk herself out of attending. She gave herself every chance to bail, but then pumped herself up with pep talks.

"You can do this. Lots of people do this. You can't meet people if you don't go out. It's just one hour. It's just one night. You can leave if it's terrible. At least you'll get fresh air. At least you'll have a painting. At least you'll get some food out of it."

She stuck to her plans, and to her surprise, she survived each outing.

She wasn't exceptionally good at any of the new hobbies she tried, but as always, she was attentive to directions and diligent in following orders, producing competent results. In cooking class, her instructor even used her as an example for others to follow... a first for Sam.

"Look," the instructor told the class, "Sam's not trying to be 'Top Chef.' She understands she is a novice. She knows she needs to master the basics. Well done, Sam. Needs more salt, but overall, good."

This made her especially popular for pair assignments. People didn't want to partner up with someone known for burning or over-seasoning dishes.

Sam's output might have been boring, but at least she was reliable.

Her most successful experience was Japanese class, which she took through an adult continuing education program. Sam enjoyed learning it in high school, and despite her recent international travel experience, still dreamed of visiting Japan. She wanted to make a good impression with her vocabulary and etiquette. She had let those skills completely atrophy since high school, but she welcomed it as a fun challenge.

In the class, the instructor appreciated Sam's rigor and dedication to getting the inflections on each syllable exactly correct. "Very good. Yes. Correct. Excellent, Sam."

She even made a few friends, Emil, Dave, and Sarita, who invited her to their informal study group outside of class, which usually took the form of an afternoon or evening at a student's home, with cheese trays and glasses of beer and wine. Predictably, studying often quickly gave way to conversation on everything from movies to families to sports and books.

Like a sponge, Sam absorbed everything the cohort discussed. She realized there was so much in life she wanted to experience, and was pleased to be part of a group of people who could spark ideas for new adventures.

As she got more comfortable with the other students, she even started sharing her own recommendations on travel, cooking, sustainability, musical movies, and other topics in which she felt moderately confident in addressing.

"Oh yes, it turns out salted butter does make a difference in baking. We're working on pastries next. You'll want to stay overnight in Cologne. My bike is perfect for both city sidewalks and paved trails. You've never seen *All That Jazz*? You must!"

Sam always expected them to turn on her and tell her that her contributions were boring or stupid, but instead, they received her with warm interest, and asked follow-up questions.

In these moments, Sam experienced the unfamiliar satisfaction of being appreciated for who she was, as she was. She still often felt the impulse to skip out on her plans sometimes, sensing the old fear that people were only pretending to like her just so they could exploit or abandon her. Pushing through her fears, Sam began building confidence that she was a likable person who was fun and interesting to be around.

Hanging out with her college friends and colleagues during this time, they commented positively on the change in her, and on her social media posts, saying it looked like she was having fun. Various people told her they couldn't wait to go bike riding with her or to try out some of her new food.

It pleased Sam to know that people noticed her making positive changes. She wondered if Tali would notice, too, and had looked forward to the next time they could have a private conversation. So when she got the invite for the "Inaugural Guy Fawkes Day Observation Bonfire and S'Mores Fest" (as it was officially named) she got carried away imagining how exhilarating it would be to match Tali as she conversation-hopped across topics, now that Sam had something of her own to talk about!

Chapter 12: The Vulnerability Hangover

NOVEMBER 2, 2019
(ONE DAY AFTER GUY FAWKES)

Other than making s'mores by a fire, the Guy Fawkes party had not gone according to Sam's plan at all. When she got home that night, she was unable to sleep at first, instead parsing every word she'd exchanged with Em. She was glad it was all out in the open, and that Em wasn't mad at her. She'd even survived her first run-in with Molly after their awkward post-wedding hookup! Sam had spent a lot of time investing in herself, and now had people who wanted to help her reach her full Sam-ness. Finally, as exhausted mentally as she was physically, she fell asleep.

Waking up the next morning, Sam felt relieved, but also overwhelmed with sudden anxiety that she allowed herself to be so vulnerable. She also wasn't entirely sure that agreeing to become a before-and-after work-in-progress was a good idea at all, and became upset at herself for agreeing to it. Sam decided to find a way to back out, but then, not wanting to think about it any more that morning, half convinced herself that Em and Tali had either not really meant it, or would not remember they'd made the offer.

More than these worries, she was preoccupied with the notion that her coming out was so easy, and berated herself for not just doing it before. Nothing bad happened: none of the judgment she'd feared, no accusations that she'd misled people about who she was, or that she'd been a coward for keeping it to herself for so long.

It wasn't a big deal after all, and was even expected. It was a little underwhelming that a moment she'd spent decades avoiding and dreading was such a non-event, but at least Em was supportive, if not surprised. Although she understood not everyone would have the same reaction, Sam felt compelled to be equally honest with the other people in her life. First, she wanted to talk to Brad.

He agreed to meet her at a bar they'd gone to when they were in their twenties, a run-down pub with poor lighting, booth benches covered in duct tape, and pool tables badly in need of new felt. She didn't remember everything being so grimy, but took comfort in the fact that it was fairly empty. While she waited, Sam ordered a pitcher of beer and some nachos and a quesadilla, thinking to herself, "Well, if it's awkward, at least we've got snacks."

When Brad arrived, she stood up and hugged him, then they slid, squeaking, onto opposite sides of the table. "Ooh, nachos!" Brad smiled, reading out to take a bite before he even finished sitting down. "What's going on, Sam-the-Eagle? You good?"

"Yeah, good. Good. I, um, I wanted to talk to you?" Sam felt herself shrinking away. Maybe this wasn't the time to tell him.

"So I gathered. What's up?"

"I wanted to tell you something. I don't want it to change anything, but I think you should know." Her insides twisted into knots. She never had difficulty talking to her brother about anything before, but she couldn't shake the fear of losing her best friend, of being rejected by her hero.

"I don't know how to say it, I probably should have rehearsed or something, but..."

"You like women."

"Yes?"

"Is that what you want to tell me?"

"Yes."

"I know. It's cool."

"You know? How?"

"I've known you literally your whole life, and I'd have to be pretty oblivious to miss the million little clues."

This was not how Sam expected the conversation to go at all, but he struck her curiosity. "What clues?"

"I don't know. Like, take all the movies we watched at Grandma Jeannie's. Remember *The Sound of Music*? All our girl cousins were swooning over the Captain, but you were angry that he'd chosen 'the frumpy nun' over the 'beeeeaaautiful baroness.'"

"I stand by that."

"Or when we watched the one with Frank Sinatra, the one where he's dancing with the blonde and the redhead at the same time…you literally said, 'Lucky guy!' You were not exactly subtle, Sam."

"That was *Pal Joey*, with Kim Novak and Rita Hayworth," Sam clarified. "And I'm still jealous he got to dance with both of them," she added, laughing at herself.

Brad chuckled as well, and continued. "There was also the time when Mark and Christine came over to our house a lot for that big project in my history class, and you were so weird. At first I thought you had a crush on Mark, but then I saw. The way you looked at Christine, how you lit up when she walked in, but also got so flustered when she spoke to you. Your face would get red, then purple, and you wouldn't make eye contact with her. You'd be so glad they were there, then you'd immediately run away and hide in your room. I mean, there were a lot of things like that. The point is, I knew."

"Well, now I feel a little like an idiot."

"Don't feel that way."

"Why not? I've wasted years—no, decades—of my life scared to tell people, and not just people, but you, my brother, my closest friend, when… when not only was it *not* a big deal to you, but it wasn't a surprise."

"You weren't ready. That's ok."

"Yeah but, ready for what? Why is it so easy for everyone else to be who they are?! I mean, I've got coworkers whose kids are in high school, and it's all so normal for them to be gay, to have gay friends. My office throws a Pride month celebration. You can buy rainbow stuff everywhere. There are allies, there are parades! All these younger adults and teenagers are out and living their lives. They aren't afraid to show the world who they are, so, why have I always been?!" She hid her face in her hands.

Brad breathed a long sigh. He shook his head, and his voice shifted to a quiet, serious tone. "It's different now. People forget how bad it was; it's changed so much and so quickly since we were kids, Sam. Of course you were scared.

"When we were younger, it *was* still a big deal, and it really wasn't safe. If you'd come out, what would have happened to you? At best, you'd lose all your friends, be ostracized and called names, have other girls act like you were contagious, ban you from parties or sleepovers or put mean notes in your locker. At best. But we both know it could have been so much worse.

"Like, I know it's not perfect now. Still, it's so different, and I think that makes it easy to look back and judge yourself, to think you were a coward. But that's glossing over the fact that there was a real threat to your physical well-being if the wrong people knew, and decided to make an example of you. It honestly physically pains me to even think about what you might have gone through.

"Remember the two lacrosse players at the high school, when the rest of the team found out? Those two guys wound up in the hospital, Sam. The hospital! When they recovered, *they* were the ones who had to switch to new schools.

"And what kind of trouble did the team get into for what they did? A slap on the wrist, and the whole community—the school, the coaches, the parents—all absolved them with 'boys-will-be boys' excuses. Don't be hard on yourself for reacting to your environment."

Sam was surprised by the emotion in his voice, and couldn't think of a response, so she let him continue.

"I'm sorry you felt like you were hiding, but truthfully, a big part of me is so glad you didn't subject yourself to any of that. I couldn't have handled it if anything happened to you." Finishing his glass, he choked up. "What if people had hurt you? What if, what if you'd hurt yourself?"

He was on the verge of tears, a condition Sam had never seen him in, not once in their lives. Brad topped off Sam's glass, then emptied the rest of the beer into his own. Sam called over the waiter for another pitcher, and as they waited, an awkward silence hung in the air.

When the new pitcher arrived, Brad, clearly trying to recover from the emotional path he had not meant to go down, poured them another round and cleared his throat, asking optimistically, "So! When are you going to tell Mom?"

"Do I have to?" Sam rolled her eyes. "I'm kidding, I know I need to let her know, I just don't really know how to do the whole heart-to-heart thing with her. That's never really been our vibe."

"If it makes it easier, she knows your not-so-secret secret, too. But yeah, you should probably let her know, that you know, that she knows."

"Ugh, it's going to be so awkward." Sam shook as if she suddenly got the chills.

"Her only concern will be the same as mine: that you find someone who treats you well and makes you happy."

"I don't think she really cares about the happy part..."

"Mom absolutely cares."

"She doesn't, though. She only cares about Kimmy, the daughter she *actually* wanted. Do you have any idea of how many memories I have of Mom being visibly disappointed in me for having a tough time at school or in my social life, and thrilled any time Kimmy did 'normal' girl stuff?"

"Yosemite Sam, be fair—"

"No Brad, you weren't there! I am telling you, after you left home it only got worse. She was so excited when Kimmy did anything that was expected for kids her age. My God, when Kimmy went to her first school dance Mom must have taken hundreds of photos in front of the fireplace: Kimmy's date putting the corsage on her, Kimmy putting the boutonnière on her date's jacket, Kimmy and the other girls with all their matching hairstyles and makeup... she used multiple rolls! She printed them out and had an entire photo album dedicated to one freaking dance that Kimmy probably doesn't even remember.

"Did she ever get excited like that for anything I did? Did she ever want to show off anything about my life to other people? For all of Kimmy's faults, at least she gave Mom the milestone moments that seemed so insanely important to her. Face it, if Mom had any feelings for me at all, she'd probably hate me, but she doesn't even give me that much thought."

"That's not true at all. She loves you. She just has a lot weighing on her, like, all the time."

"Since when are you so sympathetic to Mom?"

Pouring himself another beer, he said in a matter-of-fact way, "Since Stacey pointed out the obvious to me: that our mother is miserable, and has probably been miserable since the day she threw away her life by marrying Dad and having us."

"You think she threw away her life?" challenged Sam. She wasn't sure why this felt like an accusation directed at her, but she was taking it very personally.

"We're not here to talk about Mom," he sighed, exasperated. "We're here to talk about you. So tell her, don't tell her, do what you want. I mean, if you want, I will tell her for you. But I really think you'd both benefit from an honest conversation."

Brad paused to drain the rest of his glass. Catching the waiter's eye, he signaled for another round. He was drinking as if he was in some kind of contest. The waiter looked at Sam for confirmation, and after briefly hesitating she nodded her head. Once he returned, they continued their discussion.

"Ok, fine," Sam relented. "I'll tell Mom. What about Dad?"

"He sucks."

"Oh, that's helpful. I meant, should I tell him when I tell Mom? I assume he knows, too?"

Brad took a swig of his beer, and bit his lip. "All the credit you give him, blows my mind. You begrudge Mom over every tiny infraction, keep it all in a catalogue of her faults, meanwhile he's been an absent father our whole lives and you still believe he's the one who will give you the parental love you're looking for.

"Stop being naive, and start admitting that he sucks, Sam. I won't say he's the worst. I wouldn't dare say that, not knowing what kind of stuff Stacey had to go through, that other people go through. But, point is, he's not a good father."

"If you hate Dad so much, why'd you name your kid after him?"

"Two things. One: I told you before that was all Stace. She grew up in such chaos that she always wanted a 'typical' family," he heavily rolled his eyes and sarcastically bobbed his head, "and thought naming the first grandchild after one of the grandparents was just something we were supposed to do. We might be dysfunctional, but we're better than what she'd ever had, and she thought it would cement her permanently in our family. I wanted to name him Chuck Yeager."

"Chuck?"

"No, Chuck Yeager." Brad was beginning to slur. "Maybe hyphenated, so people would know it wasn't after Chuck Norris or something."

"And the other thing?"

"Huh?"

"You said you had two things about hating Dad."

"Right. Two: I don't hate Dad. But I do understand it's possible to love someone while still acknowledging they are an asshole."

"Now who's being hard on our parents?" Sam felt defensive, and an edge crept into her voice.

"I know you looked up to him, loved when he'd take you to a movie or to pizza, or whatever. But he wasn't doing it because he liked spending time with *you*. He just wanted an excuse to get out of the house, and you were convenient. If either Kimmy or I were as low maintenance as you, we'd have been the one he took."

He punctuated this by downing half his glass in a single swallow. The words landed like a weight on her chest. What he said hurt Sam, not because it was harsh, but because it was true. Feeling emotionally neglected by her mother, she took any attention she could get, and her dad, whatever his motive, had provided that at least on occasion.

Brad could see he'd wounded his sister, and as he served them each a fresh beer from the third pitcher, he apologized for going too far. "I'm not saying don't tell him. I just don't want you to be disappointed when he doesn't hug you and tell you he loves you and he wants to join PFLAG or something. Just do yourself a favor, and lower your expectations."

"And Kimmy?"

"Fuck Kimmy."

"Brad." He never swore like this. Clearly she made a mistake agreeing to the third pitcher. "Maybe that's your last glass. We should go."

"Sorry. You can tell her, but be ready for her to be shitty about it. Or, maybe she won't be. She's so self-absorbed she'll probably immediately forget, because we all know she only cares about things that directly benefit her."

"On that, we can agree." Sam signaled the waiter and reached for her wallet. "I'll just focus on telling Mom and Dad for now. It's not like I'm going to see her any time soon, anyway. We aren't in touch, so it won't exactly have a reason to come up. You know I don't even have her phone number?"

Brad fumbled for his own wallet as he protested, "Nope, nope, I got it." With a careless flick of his wrist, he tossed a card onto the table.

Sam relented. "Thanks. And thanks for meeting me. It means a lot. And you know if you ever need to talk to me about anything in *your* life..."

Sloshing his beer a bit, and staring past Sam into the distance, he cut her off. "Look Samwell, life is hard, you know? There are so many terrible, difficult, awful, fucked up things in this life, I don't know how anyone can be expected to make it on their own. It's a hell of a lot easier to survive all the bullshit when you can do it with someone you love, who loves you. If that person happens to be the same sex as you, who fucking cares? Live and let live. Anyone who says otherwise is a hateful asshole that is both incapable and undeserving of love. No one should have to face this world alone."

It was only now, without the distraction of wondering how he'd react to her announcement, and cooling off from the debate over their parents, that Sam fully absorbed how tired he looked. In fact, he looked unwell.

"Are you ok?"

"I told you, Sam, I've known forever. Nothing you do could ever make me stop loving you. Unless you started rooting for a Philadelphia sports team. Then we'd have a problem. Please don't fall in love with an Eagles fan."

"No, I don't mean how are you feeling about me. I'm asking—is something the matter? Did something happen with Stace?"

"Stace?" By this point he was fully slurring. "No. She's the best. Better than the best. She's a fucking queen among women. A queen who decided, I don't know why, to marry this jackass."

The waiter returned with the card and receipt. Sam quickly scrawled her brother's name at bottom, and set down a cash tip on top of it. "I'm going to drive you home now."

"Boooo."

"Good talk, bro."

Waking up the next day, Sam couldn't remember the last time she'd ever slept so late. "I guess my body knew what I needed," she reasoned with herself, and headed toward the bathroom. As she luxuriated in the steaming hot shower, she ran through the last few days in her head: the conversation with Em and Tali, drinks with her brother. She thought she'd feel significantly different after these revelatory talks, but she was surprised to feel like her normal self.

Stepping out of the shower, she remembered how her brother seemed upset the night before. Sam texted him to ask if he was all right. She didn't get a reply from him, but a few hours later, Stacey sent a message from her phone.

"Hey! Brad's really tired, he's not feeling well."

"No surprise there, given how much he drank," Sam thought to herself, before replying. "Oh no. Sorry to hear that. I'm sorry I let him drink that much, and dropped him off to you in that condition."

"That's ok, I already have a toddler to deal with, what's one more?"

The winky face emoji might have bothered her coming from anyone else, but from Stacey she knew it was a genuine attempt to lighten the mood. "Can you let him know I hope he's ok?"

"Of course. And Sam, I'm proud of you."

"Thanks Stace."

"Love you, girl. I gotta go take care of my two toddlers now lol."

Sam decided that was enough interacting with people for now, and became aware of her hunger. With all her nerves the night before, she'd barely touched the food. She ordered a massive burrito and potatoes, smothered in sauce and cheese. She mindlessly watched reruns of her favorite sitcoms for hours in a row, becoming a zombie until her phone buzzed, alerting her to new messages from Em.

Chapter 13: A Personality Makeover

NOVEMBER 3, 2019
(TWO DAYS AFTER GUY FAWKES FEST)

Em texted Sam to let her know they were on the way to Sam's apartment. She wasn't going to get out of it, after all, but to her surprise, she was becoming comfortable with the idea of letting Em and Tali take the lead. That was what normal Sam would do. Let others lead, so she could follow. She felt safe again.

Although Sam knew Em and Tali had only good intentions, she couldn't completely shut out some of the apprehension the notion of a makeover raised in her mind. She'd always been sensitive to how she looked. Her parents were of such varied and mixed ancestry that, while she didn't naturally present as any one discernible ethnicity, she also didn't read as entirely white.

She didn't even match her own siblings, with Brad and Kimmy's olive skin contrasting against her own pink flesh. They did all share dark, bushy eyebrows and thick, unevenly textured hair on their head, which caused Kimmy great frustration, as she'd tried many times to look more blonde to match her friends. It never worked out; her hair wouldn't allow it. To compensate, Kimmy joined her friends in tanning beds so she could at least match their oompa-loompa orange complexions.

When they arrived, Em and Tali looked around, taking in the apartment for the first time. Sam was suddenly self-conscious of how plain and unadorned it was. Still, if they judged it negatively, neither said anything, launching immediately into their mission.

To Sam's relief, her friends had no intention of giving her a movie montage-style makeover. They just wanted to help her learn to be more comfortable in her own skin. Instead of trying to make her look like everyone else, they asked her how she wanted to look.

"Can we start with accessories? What about jewelry? You never wear jewelry. Is that because you don't want to, or because you don't have any?" Tali asked this as she poked around Sam's nightstand, finding a small velvet box. "May I?"

Sam nodded, and Tali opened the lid to reveal a tiny pendant, about the size of a dime. It was in the shape of the letter "S," attached to a delicate gold chain. "Aww, this is pretty! Why don't you ever wear it?"

Smiling, Sam took the box from Tali. "I got this from Arvind one year for my birthday. His family was new to the U.S., and were having a tough time adjusting and feeling accepted. Arvind's parents were worried about how he'd fit in at school. They were so excited whenever he got invited to a party that they always gave these gifts that were way too nice for elementary school kids.

"Anyway, I had never gotten jewelry before—well nice jewelry. I had a plastic watch and some beaded necklaces and those woven friendship-style bracelets. Never anything as fancy as this, though. I was so excited, and told him I would save it for a special occasion.

"I could tell it meant a lot that I liked his gift so much. It was so sweet, but of course my sister immediately ruined it by making a scene about how he liked me and wanted to kiss me and marry me. She embarrassed us both, and he got tired of trying to explain how jewelry is important in his culture.

"She ruined my desire to wear it, but I used to take it out of the box every night just to look at it. I'd hold it up, let it dangle and watch it catch the light. One night Kimmy caught me and she made so much fun of me. For weeks after she relentlessly mocked me about it to my family, and eventually I grew sick of hearing about it, so I shoved the whole thing away.

"The rest of my family, I think, just assumed I didn't like or want jewelry. I don't know. I'd wear some if I had any, but I don't know what would look good on me, or how to know what would go with different outfits."

"Dude, your sister is truly the worst." Em gave a disapproving face. "I changed my mind, I definitely hope I never meet her."

"She's not fun, that's for sure."

"I had a girlfriend once whose family was the same way as your friend. Gold was really significant and jewelry conveyed a lot of meaning in her culture, too. She gave me a stack of gold bangles once. They were stunning. Entirely too elegant for me."

"Wait, what bangles?" Tali interrupted. "Where are said bangles? I've never seen gold bangles!"

"That's because I don't have them. I gave them back."

"Why would you do a silly thing like that?" Tali acted as if it was incomprehensible.

"Because, Natalia, unlike Sam's sister, I'm not an asshole. Those bangles belonged with her, until she found someone who really deserved them."

"But I would look so cute in bangles!" lamented Tali, staring intently at her naked wrist with an exaggerated pout.

"Well then, I guess I know what you're getting for Christmas."

"Don't tell me! It has to be a surprise!"

Em rolled her eyes, and turned back to Sam. "Why don't you wear it now?"

Laughing, Sam took the necklace and held it up to her, demonstrating the chain was too small. "I've grown just a little since then."

"That's no problem," Tali assessed. "We'll just get you an extender. Now, on to clothes! Emilia, my love, you're up!"

"First, I need to understand what's going on with your current clothes, Sam. Your style is what I might call, 'menopausal malaise.' You've said you aren't content with your wardrobe, so why do you dress this way?"

"It's pretty much what my mom has always worn, so in my head, this is what a professional, adult woman wears. I also never know what's cool, or for how long anything is on trend, and don't want to invite criticism that I'm behind the times. I guess, I figured this is all safe, no one can judge me."

"Don't worry about trends or what other people think." Em gestured back and forth between herself and Tali. "Look at us, we dress so differently that even if we had remotely similar figures we could never share clothes. We each feel true to ourselves in what we wear. When you dress for yourself you feel more confident, and other people pick up on that energy."

Sam was surprised Em thought so much about fashion. She always looked so at ease in her clothing, Sam had assumed it was effortless.

Em continued, "It makes people respond positively to you. Dress in whatever makes you feel self-assured and happy. So, what makes you feel happy to wear?" Sam honestly didn't know, as she'd spent years paying minimal attention to her appearance.

With Em's help, she pulled everything she owned out of her closet and drawers. It was a sea of neutral and drab colors, the uniform of a woman begging to fade into the background. As they sorted the small pile of clothes she really liked versus the mountain of those she had because she thought it's what she was supposed to wear, Em kept prompting Sam with questions to help narrow down ideas. Unfortunately, Sam didn't even know if she wanted skirts, dresses, pants, sweaters, anything in particular, really. She was a sartorial blank slate.

Em proposed they go to a thrift store, explaining it was a cost-effective way to try out a wide variety of clothes. As a bonus, it meant not supporting fast fashion, which was important to environmentally-conscious Sam. Plus, they could donate the current, unwanted clothes while they were there, so Sam didn't have to deal with them anymore. These were all good points, but Sam hesitated, mumbling that she hated shopping and wasn't sure she felt up to going anymore, that perhaps this was all a mistake.

"What's got you so worked up?" Em pressed. Hesitantly, Sam confessed to all the negative feelings about how she looked, telling them about the failed band makeover. In summation, she explained how she never wanted to waste the effort trying to fix something she knew was utterly broken beyond repair.

Tali looked at her sympathetically and threw her arms around her. "Poor Sam! I can't believe they did that to you. I wish I could travel back in time and stop them. What a bunch of jerks. Oh, you poor poor thing, that's so sad!"

Em was far less coddling. "That's the problem? That was, what, twenty years ago? You can't let anyone have that kind of influence over you... especially those fucking people. For crying out loud, they probably don't even remember you, and you're still letting them dictate how much you like yourself? Not to sound harsh, but it's time to grow up and get over that high school shit. Deal?"

Sam agreed to try, and for the next few hours she allowed herself the hope of someday feeling more confident in her own body. In spite of herself, she even had a little fun. She discovered she was unexpectedly drawn to cheerful colors and bold prints. She was not used to seeing herself in some of the patterns and silhouettes, so it was an adjustment not to feel like a stranger stared back from the mirror.

When Em and Tali told her that something was flattering or that a color looked great with her skin tone, she initially had a hard time accepting they meant it. Eventually, she realized it wasn't fair to them and that she had no reason to be suspicious of their motives. Maybe the clothes really did look good on her. Before long, she had a respectable assortment of clothing, and felt satisfied seeing each item again as the cashier scanned and bagged them.

"I'm staaarving! If I don't eat soon there will be a serious problem," threatened Tali, with her typical degree of histrionics. They decided to go to a Thai restaurant Sam frequented. As they settled into their table, Sam realized all day had been about her, and felt like she was dominating their time. She decided to turn the spotlight on her friends.

"You know, I don't actually know how you two met. I know you got together at some point junior year, but sometimes it feels like I've always known you as a pair." Over appetizers, they told her the story, in the way that long-term couples do, finishing each other's sentences and disputing irrelevant details. Sam was able to follow the general story.

Back in college, Tali was hanging out with a bunch of people in a part of the campus that no one really used. Most students forgot it existed. The group she was with ordered pizza, and Em showed up right as it was delivered.

Em immediately noticed the cute tiny girl with the big curls, so she was already observing Tali when the awkwardness occurred. Tali pulled a slice of cheese pizza from the box, and the moment she took her first bite a guy confronted her as if she was a criminal.

He asked if Tali was a vegetarian, and when she said no, he chastised her for taking a slice of plain cheese when there were vegetarians present. Tali told him she didn't realize it was wrong, that cheese was her favorite, and that she had pitched in cash so she didn't realize it wasn't ok to take what she had ordered and paid for.

He insisted she should have taken the pepperoni or the ham and pineapple, and when she said she didn't like pepperoni or ham on pizza, he raised his voice. "Then pick it off! The point is, you eat meat, vegetarians don't. You can pull the meat off and still eat it; they can't!"

That's when Em stepped in and saved the day, coming to Tali's defense and putting the pizza warrior in his place. As Tali told this part of the story, she stared up at Em with utter affection.

Sam enjoyed seeing them interact and being in their company. She recalled what Em had told her: that spending time with Tali was erasing the mystique that had kept her crush burning all these years. Tali was a fun and exciting person to be around, but so was Em, and they were so good together. She was grateful Em had given her this opportunity to develop a friendship.

After dining they returned to Sam's apartment, full and triumphant. Clothes were settled. Sam had plenty of new looks to test and see what she liked wearing when she was out and about.

"Ok, but what do I do with this?" Sam asked, pulling at her hair.

Running her hands through her own short pixie cut, Em laughed "You got me there. Hair is Tali's department."

Tali was more than happy to give advice. "Honestly, you should treat yourself to a full service hair appointment, at a really good salon, just this once, at least. I know some amazing stylists, who will embrace your natural texture and work with it, not against it. You can ask them for a consultation and they can help you figure out what you like best and teach you how to maintain it. Some things are worth leaving to professionals, and I firmly believe hair is one of them!"

This made sense to Sam, and she wrote down the names Tali rattled off. "Now, let's talk skin care." Tali pivoted. "It's all about moisturizer."

Em and Sam groaned in unison, then laughed. They had hit a wall and were tired. They all agreed it was a good stopping point. The three friends said goodbye with hugs. Em and Tali said they looked forward to seeing Sam in her new duds the next time they got together.

As Sam got ready for bed, she couldn't stop smiling so much that it hurt her cheeks. It had been a long and successful day. Sam felt fulfilled at having deepened her friendships with this new bonding experience. She felt inspired to take steps to take control of her life, and empowered to focus on her own well-being and happiness, independent of a romantic partner.

Sam made a commitment to herself. If she changed up her wardrobe, styled her hair, worked out, ate right, took up a new hobby or decorated her apartment, it wasn't going to be for anyone but herself, for the sole purpose of her own satisfaction.

Chapter 14: Black Friday

NOVEMBER 27, 2019

Later that month, Sam prepared to return to her childhood home for Thanksgiving. Since she lived a reasonable driving distance, Sam usually didn't sleep at her parent's house, preferring to return to her own apartment when she hit her limit of family frustration.

Feeling ready to embrace the possibility of change as part of her personality makeover, this year, she decided to stay over. When she asked her mom if she could sleep in her old room (which her mother had partially converted into a scrapbooking and crafting room), Bev actually sounded almost pleased at the idea.

"You're always welcome to stay, Samantha. All of you are."

"When is Kimmy getting in?"

"I didn't tell you? She's not going to make it this year. She just started a new job and doesn't have enough leave yet to take off for the drive all the way up from Florida."

"Florida?! I thought she was in Louisville?"

"No, she moved to Tallahassee, and she waited too long to find tickets for a direct flight. All that was left were connecting flights through Atlanta, and no one wants to go through that airport around the holidays. Maybe next time I'll just buy the ticket for her. But Brad and Stacey will be here starting on Wednesday night, and I know your nephew will be excited to see you. I got some new coloring books and crayons for you all."

As relieved as Sam was to have a holiday reprieve from Kimmy, she was anxious as she packed, still shaken by some of the uneasy feelings that lingered after her conversation with Brad at the bar. Sam hoped the extra time with her family would help her reevaluate her relationship with her parents, and give her an opportunity to come out to them, without making the actual holiday all about her.

When Sam arrived on Wednesday morning, her mother was already busy in the kitchen, a one-woman assembly line tackling dessert prep. Bev barely looked up from her work long enough to greet Sam, who immediately felt discouraged and walked to her room to get settled. It was going to be a very long holiday.

When Sam came back downstairs, Beverly stood hand on her hip, face scrunched, looked both preoccupied and annoyed, as if she was trying to figure something out.

"What's wrong?" Sam asked.

"I thought I bought a new almond extract, but I can't find it…" Bev trailed off, holding up a nearly empty bottle as evidence.

"I'm sure it's around somewhere, let me help you look."

"No it's ok, you don't need to do anything." Her mother's brusque dismissal was too familiar to Sam, and it activated something in her.

"Actually, there is one thing I need to do. I need to let you know that I am gay. I think you already knew that, but I'm confirming it. So. There it is."

This wasn't how Sam planned to broach the topic, but the brief pause that followed was not exactly surprising.

Finally Bev spoke, collected and poised. "I see."

"You knew, right?"

"I suspected, but you can never really know unless someone tells you."

"You never asked, though."

"Your brother encouraged me to mind my own business. He said when you were ready you'd tell us in your own time and asked me not to pressure you."

"Oh. Well, ok. I guess he was right."

"Yes."

It wasn't going badly, but Sam still felt suffocated in her mother's presence.

"So that's all. Just wanted to make sure you knew, so if I bring a lady home some holiday, you aren't surprised."

"I'd be happy if you did. I hope you find someone very nice."

"Thanks."

"Just, please don't settle. You don't have to rush to find someone. Take your time and make sure when you find a partner, it's somebody who values you."

"Got it. I will not settle."

The kitchen was filled with the silence of two women who don't know each other very well, neither sure of what to say next. Sam broke the ice first.

"Since I was going to run to the store anyway," offered Sam, "I can grab some more almond extract for you while I'm there."

"You don't want to go to the store today; it'll be a zoo."

"I know, but I need a few things. Really, I don't mind."

"I appreciate that." Her mother reverted to her usual stiff, distant self. "I'll get you some money."

"I got it. And if there's anything else you think of while I'm there, just text me."

"You're sure?"

"Yes."

As she left the kitchen, she heard her mom's voice. "Samantha?"

"Yeah?"

"Thank you for telling me." Before Sam could respond, Beverly turned back to the pantry and began to rummage for other ingredients.

From the outside, the store looked the same, but inside it bore no resemblance to the grocery market she'd grown up with. Sam had no idea where to find anything. She must have looked visibly confused as she wandered the aisles, because suddenly someone asked "Can I help you find something, ma'am?"

Sam turned, expecting an employee, but finding instead Courtney, her younger sister Kimmy's friend. Sam froze.

"Sam, it's me! Courtney! Do you remember me?"

"Yes, Kimmy's friend. I remember. How are you, Courtney?"

"I'm great! Home for Thanksgiving, and I *had* to get out of the house, so I offered to do all of my mom's shopping for her. Turns out, she hasn't even gotten a turkey yet!"

Sam chuckled, "Well, I hope she likes chicken."

"I know, right? Who waits this long to get stuff? Anyway, how are you? You look great!"

Comments on her appearance were still a discomfort zone for Sam, so she deflected, asking, "Hey, have you heard from Kimmy lately?"

Courtney's face fell into a grimace, her voice suddenly strained. "Look, I wouldn't normally say this about someone to their own family, but I know you understand better than most people how she is. I've kind of been avoiding her the past few times I've been back in town. We all have, actually."

This was news to Sam, and a surprise to hear coming from one of her sister's oldest friends. "I had no idea. She doesn't talk to me about anything. Whenever she's here I don't know what she gets up to, so I just assume she's catching back up with you."

"No, I don't even try to find out if she's coming home anymore, to be honest."

"Did something happen?"

"Not one thing, but you know your sister. She's always been self-centered, and well, mean. She's a mean person. When we were young, she was fun enough to balance that out. She made it amusing to be on her side, as long as you weren't the target of her terror. But that was immature then, and it's even worse now. We're all too old for that."

"I know what you mean," agreed Sam, wishing they weren't having this exchange in the middle of the baby supplies aisle of the supermarket.

"Yeah, it's just like, the last few times we saw her, she had nothing going on in her own life, so she had nothing to talk about, except gossip about other people. Mutual friends. She wasn't just judgmental like usual, though. She was sharing deeply private information she shouldn't have: people's financial problems, infidelities, depression from broken engagements and miscarriages, *really* personal stuff. Stuff we didn't want to know about, and felt guilty hearing. It was not cool at all."

"Geez, that's terrible." As she so often had throughout her life, Sam felt ashamed by her sister's behavior. "I had no idea she'd gotten that bad."

"Yeah, the last straw was one night at a happy hour to celebrate our friend Kendra's promotion to partner at her firm. Out of nowhere, with no prompting, Kimmy revealed one of our friends is pregnant. This friend used to have a really bad eating disorder. Your sister started gloating about how our friend was going," and here Courtney used emphatic air quotes, her shopping list still flapping in one hand, "to 'get fat and stay that way,' and her husband would probably divorce her once he realized he'd married a 'secret fatty,' leaving her with 'nothing but a fat ass and a stupid baby.' Then she threw up, so Allison drove her to your mom's, and when Allison got back, we all agreed we were done with Kimmy. For good."

"I'm so sorry you all had to deal with that."

"It's our own fault, we should never have tolerated that behavior. Let's be real, we didn't just tolerate. Since elementary, school we encouraged and rewarded it. The first time my husband, Steve, met her, he told me he thought she was a genuinely awful and cruel person, but it took me a little longer to admit that I agreed with him."

"Hey ladies!" A loud voice honked at them. "This is a grocery store, not a reunion. Get out of the way and let other people shop!" A stocky woman in an absurdly-puffed parka held her hands gripped tight on her cart handles, impatiently tapping her foot.

Sam and Courtney looked at each other, trying not to laugh, and moved away toward a quiet part of the store. Sam offered words of apology. "I'm so embarrassed. I can't believe she did all of that to you."

"You have nothing to be embarrassed about, Sam. If anything, we all owe you an apology for not standing up to her when she bullied you in front of us. I'm sorry we were little jerks. And you were always so nice to us, too. Man. I'm an asshole!" She shouted this last statement dramatically.

"LANGUAGE!" snapped a man pushing his two young children by in a shopping cart, shaking his head at them in disapproval.

"Sorry, sir," demurred Courtney. "Look, I need to go buy the fifty-three things on this impossible list, but do you want to hang out? A bunch of us are going to hit up some breweries for Black Friday tastings… you should come!"

"You know what? Yes. That sounds fun. Text me the details?"

They exchanged numbers and wished each other luck in their shopping quests.

Back at the house, Sam waited for an opportunity to talk to her father, which was difficult, as Ray made himself scarce enough that she didn't see him at all on Wednesday. Instead, she made herself useful in the kitchen, impressing her mother with some of her new-found cooking skills. "Look at you, Chef Sam!" If Sam didn't know better, she would have mistaken it for parental pride.

The next day, Brad, Sam, and Stacey all helped Beverly, while Ray-Ray played with his toys and watched the Thanksgiving parade on the TV. During one of the commercial breaks, a regional reporter teased an upcoming news story:

"Should this local landmark known to area children as 'Suicide Hill,'" she deepened her voice at the name, "finally be closed by authorities? Hear what residents have to say." Turning her head from the TV, Sam tried to avoid eye contact with her mother, hoping not to draw attention to an event that Bev had never forgotten.

Unfortunately, Brad tried to do the exact same thing, and when Sam's eyes met his, they both struggled not to laugh. They clenched their mouths shut and tried to turn down their smiles, but to no avail. Finally overpowered by the urge, they both fell over laughing.

"It's not funny, Bradley!" Beverly was beyond unamused. "How would you like it if Ray-Ray came home completely mangled—scarred for life, disfigured—because he wanted to be one of the cool kids? Stop laughing. Samantha, don't encourage him. Shame on you both."

Stacey gave them a look to pull themselves together, which they did. The siblings resumed helping, only occasionally whimpering a suppressed snicker.

When Sam finally found a moment with her father, he was in his armchair, completely engrossed by his tablet, mindlessly tapping the screen in a repeated motion. Ray didn't raise his head up from the screen, but all the same, Sam worked up the courage to just say it.

His response was simply, "Yep. Your mother thought so. Do you... need anything?"

"Like what?"

"I don't know. I'm not sure what to say here."

"There's not exactly a script, Dad."

"Ok, ok. Well, you know I love you, always have, always will. You're still my little sidekick, right?"

"Of course."

"All right then." Ray's nod indicated he had nothing more to contribute to the conversation. Taking the hint, Sam walked back to her room, glad it was done.

The rest of Thanksgiving Day went well. Sam was relieved she finally spoke with her family, and even more that she hadn't needed to talk to her sister.

On Black Friday, she met up with Courtney and her crowd, some of whom she recognized as Kimmy's childhood friends. The rest were spouses and acquaintances who had joined the group over the years.

Everyone who knew Sam embraced her, remarking how well she looked and that they were happy to see her again. Several people who only knew Kimmy expressed disbelief that she and Sam were related by blood, and questioned how two people who grew up in the same house could turn out so different.

Steve asked, "No offense, but you seem, normal. And... nice. How did that happen?"

A few of Kimmy's friends took the opportunity to apologize to Sam for the part they'd played in enabling Kimmy's bullying over the years. Sam didn't want to dwell on the negative, so she quickly expressed forgiveness, then changed the conversation.

At the end of the night, Sam started toward her parents' home, finding that she couldn't stop grinning, replaying all the pleasant little moments and interactions in her head. She had more fun than she'd expected, and felt pleased with herself for saying yes and putting herself out there.

Sam's serenity was interrupted by frantic texts from Stacey.

"Have you seen Brad? Sam? Please answer."

"No, I've been out with friends."

"He hasn't texted you?"

"No. What's up?"

"I was taking a shower and when i got out hw was gone." The typos from the usually precise Stacey betrayed her level of worry.

"OMW. Will try to get a hold of him."

"Please let me know."

Sam recalled how her brother's recent behavior seemed inconsistent and out of character. Texting and calling him as she finished her trip home, Sam was overcome with a choking feeling in her throat and tension in her jaw, like she wanted to scream but couldn't unlock her mouth to yell for him.

Arriving at the house, she checked in with Stacey, and together they rushed from room to room looking for a sign of Brad, for any clue where he may have gone. In the garage, Sam noticed something out of the corner of her eye wasn't quite right. Something had been misplaced or taken...and then it hit her.

"Stay put," she directed Stacey. "I have an idea where he might be, but in case he comes back you should be here." She hugged her sister-in-law with a reassuring squeeze, then ran out into the snow. Sam tried to remain steady as she jogged toward the woods, but patches of ice made her way difficult.

Finally, out of breath and spent from the effort of keeping upright, she came to the top of Suicide Hill. Suddenly, she was a little girl again, terrified, staring down. There he was. Brad's motionless body sprawled next to the creek, surrounded by smashed pieces of an old, wooden sled. The voice that came from Sam's mouth as she screamed his name was unrecognizable even to her. As gravity and ice combined to win, she slid down the hill, tumbling, landing next to her brother.

To Sam's immediate relief, she heard him straining to talk, and saw him trying to lift his head. Through tears, she reassured him he was ok, and with tremendous effort managed to help him sit up. She could tell he was still trying to speak, but then he gave up, collapsing the full weight of his body onto her shoulder. They sat there in the snow as he unleashed a torrent of sobs. She was so focused on her brother that she hardly noticed the cold from the ground.

After Brad collected himself, Sam asked what was wrong. She understood that the idea of Suicide Hill probably came into his head after the news report, but what on earth possessed him to do this, by himself, at night with no one to help him if he got hurt? At first, he tried to brush it off, saying that he had never completed the sled run, and needed to get it in before the hill was closed off forever. Sam didn't relent, though, and insisted he be honest with her.

It took some time, but eventually he managed to share what had happened. Earlier in the year, Devon, one of the men he'd served with years ago during his second deployment, committed suicide.

Not only was Brad devastated by the loss of his friend, who left behind a wife and small children, but he was also disoriented by the shock. They had been in frequent touch over the years. Devon was employed, married, gave back by volunteering at a non-profit for veterans. To Brad, he seemed happy and well-adjusted, thriving in civilian life.

During Devon's funeral, Brad had the added difficulty of everyone asking him if there had been any signs—questions that caused Brad to feel like he was to blame, as if there was something he should have seen or noticed. He wasn't just in mourning, but also fighting off mounting guilt at not preemptively saving his friend. His guilt was compounded by the men who stood up to share stories about how Devon had saved them at various times overseas. Brad was convinced he'd let down his friend, his friend's family, and an entire community.

Ever since, he had been privately nursing his conviction. He knew he'd been drinking too much, but it was the only thing that numbed him enough to help him forget. Brad explained to Sam that anytime his brain was clear, all he could think of was Devon, and how he should have been able to help save him from himself.

At last, Sam understood the weight Brad had been carrying all this time. Sam looked around, at this place of her brother's greatest triumph, and finally saw him not as the hero she'd long revered, but as a man in need of help. She'd known him all her life, but had never seen him so defenseless.

"We need to get home, Brad. Stacey is out of her mind worried about you."

"I know, I know. I just…"

"You need help."

"I don't want to hear it."

"Too bad. You can't carry this on your own, it's not fair to you. It's also not fair to Stacey, or to your son. You can't care for your family if you can't even care for yourself. You need to talk to someone."

"Right now what I need is to change into not-wet clothes."

"Okay, but this conversation isn't over. Consider it paused."

"Okay, pause. Now help me stand up."

Slowly they pulled each other up, and brushed off as much snow as they could from their clothes. Sam put her arm through her brother's, starting to steer him home, when he stopped. Gesturing at the splintered wood, he asked "What about the sled?"

"I think that belongs to the creek now."

To her relief, he let himself chuckle a bit. "Well, Sam-I-Am, say goodbye to Suicide Hill."

"Good riddance. I never liked this place, anyway."

"Hey, it helped us when we needed it."

Acquiescing, she said with a sigh, "Goodbye, Suicide Hill."

They walked home in silence, with only the crunching of ice and snow as a soundtrack to their journey.

Stacey, understandably, was beside herself when they got home. Sam couldn't zero in on if her sister-in-law was more angry or relieved or worried, but she felt glad she'd been able to return Brad safely. Well, safe enough. Alive, at least. Beverly prepared some hot chocolate for them, and asked Sam what had happened.

Sam quickly tried to tell both Stacey and Bev about the guilt Brad felt at letting down his friend, but he attempted to prevent her from sharing details. Before shepherding Brad to sleep in his childhood bedroom, Stacey pulled Sam aside to hug her. As she did, she whispered, "I'm going to need your help in the morning, Sam." Beverly gave Stacey a huge embrace, patting the back of her hair.

Exhausted, Sam realized all at once that she didn't know what time it was, and also that there was nothing more she wanted in this moment than warm pajamas and the comfort of a bed. On Bev's advice she rinsed off with a hot shower. She quickly changed into a matching set of flannels and got ready, fighting off sleep while standing at the sink to brush her teeth. She hardly remembered getting into bed. She had a vague impression of Bev helping her, even tucking her in.

The next morning, Sam woke to find Stacey already sitting in the kitchen with Beverly. Calmly, Bev and Stacey laid out for Sam the plan: they were going to have a mini-intervention with Brad, giving him an ultimatum to get therapy, and—if the therapist recommended it—to stop drinking, and start attending Alcoholics Anonymous meetings. Sam was bewildered that both her mother and Stacey seemed confident this would go smoothly.

"You actually think we can make him do anything he doesn't want?" Sam asked, incredulous, hoping to make them understand their expectations were unrealistic.

"We do. He doesn't want to keep hurting himself, and he certainly doesn't want to keep hurting his family." Beverly looked Sam directly in the eye, while holding Stacey's hand in support. "He's a good man. He just needs a little direction. We can give that to him, together, and he'll hear us."

Stacey added "Aside from Ray-Ray, there is no one in the world who loves him as much as the three of us, and no one whose opinions he values more. He might try to dismiss it, but he'll get there, you'll see."

Sam understood, and began to share their optimism. Noticing Ray's absence, she asked after him.

"Your father isn't interested in participating, Samantha." Beverly was not bitter when she said this, but she did convey a sense of being wounded by it.

"He thinks we're being hysterical and need to leave Brad alone. So he went... I don't know where, I don't really care." Stacey punctuated this declaration by raising her hand to wave away the phantom of Sam's father. "If he's just going to disagree and undermine, I'm happy he left."

"Well," Sam took a breath. "Tell me how this goes, then. What do I need to say?"

By the time Brad walked into the breakfast nook, they were ready. Sam was shocked at how bad his injuries looked in the light of day. She whispered to Stacey, "Does he need to go to the hospital?"

Stacey responded "I tried, but he put up a fight about it. So let's get through this, first."

Brad did indeed resist the intervention. He tried every tactic: underplaying the severity of his injuries from the night before, relativizing his drinking as "less than most people," arguing that he'd never needed therapy before, even after his deployments, so he certainly didn't now. He told them they were all feeding off each other's worries, that he wasn't really that sad, and that it was much ado about nothing.

The three women held fast, though, and as a team, they took turns being persuasive, firm, and when needed, confrontational. Still, they couldn't convince him he wasn't to blame for Devon's death. Brad grew angry. "What exactly makes you experts," he stared down Sam and Beverly, "and why is this any of your business?"

Stacey was a force and stood her ground, repeating that she loved him, and because she loved him she wanted him to heal. "It's not cowardly to get help. It's brave to face your problems."

Somehow, Stacey got through to him. Brad listened obediently as she instructed him, "You're going to therapy. You can never be whole or present for your family as long as your mind is still stuck in a desert ten years ago, or a funeral ten months ago. Between raising Ray-Ray, and your desire for another kid in the future," (news to Sam) "it's not fair that I'm going to have to look after you, as if you're a child, too. I need to be able to rely on you to help me as a fellow parent. My partner."

At last, he relented and agreed with them. Brad promised to lay off drinking for a while, and to start seeing a therapist, one who specialized in veterans' issues, to help him deal with his various levels of grief. Sam felt relief for her brother, and reassured him that he was making the right decision. She gingerly gave him a hug, waving goodbye as he and Stacey left for urgent care.

Left alone with Bev, with whom she'd never spent much one-on-one time as an adult, Sam quickly packed her bag and said goodbye. She had felt so close to her mother during the morning, the unusual feeling of being united, a team. When it was over, the old dynamic returned, and Sam felt lonelier than ever in Beverly's presence. She didn't bother leaving a message for her father, with whom she felt disappointed.

Heading home, Sam was inundated with moments from the holiday agitating around her head. She anticipated that her coming out would be the cause for drama, but instead it seemed expected, and not a big deal to anyone. No, it was her brother who had been the source of concern.

She reflected on the high of reconnecting with old acquaintances and the release of forgiving them, and the low of feeling her father's indifference toward her family. At least Kimmy hadn't come home this year.

Sam could only imagine how much worse it would have been with her sister provoking them all.

The thought of Kimmy soured her, causing Sam to involuntarily recoil and screw up her face in disgust. She decided she needed to take a little time away from worrying about her family. Brad had a plan to get his life in order, and had an incredible partner in Stacey to help him. It was time for Sam to get back to her project, pursuing the life she wanted for herself.

Chapter 15: A Gallery of Broken Hearts

NOVEMBER 29, 2019

As Sam had grown closer with Em and Tali over the past few weeks, it occurred to her that she'd always expected other people to reach out to her. She was so scared of rejection that she never initiated anything, and that was a major contributor to her loneliness. She saw that when she actually made an effort, people were willing to make time for her. She'd been making small strides with people from various parts of her life, and finally felt confident enough to host an event that brought them all together.

On Saturday night Sam threw a small Friendsgiving for her college friends and coworkers who stayed in the area over the holiday. She also invited new friends she had made in her classes. It was a last-minute invitation, but to her delight people accepted. She was nervous at the notion of having to facilitate conversation, but luckily, most people she invited were pretty outgoing. To Sam's relief, everyone got along without needing her to prompt them, and she was able to focus on perfecting the details of her dishes as she set them on the table.

Her guests were more than happy to sample some of the new recipes she'd learned. The meal was a success, and Sam felt content at hosting a social event for the first time in her adult life. Caught up in the wave of happiness, over dessert and coffee, Sam announced that she felt like she had her feet under her, and was ready to make her entrance into the dating world.

With hugs and cheer, Sam's friends said goodbye and departed from the Friendsgiving feast, happily toting leftovers. While she finished cleaning up from the gathering, Sam immediately regretted declaring her intention to enter the dating scene. Although Sam felt confident in the moment she made her announcement, it unleashed a series of memories she had to work her way through, whether she wanted to or not.

Throwing herself into dating forced Sam to confront the lifelong struggle she'd had in forming lasting platonic relationships, let alone aspiring to a romantic relationship. Even before the added complication of navigating her sexual orientation, she'd never managed to have a close, lasting friendship.

As she got ready for bed and settled under her covers, she tried to focus on the wonderful evening she had just hosted. Still unable to dismiss uninvited recollections for the majority of the night Sam was trapped as an unwilling participant in one bad memory after the other.

[1995]

First, there was Delara. Gretchen's party had effectively ruined elementary school for the most part, but Sam did get a several-week reprieve in fourth grade thanks to a new international student, Delara, to whom only Sam paid any attention.

* * *

As the negative nostalgia booted up, Sam groaned, and actually spoke out loud to herself. "Ugh, no, please brain, I *do not* feel like reliving my greatest hits of failed friendships tonight. Please not tonight. I just had an incredible Friendsgiving that couldn't have gone better. Please, just this once, can't I just have one night without your torture?"

Pleading with herself in the present was useless once Sam's memory kicked off, though. She'd have to go through it all again.

[1995]

Sam walked through the halls of her elementary school, marching from the front office with a special mission: make a new student, Delara, feel welcome. Her teacher had urged the entire class to do this, but most of her classmates laughed in response.

Not Sam, though. She saw this new student as an opportunity. Sam wasn't just going to make the new student feel welcome, she was going to become her best friend! Maybe she'd even invite the girl to have a sleepover... no, Kimmy would ruin it... but maybe this new girl would invite Sam for a sleepover at her house! Then, once she had a positive sleepover experience, it would naturally undo all the harm she'd experienced since Gretchen's.

Determined to make this friendship work, Sam even checked out a Persian-English dictionary from the library to teach herself Delara's native language, which her new friend appreciated. They were inseparable at school, and Sam's teacher commended her for making such an effort. Delara invited Sam over to her house each weekend for one-on-one hangouts at her house. Sam was exhilarated by developing a close friendship, and even felt good about herself when she used her language skills to impress Delara's parents.

Things were going well, until Delara's birthday party. Although most students no longer threw co-ed parties at that point, Delara's parents invited the entire class in order to maximize their daughter's chances of developing a thriving social life. Sam didn't understand why she wasn't enough for them, but was sure if everyone saw her standing next to Delara when she opened her presents or blew out the candles on her cake, they'd understand that Sam was her best friend. Her classmates would see that even if they didn't agree, Sam mattered to at least one person.

Half out of curiosity and half out of obligation, nearly every invitee accepted, turning up to Delara's house in trendy party clothes with gifts in hand. That's when the class discovered that Delara might be the newest kid in school, but she was also easily the wealthiest. Well, her parents were, but that was close enough for the superficial kids in the class. Now they finally cared about getting to know her.

Sam felt the tide change in real time, and she couldn't stop it. Her classmates crowded Sam out during gifts and cakes, and even Delara's parents didn't seem to pay much attention to her presence as they focused on their hosting duties

Everything changed after that, and as the friendship waned, Sam realized it had been based on Delara's scarcity of options, rather than any affection for Sam. Delara started getting invites to other parties which didn't include Sam.

As sad as it made her, Sam couldn't begrudge the girl for accepting. No one wants to be an outcast. As Delara showed up to school each week dressed and styled more like the girls who tormented Sam, she wasn't mad. She envied Delara for succeeding in a matter of months when Sam hadn't been able to over years.

Seeing no point fighting for the affection of someone who moved on so quickly, Sam let go and returned to her outcast status.

* * *

Seeing the last glimpse Delara fade away, Sam tried to focus on how tired she was. Squeezing her eyes shut as hard as she could, she begged her brain to let her fall asleep. No such luck, and instantly she was on to the next lowlight, starring Sheila.

[1996]

During one of Sam's summers with her grandparents, Brad also visited, while Kimmy stayed at home with Ray and Bev in the hope that dedicated time to their youngest daughter might reduce her need to act out for attention. Sam felt slighted that once again her parents prioritized Kimmy, but at least Sam would get to be with people who always made her feel special. Between her grandparents and her brother, there was no one else she needed.

Due to some untimely and urgent home repairs they needed to take care of, their grandparents spent much of the first two weeks dealing with the contractors. Apologizing for the mess and noise, Grandma Jeannie and Grandpa Tony encouraged Brad and Sam to play with other kids on their street. Some lived there year-round, while others were also just making summertime visits to family.

Shy little Sam, fresh off the sting of her lonely fourth grade year, agreed to go with Brad to meet some of the other kids. As they walked toward the nearby park, Sam reasoned with herself. "Maybe if they like Brad enough, they'll like me a little, too… I wonder if they have a hill he can hop?"

Shortly after arriving, Brad hit it off with a girl his age, and luckily she had a younger sister, Sheila, about Sam's age.

Brad encouraged his sister to give Sheila a chance. "Go on Sam Spade, she seems like a lot of fun. Meet me back here at dusk and we'll go back to the house."

Sam hesitated, but Sheila was a ball of enthusiasm and energy who embraced Sam and immediately launched into conversation.

Sheila was only there for the summer, too, and instantly made herself part of Sam's routine. Every morning, Sheila came by to collect Sam for another adventure. They went to the playground and the creek, read books, colored, made friendship bracelets, played games, spied on their older siblings (they caught Brad and Sheila's sister kissing more than a few times,) and shared snacks.

Sam couldn't believe her good luck, especially when after only two weeks of knowing each other, Sheila surprised Sam with a gift. It was a plastic "best friends" half heart necklace, with the other matching half that Sheila kept for herself. There it was, in Sam's hand, around Sam's neck: physical proof that she was neither invisible nor unloveable. She was a friend, a Best Friend.

Sam wore the necklace with pride every day. She even slept with it on, and throughout the day fidgeted with it, reassured by the tactile reminder she had a friend, and that her friend wanted everyone to see how much Sam meant to her.

At the end of the summer, Sam and Sheila exchanged tearful goodbyes and home addresses. Sheila promised to write regularly.

After returning to Virginia, Sam wrote first, and often. She must have written too often, because one day the first letter finally arrived from Sheila, and inside the envelope Sam found the other half of the best friend necklace.

* * *

"FUUUUCK!" Sam pulled the comforter over her face, stuffed part of it into her mouth, and screamed into the wadded fabric. Whatever afterglow Sam had felt from Friendsgiving was officially gone. She just wanted to sleep, but this wasn't her first retrospective rodeo. She knew what was up next, the double-trouble nightmare of Lianne and McKayla.

[1998]

Sam was impatient to get out of elementary school and eagerly awaited the fresh start promised by seventh grade. Five or six local elementary schools fed into the intermediate school. Not only would it help decrease her interactions with her longtime classmates, but she would also get to meet new people who didn't have opinions of her yet. During her first day of school, she met Lianne and McKayla, girls from a different elementary school.

Their lockers were near Sam's, so she'd already seen them before they all officially met in gym class. They were polite when she introduced herself, and didn't seem to have any idea who she was. Just as she'd hoped, she finally got to make a new impression on people who didn't know her baggage. The two new friends were a package deal who were fairly insular in their friendship with plenty of inside jokes and slang, but Sam was grateful to be a third wheel, if it meant having someone to share lunch time with.

Lianne and McKayla were more than happy to include Sam in their activities, as long as she didn't express an opinion counter to theirs, or a preference they didn't approve of. They were very vocal in correcting her over trivial verbal missteps, and even shamed her for some of her food choices in the cafeteria. Sam accepted this as early friendship growing pains, and hoped that over time they'd warm up to her more. She also hoped that if she could show other new classmates she was capable of being a friend, maybe more people from the other elementary schools would also want to hang out with her.

Desperate not to lose her only close approximation to friends, she conformed to Lianne and McKayla's desires and lost any sense of her own identity, but it didn't make them appreciate her more. After a while, Sam realized the friendship wasn't actually as fun for her as she wanted it to be. It wasn't any fun at all, most of the time. Sometimes started to feel like she was only there so they had someone to feel superior to.

She considered breaking off their friendship, and suspected they would welcome her departure. Sam's suspicion proved accurate during a field trip to an amusement park. When Sam boarded the bus, she saw Lianne and McKayla already seated together, and surveying the full seats around them she understood they had made no attempt to save her a spot near them.

Sam was familiar with this embarrassing position. During elementary school she'd often had to ride next to a teacher or a chaperone, and she knew her classmates would vocally judge her decision. Sam looked around and weighed her options, trying to remain calm and hope that no one would call attention to her situation.

For this ride, her choices were not appealing. She wasn't close with their teacher, and she knew the teachers preferred to be alone, anyway, to save their energy for the day ahead.

There were two dads on board, but one had been rude to her at a class picnic the year before, so that ruled him out. The other was the parent of a kid she didn't have any particular issues with, but she knew she'd get teased for having a crush if she sat with a man.

That just left the third chaperone, a mom of one of the girls from Gretchen's sleepover. She decided the mom was the least objectionable option. As Sam sat down, she realized the mom didn't recognize her at all. Sam considered filling this woman in on her daughter's role in making Sam's life unbearable, but couldn't count on the mom to be any nicer than her daughter.

Since it was going to be a long bus ride, the school had rented a fancy coach bus with a bathroom and television monitors. Their teacher put a movie on that everyone else was already familiar with and quoted along to, but Sam hadn't seen it. She often missed movies that came out during the summers she stayed with her grandparents, and didn't exactly spend a lot of time with her peers during the school year to catch up on the latest in pop culture.

The field trip was miserable from start to finish. Lianne and McKayla kept her at a distance the whole time. Sam didn't like rollercoasters in the first place, but especially not when having to sit strapped in next to a chaperone or the teacher. At lunch time, she ate by herself, watching everyone else compare souvenirs and plan their next round of attractions.

She regretted coming along on the field trip at all. She'd faked Beverly's signature for nothing! (Bev and Ray both forgot to sign her form.) At least when class outings were to museums or the zoo she could take her time and enjoy the exhibits solo, without the reminder that she was a loner.

At last, the teacher collected them all and corralled them back onto their coach. During the bus ride home, Sam voluntarily sat in the very back of the bus next to the bathroom just to have some solitude. No one else wanted to sit in the odd seat, and most kids fell asleep on the ride so Sam was able to be by herself. To encourage the quiet, the teacher didn't put on a movie, and even asked the driver to turn down the lights, so Sam had nothing to distract her thoughts.

She couldn't help letting a few hot tears slide down her face, hoping no one would notice if they passed her to use the restroom. Sam had a chance to reinvent herself and make a new start, and instead she let other people direct her behavior. Plus, she was so focused on keeping them happy that she hadn't worked to cultivate any other friends, so she was back where she started.

She didn't bother seeking out Lianne and McKayla after that day, and they didn't seem to particularly miss her company. She'd completely changed who she was just to earn their acceptance, and in the end it was as if she hadn't even been a blip on the radar of their friendship.

* * *

Sam never liked thinking of those two girls, even now that it was decades after the fact. Thinking of all the time she wasted trying to earn her way into that friendship for nothing was excruciating, and yet it still wasn't even the worst memory of middle school.

[1999]

In eighth grade, her hope at a new friendship lasted even less time. When Willa arrived from Los Angeles, everything about her California style was exotic to Sam and her fellow Virginians. She wore colorful West Coast surfer clothing and vibrant, shimmery makeup, and her hair was streaked with comic book color streaks. She layered jewelry on her arms and neck, and even had an expensive designer handbag! (Or so Sam heard someone say; she didn't know one logo from the next.)

Exciting, yet unfounded rumors involving various celebrities Willa knew personally swirled about her immediately and everyone wanted to be her friend to get the inside scoop. Sure, many kids at the school knew politicians or diplomats or even professional athletes, but nothing like the movie stars they were sure Willa must know. They were sure she must have lots of stories to tell about movie stars, musicians, and models.

Willa was assigned to Sam's home room, so their teacher asked Sam to be Willa's buddy. Sam was not in a rush to have an assigned interaction, especially since she was intimidated by this glamorous, gorgeous girl.

"Hi, I'm Samantha, I'll show you around today."

"Hi, I'm Wil!"

"Oh, heads up... when I told people I prefer 'Sam,' I got some nasty comments about why I wanted to go by the boy version of my name, so you might not want to go with 'Wil.'

"But that's what I go by. No one calls me Willa. And who cares if people don't like it? Other people's opinions don't matter to me. And I can't imagine anyone being nasty to you—you're so nice. I can tell we're going to be best friends. So where do we go now, Sam?"

Wil popped a huge chewing gum bubble and gave Sam a disarming smile, allowing Sam to feel cautiously open to the idea that maybe she could have a friend. Noticing Wil's shocking blue nail polish, Sam complimented the look.

"Thanks Sam! It's Urban Decay, I'll bring it in tomorrow so you can use it, too. I have some other colors that might look good on you, too!"

"Sounds great!"

Sam walked Wil to her locker and showed her how it worked, keenly aware that everyone was watching them. Sam liked Wil, but wished she'd been assigned a buddy with a little less visibility. Wil didn't seem to mind at all. Maybe she was used to hanging out with celebrities, and had learned to ignore the press. Sam explained the alternating daily "block schedules" for classes, and comparing their schedules they saw that they had a lot of overlap.

"Perfect! You have to promise to save me a seat next to you every day, ok Sam?"

"I promise, Wil!"

At lunch, Sam and Wil walked into the cafeteria to find all eyes on them, waiting to see where they'd choose to sit. The girls settled at an unoccupied table, and before even unpacking their lunches found themselves surrounded by people asking if they could sit with them.

"Sure, whatever Wil wants," Sam replied, even though they weren't really interested in her response. Sam registered a number of her old elementary school bullies at a nearby table staring at her so intently that it made her physically uncomfortable. During lunch, Wil loudly made it clear to their dining companions that Sam was her friend.

"Sam's coming with me to Miami for Spring Break!" Sam wasn't aware of this plan, but nodded along since it seemed to impress their lunch mates. "I told my parents I can't wait all summer to go to a beach so they said I could bring some friends, our treat!"

"Oh," Sam piped up, unused to speaking in a crowd. "We have beaches in Virginia!"

"No, like, real beaches. Virginia has no waves."

"We have waves, every beach has waves."

"No silly, for surfing!"

This prompted the guys to fall over themselves explaining how they all wanted to surf, and that they could skateboard, and she should come watch them skate after school. One boy tepidly offered Sam an invitation to accompany Wil.

At the end of the day, Sam was tired from all of the interaction with her classmates. She wasn't used to so much talking and listening. Having a friend was going to be a lot of adjusting, but she was willing to change.

On the second day, Sam tried her best to look good for school. She'd never painted her nails before, so she hoped Wil might help her with some of the polishes she promised to bring. In the morning, Sam saved Wil a seat in history class. Wil had just slid into her desk next to Sam when Gretchen walked in. Usually, she sat as far away from Sam as possible, but today she walked right over and sat in front of Wil. Sam watched Gretchen pull out a marker and write on her the palm of her hand.

At first she couldn't make out what it said, until Gretchen lifted her palm and showed it to Wil.

She pointed her finger tips at Sam, who could just make out the scribbled note: "I hate that girl."

Wil drew back at first, unimpressed, and responded, "'I don't know you, and I don't know what your deal is, but leave me out of it. Sam's cool with me." She gave Sam a reassuring wink and tossed a fresh piece of gum in her mouth before offering one to Sam.

Dissatisfied, Gretchen pulled out a sheet of notebook paper, and spent half of the class hastily writing before passing it to Wil. Reluctantly accepting it, Wil slowly read it, occasionally looking over at Sam, her face showing increasing confusion and discomfort.

Sam didn't know what Gretchen could possibly have written, as they rarely interacted at all, but whatever it was clearly made an impression, because from the moment class ended, Wil started to ignore Sam.

The one-day best friendship was over. With a single piece of paper, Gretchen erased Sam, and took her place as Wil's best friend. Sam watched Gretchen and her friends dress more like Wil and adopt her West Coast slang. She tried not to pay attention when she heard them talking loudly in class about how much fun they'd had in Miami. For the rest of the year, Wil avoided talking to Sam again unless it was necessary for an in-class assignment.

Then, in high school—

* * *

"Nope. No. I don't want to think about high school." Sam insisted on arguing with herself, even though she always lost this debate. "Ok, I can stop this. Let's name countries, in reverse alphabetical order. You can't remember high school when I'm focused on Zimbabwe and Zaire, now can you, brain? Huh?!"

Sam was correct, her brain could not multitask. It chose high school memories over geography.

[2000]

In high school, Sam tried out for and made the marching band. It had been Brad's idea. "Come on Samantha Stephens! High school can be rough, but if you join a team or a club you'll have built in friends. Plus, it will guarantee you're out of the house and away from Kimmy. How can you turn that down?"

Each day, Sam tried so hard to make small talk during practice, but felt flustered when feelings of physical attraction to any of the girls flared up, causing Sam to trip over her words. Conversations never lasted beyond a few sentences exchanged politely, until whichever girl she spoke to grew tired of humoring Sam and turned to someone less awkward.

Once, trying to commiserate about the heavy uniforms in the early September heat, Sam pulled at her shirt collar and shared loudly, "Phew, I am HOT!" Two boys from the percussion section walked by at that exact moment and one responded, "No, you're not!" The other boy high-fived him as they walked away, laughing.

This was only a few short days before the dreadful kidnapping-turned-makeover team building disaster, which set her sadness in stone.

* * *

Sam sat up in her bed, rubbing her temples with her hands and exhaling a massive, pained sigh. The makeover memory always crushed her. She'd hoped her recent positive experiences would ease the pain, but apparently not yet. She was in for another long, long night. So much for sleep, when there were still more disappointments to revisit. "At least Scrooge only

had to deal with his series of ghosts for ONE night,"
Sam grumbled to herself.

[2000]

After the night in Eileen's basement, the only other
time Sam tried to be friends with someone in high
school also ended poorly. For whatever reason,
Sam could not guess, an intense girl named Crystal
decided they were going to be best friends.

At first, Sam enjoyed having someone to talk
to between classes and sit with at lunch time.
During the week, Crystal called her at night just to
talk, and they'd chat for ages until Kimmy forced
Bev to intervene and stop tying up the line.

After the Friday football games, Crystal
waited by the locker room for Sam to change out
her marching band uniform, then would take Sam
out for a late slice of pizza or some frozen yogurt at
TCBY. Crystal made Sam feel special... until she
made Sam feel suffocated.

They'd only hung out over a couple of
months when Crystal turned possessive and
controlling. She acted jealous of Sam sharing her
attention with anyone else. Between classes in the
hallways, Crystal would demand of Sam, "Why are

you talking to him? What does she want from you? What are you two hiding? What were you saying about me?"

Usually Crystal's seething scared off whomever Sam was chatting with, which Sam resented. One day her classmate TJ, who had been asking Sam about a pop-quiz they'd just survived, did not back off, instead responding directly to Crystal. "Hey, this is a Mickey and Minnie conversation, so see your Goofy ass out!"

Furious, Crystal glared at TJ before grabbing Sam by the wrist and yanking her away. Crystal didn't seem to notice or care that she'd hurt Sam. As Sam massaged her wrist, Crystal raged.

"You just aren't focused on this friendship at all, Samantha! I feel like I'm the only one doing any of the work! It's all one-sided and just me giving myself to you constantly, while you never give any of yourself to me. You are so selfish!"

Terrified of losing her only friendship, Sam apologized profusely and tried to figure out a way to salvage her relationship, but Crystal met her attempts with new criticisms every day.

When Sam experimented with braiding her hair, Crystal told her not to do it again without consulting her first. Then there was the time Sam's mom bought her a new shirt. No, it wasn't really Sam's would have picked out for herself, but she so rarely got anything from Bev that she wore it to school anyway. As soon as Crystal laid eyes on Sam she relentlessly mocked the shirt until Sam changed into a spare she kept in her gym locker.

Sam knew she needed to end the friendship, but feared the volatile response she'd likely receive. Unbeknownst to Sam, their vice principal and the freshman guidance counselor had been tracking Crystal's academic and interpersonal difficulties all semester, issuing multiple written warnings about her low grades and high volume of complaints made by classmates and teachers. When they tried to speak to Crystal about it in person, she was hostile to the point they felt unsafe.

Before long, Crystal was gone, transferred to the district alternative school for students needing extra emotional and behavioral support to complete their public school education. Once Crystal left, she never reached out to Sam again.

Sam was so relieved that she didn't even mind being plunged back into a solitary existence. If that was the best she could expect of friendship, she'd rather take her chances being lonely than being controlled.

* * *

"Ok, we've made it through Crystal." Sam allowed herself an exhausted yet eager cackle. "That just leaves college, then I should be done with this and can finally, FINALLY, get some sleep. At least college wasn't traumatic... just... not special. I wasn't special."

[2004]

Sam entered college with no expectations of friendship, and hoped at best that she'd make it through four years without any major relationship mishaps. Despite her cautious approach to letting people into her life, Sam was grateful to be included in a group that organically emerged from the assigned housing in their co-ed freshman dorm.

She was happy to tag along, as long as she didn't cause anyone a reason to dislike or exclude her. She contributed money for shared adventures, offered to be the designated driver and make sure

224

people got home safe from parties, and didn't get sloppy drunk so she could maintain self-control and not make a fool of herself.

During her college experience, Sam managed to stay part of the group as it grew and evolved. She developed a reputation as a quiet, but reliable friend. Sure, she realized she was an outer planet in her friends' orbit, as she never really got invited to hang out with anyone one-on-one, but still, she managed to build a solid circle of acquaintances over four years.

As a bonus, she actually liked spending time with them. Sam had always been so desperately focused on if other people liked her that she'd never had friends that she actually liked before. They were good people, and she felt fortunate she'd been able to maintain their relationships through graduation. She did long for deeper companionship, and perhaps it would have been nice to go on at least one date, one time, but hey, she wasn't a loner anymore, and for her that was enough.

* * *

Relief washed over Sam. The college memories hit differently for her after her recent interactions with Em and Tali. She understood now that she had been so guarded that her friends couldn't get close to her. She hadn't let them. She was annoyed with herself for preventing those friendships from being more intimate, but that wasn't as bad as when her undergraduate memories previously played out as if her friends had simply decided that she wasn't worth their time.

Now that she'd relived college—which wasn't so bad after all—she could get to sleep. Or so she thought. But she was still awake... something new was stirring in her.

Sam had never been sure if her awkwardness around dating was due to her desire to hide her sexuality, or that she'd always been terrible at forming bonds with anyone. But her newly-declared intent to date, combined with her unexpected run-in with Courtney, brought up a memory she'd long buried, and had even convinced herself wasn't real.

[2001]

The night in the laundry room with Mari comprised the entirety of Sam's romantic experience, and realistically it wasn't even a night. It wasn't even more than a few minutes, at most.

* * *

Sam flung her body violently back against the mattress. "Oh come on! MARI? You're going to make me think of Mari?! What are you doing to me?" Sam really didn't like herself sometimes. The night felt like it would never end, and Sam accepted that she would never get any sleep at this point. She didn't dare look at the clock. "Fine. Let's think about Mari."

[2001]

It was a Saturday night and Sam was at Mari's house, having been forced by her parents to babysit Mari's younger sister Allison. Unfortunately for Sam, Allison happened to be best friends with Kimmy, who was also under Sam's care that night, along with a few of their other younger girls, including Courtney.

The evening was a nightmare from start to finish, with the little hellions teasing Sam mercilessly. They ate food they weren't supposed to, drank soda that was off limits, and refused to go to bed, all the while explaining to Sam the many ways in which they thought she was a loser. When Mari unexpectedly showed up, Sam ran to hide, but Mari found her.

Mari was popular, but also very sweet. Although Sam had never spent time with her in a

227

social setting, they'd been partnered on a few projects in their history and English classes. Mari was always kind to Sam, and pulled her weight on the projects. Initially skeptical, Sam assumed she'd have to do all the work, but Mari's efforts elevated their projects and her presentation skills earned them praise in addition to their good grades. Sam developed a little crush on Mari, but knew it was silly because Mari was attached to a different football player every other week.

Still, Sam didn't want to run into her like this, hanging out with obnoxious children instead of partying with people her own age. "Hey Sam! Whatcha up to in here? taking a break from the little monsters? My parents better be giving you a biiiig bonus!"

Mari made herself laugh as she stumbled into Sam, who tried to steady her before quickly pulling her hands away. Sam smelled cigarettes on Mari's breath, which was a little revolting, but she also smelled her fruit-scented conditioner, the one she'd grown fond of during their classes together.

Sam smiled at Mari, unsure of what to say, and before she could think of anything, Mari's mouth was on hers.

They were kissing. This was Sam's first kiss. A million thoughts raced through her brain as she tried to understand—but also enjoy—what was happening. Mari pulled away, grinning, and cupped Sam's chin in her hand.

"I've always liked you, Sam. You're not an asshole. You're, like, nice."

"Thanks, you're nice, too.

"I have to sleep now, gotta brush my teeth before the parents get home." She tottered out of the laundry room, and as she reached the door to leave she turned and blew Sam a kiss.

Sam stayed frozen in the laundry room, flush with the excitement of her first kiss, and filled with the dread of what would happen next. Would Mari remember? Would she regret it? Would she trust Sam not to say anything? Or would she try to get out ahead of it and spin some cover story, perhaps accusing Sam of coming on to her? Adrenaline and anxiety spread across her body, preventing her from sleeping for the rest of the weekend.

When Sam ran into her at school, Mari made no mention of what had happened, but to Sam's relief, she also didn't keep Sam at a distance.

Mari greeted her with her usual smile and wave, as if the laundry room hadn't happened at all. That was fine by Sam, who didn't really want to discuss the fact that she, a girl, had kissed another girl. Or let another girl kiss her.

Whatever had happened, she knew it wasn't something she was ready to deal with. Their relationship as classmates didn't change, for better or for worse, and they never saw each other again after high school. Sam decided it was best to never think on that kiss again, just forget it happened.

* * *

Sam was glad her first kiss was with Mari, even if it did taste like cigarettes. She just wished it hadn't been her only kiss all the way into the present. Shaking off the negative memories of relationships gone wrong, Sam told herself that wasn't how it had to be anymore.

Now it was different. She was different. She had maintained her circle of friends from college, and felt truly close with Em and Tali. Through consistently putting herself out there, she was strengthening existing friendships while making new ones at work and through her hobbies. And she was even making friends of Kimmy's friends, something that never would have occurred to her as a possibility.

230

Thinking of Em, Sam thought back to her advice from the makeover day: "For crying out loud, they probably don't even remember you, and you're still letting them dictate how much you like yourself?"

Sam had to let go of the memories, or at least not give them attention beyond when they recurred. For the first time in her life Sam truly felt she deserved to be present in her own life. She was working hard on herself, and was capable of growing and making changes.

Opening herself up to her friends, new and old, was making her life fuller and increasing her confidence. Sam was letting people get to know her, really know her, and they liked her for who she was. Defiant, Sam decided that even if she couldn't stop her memories, she wasn't going to let them stop her.

Chapter 16: A Series of Unfortunate Dates

DECEMBER 2019
(ONE MONTH AFTER GUY FAWKES)

Sam's friends were very ready to assist her in finding a match. They took over updating her profiles on multiple dating apps, and Sam even allowed them to make matches on her behalf.

The disastrous result was two weeks in a row of first-date marathons. Back-to-back, her nights and weekends were so packed that she hardly had time to process one disappointment before heading to another.

The perhaps predictable outcome of throwing herself into online dating as if it was a Whitman's sampler box of single women was that Sam became something of a one-date wonder. Her encounters weren't just slightly off, but catastrophically bad. She began to wonder what she had put into the universe to deserve this.

In fairness to Sam, it wasn't just that she was being picky. She was a total rookie. After decades of hermetic life, she didn't know where to begin with dating. As she'd never fully formed her own personality, she wasn't sure how to present herself on a first date, and was also unsure how to gauge with whom she was compatible.

Sam worked her way through a rogues' gallery of women who left her increasingly convinced that not only was she meant to be alone, but perhaps would be better off that way.

There was:

- The woman who made it clear she wasn't interested in "being godmother to a baby gay," telling Sam to call her back in a few years when she had more experience under her belt.
- The woman at the taco bar who spent the entire meal telling Sam her horoscope, all the while with giant chunks of elote stuck in her teeth.
- The woman who showed up at the gelateria with her kids, despite listing herself as child-free on the apps.

- The woman who brought a friend with her, in case she got bored.
- The woman whose ex showed up and threatened Sam, Sam's date, their waiter, two bus boys, a hostess, and half of the other patrons.
- The woman who spent an entire concert loud-whispering criticisms of the orchestra.
- The woman who insisted the museum would be better if they got high first, and became impatient when Sam opted out of gummies.
- The woman who was very passionate about her gun collection.
- The woman who wanted to go on a hike, but spent the whole time complaining about her new shoes getting dirty.
- The woman who kept calling Sam, "Sammy," despite Sam asking her not to. *(Only Grandma Jeannie got to call her that!)*
- The woman who used happy hour to catalogue everyone she'd ever dated, and their key faults.
- The woman who was entirely too into fitness, forcing Sam to watch her amateur workout videos over brunch.
- The woman who compulsively licked her fingers before touching their shared food.

After surviving this gauntlet, Sam updated her friends
that she needed an indefinite break from the dating
scene.

Chapter 17: Otherwise Known as Ajax the Great

DECEMBER 14, 2019

Sam decided that her shift away from finding human companionship was the perfect time to seek out animal companionship by adopting a dog. Sam had always wanted a pet, but her siblings' constant fighting had made the request a non-starter in her childhood home. Beverly said the last thing she needed was more responsibility and more noise. Anticipating her new dog prompted an unwelcome memory from middle school.

[1998]

Sam walked her neighbor's dog as a favor while the neighbor recovered from surgery. Sam adored the dog, a female mystery mix named Cookie. She was an intrepid canine, and Sam was happy to let the sweet powder puff of a pup take the lead on their walks.

One afternoon they came upon a blacktop where teen boys played basketball. She heard yelling, and realized it was at her. They were mocking Sam, asking who was walking who, because it was hard to tell which one was the dog. "Two bitches on a leash!"

It destroyed her. Sam was used to abuse from her sister, but these were strangers. How ugly must she be to elicit this reaction from people the very first moment they saw her? She could hear the insults as clearly now in her head as she heard them that day, and—

* * *

"You know what?" Sam spoke out loud to herself, interrupting her own memory. "I don't have time for this. I don't know those guys, they didn't know me, and they don't matter. I have a dog to prepare for."

237

Em and Tali agreed to pick her up over the weekend so they could all go to the local animal shelter together. Ever the planner, Sam made a list of everything she would need for a dog—beds, toys, bowls, collar, harness, etc.—as well as what she was looking for in a match. She wasn't interested in a dog that was too outgoing or rambunctious. She wanted a chill dog to complement her own energy. As they pulled up to the shelter, her enthusiasm was matched—surpassed, actually—by Tali.

Inside, Sam was overwhelmed by the number of pets needing homes, feeling terrible she couldn't take them all. While they slowly walked down the long aisle of adoptable dogs, she heard Em talking to the volunteer named Sandy, running through pertinent information:

"She's a first-time dog owner, definitely not ready for a puppy, preferably an adult who is already housebroken, likes being outdoors but also looking for a fellow couch snuggler, needs one that will thrive in an apartment," and so on.

At once, Tali and Sam both stopped short and locked eyes on a cage with two small dogs, named Buster and Bluto. Tali engaged Sandy, and before she knew it, Sam was holding one in her arms, Tali cradling the other.

The dogs were of no identifiable breed. They were brothers, surrendered together, and because they weren't puppies, no one had expressed any interest in them. They were healthy, but understandably anxious from having been in the shelter so long.

Sam was smitten, but knew two dogs was too much for her to take on. She also felt guilty at the notion of splitting them up.

"I know!" Tali reinforced Sam's concerns, and then offered a solution—they each adopt one.

Em tried to shut this idea down before Tali got carried away. "Noooo, I told you, Natalia. I told you before we came here, no."

"And I told *you*, Emilia, that if we came here I would talk you into it. You knew the risk, yet here we are."

Directing her attention to Sandy, Em explained, "Our 13-year old Chow mix died last year. My wife's clearly ready for another dog, but I don't know if I can go through it all again. Not yet."

Sandy, visibly moved, expressed sympathy, agreeing."Everyone heals in their own time; you'll know when it's right."

Tali twirled around to Sam. "Sam, you won't take them both, right? And you don't want to split them up?"

Sam nodded, but before she could say anything Em repeated, "Tali, no, I'm not ready."

Without a moment's hesitation, Tali transferred the dog from her arms into Em's, and Sam could see it had an immediate effect.

"I don't know, Tal."

"But if we don't adopt them, they'll die!"

"Ma'am, we're a no-kill shelter." Sandy was trying her best.

"If we adopt him, then Sam can take his brother, and they'll still get to hang out. They won't have to miss each other, and they won't have to rot here in this prison!"

"I assure you they are very well taken-care of." Now on the verge of becoming offended, Sandy started to lose her patience.

"Come on Em! We can name our's Achilles, Sam's can be Ajax the Great, they'll see each other all the time and we'll all be sooooo happy!"

Em didn't respond right away, lost in the eyes of the little dog who was making himself at home in her embrace. "Isn't 'Ajax the Great' a bit of a lofty name for a dog?"

"Well, we wouldn't want anyone confusing him for Ajax the Lesser, am I right?" She looked to Sandy for reinforcement, but Sandy was immune to Tali's charm, and not prepared to engage in this level of decision-making.

"Ok. If Sam says yes, I say yes."

"Sam?" Tali's eyes were pleading, but also lit up because she already knew what the answer would be.

"Of course. Let's do it."

"Let's get you some forms." Sandy guided them toward the office.

"Do we have to leave them here, or can they come with us?" Tali didn't want to let the pups out of her sight.

"They can come, too. Follow me."

On the ride home, Tali cradled Achilles on her lap in the front seat, and Ajax fell asleep on Sam in the backseat.

Ajax immediately made Sam's apartment his own. It took Sam a few days to not be startled each time she realized she wasn't alone, but they quickly fell into a routine and in no time were bonded as if they'd always been family. As promised, the three friends made sure the brothers saw each other frequently, and the dogs thrived with their new families.

Throughout the day, Sam found herself talking to Ajax like he was the best friend she'd always longed for. She surprised herself each time a new nickname for the little fellow popped unexpectedly out of her mouth.

For someone who had never felt creative in her life, these spontaneous terms of endearment caught her off guard.

She loved falling asleep to his loud snoring, and being awoken by snuffly kisses on her forehead in the morning. He was a sweet boy, but very insistent on prompt walks before breakfast.

Whether Sam was just impressed by the novelty of having a dog, or enamored with Ajax in particular, everything he did was adorable and noteworthy in her eyes. Her phone was filled with Ajax photos and videos, and her social media feeds became almost exclusively Ajax content. She didn't feel silly about this, as Em and Tali did the same with Achilles.

She tried not to spoil Ajax, but he was so cute with his toys and so appreciative of treats that Sam couldn't help herself. She rationalized it by saying that it was making up for the time he'd spent in the shelter.

Ajax became her shadow, following her from room to room, bringing toys to invite Sam to play games with him. On their walks, she liked to let him pick a path and follow him. He stopped to sniff every few feet, taking in all the smells of his new neighborhood, growing more confident each day. He was everything she'd dreamed of in a canine companion.

Sam's days felt more complete with her new little buddy. She'd had no idea how caring for another living creature could make her heart so full.

Chapter 18: In the Bleak Midwinter

DECEMBER 24, 2019

"Great, we'll see you there!" Courtney and her crew would be home again over Christmas, and Courtney reached out to invite Sam for Christmas Eve drinks. Sam and Courtney had been texting regularly since Black Friday, and several others had connected with Sam online. Seeing them had turned out to be an unexpected high point of Thanksgiving, so Sam decided she would stay overnight again at her parent's house for Christmas.

This time, she packed up supplies for Ajax, too. "You're sure you don't mind me bringing him?" Sam was incredulous her mom didn't object to him being at the house.

"Your nephew would never forgive me if I made him miss an opportunity to play with his new canine cousin."

"I can't wait to see them together, it's going to be so cute. You'll love it."

"I'm sure I will. Drive safe."

As they drove, Sam listened to the local radio station that played only Christmas music from Thanksgiving to New Year's, singing along loudly to serenade Ajax. He was good in cars, and the trip was off to a smooth start.

Her excitement plummeted the moment she entered the house.

Kimmy.

No one told Sam she'd be there. How had Bev neglected to mention this? Sam hadn't seen her sister in nearly two years, and was not mentally prepared to face her. Her heart both raced and sank. While she wanted to turn and leave, she was frozen in place, hoping somehow this would ensure her tormentor couldn't spot her.

From her perch on the couch, Kimmy instantly noticed her sister, and her sister's new dog. "Looks like Samanth-duh finally managed to bring a man home for the holidays."

Sam had no response. What was happening? Sam was a new, improved version of herself. She was taking care of herself. She had new clothes, nice hair, she had friends and a life. She was a good person. She was a fully-realized functioning adult who worked hard and engaged in continuous learning. There was nothing to criticize about her existence, and yet she knew that in her sister's eyes, she was a complete failure.

"Sam doesn't need a man. And I haven't noticed you bringing anyone home either, Kimberly-Anne." Thank goodness, Brad was there, walking in the front door. He was loaded down with a comical amount of presents and luggage in his arms, Ray-Ray clinging to his leg making dinosaur noises, and Stacey trailing behind with even more food and gifts. Seeing Ajax, Ray-Ray released Brad and ran to him.

"What did we say about meeting dogs, buddy?" Stacey reminded him. Ray-Ray politely held out his hand for an introductory sniffing. The little dog welcomed the attention, and the two were instantly adorable together. Sam came back to life at once, setting down her bags and kneeling to play with her nephew and her dog.

Kimmy made a disgusted noise. "Is that mutt safe around kids?"

"Seems to me you're just jealous that Sam has something new in her life." Brad was heating up. "We all know you can't stand when anyone else is more interesting than you."

"Shut up, Bradford." Kimmy was clearly feeling the holiday spirit and bringing the attention back to herself, using the name she'd made up to annoy him as a child.

Stacey tried to ease the mood. "I didn't know you would be here, Kimmy. It's nice to see you."

"What, I have to get permission to come to my own house?" With a fake salute, she rolled on. "Ma'am, yes ma'am. Do I need your clearance to stay in my own room? Is there a form I'm supposed to fill out?"

"No one suggested that. We're going to get settled now." Giving up, Stacey called loudly for Sam's mother. "Beverly, we're here!"

Sam saw Kimmy gearing up to go after someone, anyone, again. Before she could, Sam quickly asked Ray-Ray to help her bring Ajax's toys and supplies to her room. He obliged, and then joined them for a stroll around the neighborhood. Sam pulled herself successfully out of the line of fire, at least temporarily.

Getting dressed to go out, she realized she was about to see all of Kimmy's friends. Did her sister know? Had she been invited, too? If she was, they hadn't said anything. She texted Courtney. "Guess who was here when I got to my parents' place?"

Three animated dots flickered on the screen, followed by, "My condolences. I hope she doesn't ruin your holiday. Did you tell her we're meeting up?"

"No. I wasn't sure if you knew she was here."

"I didn't. I hope it's not too complicated for you to get away without her knowing. Are you still coming?"

"Of course. I'll be stealthy."

"LOL perfect. Gotta finish getting ready, see you in a bit."

By this time, Kimmy had removed herself to her own room, sulking at the lack of engagement. Trying to get out of the house before her sister emerged again, Sam quickly fed Ajax, and went over instructions for his care with Beverly and Ray. "It's all written down here. Remember: no human food, no matter how cute he is when he begs, and if there's an emergency call me right away, ok?"

"I think we understand how a dog works, Samantha. He'll be fine. Matter of fact, he can come keep me company in my study. It'll be nice and quiet for him in there." With that, Ray scooped Ajax up and walked off. Sam realized she'd given her father the perfect excuse to avoid his family.

Stacey came out with her purse and keys. "Ready?"

"Ready for what?" A harsh voice demanded from the top of the staircase. Kimberly-Anne, ready for round two.

"I'm dropping Sam off to hang out with some of her friends."

"Sam doesn't have friends."

"Regardless of your assessment, she indeed has human friends, with whom she has real plans, to which I am taking her myself. Bev, I'll be back soon to help wrap things up before church."

Kimmy now cast a glare at her mother. "You're all going to church?"

Stacey fielded the question, sparing Bev the frustration. Bev threw up her hands and walked into the kitchen.

"No Kimmy. Your mom and dad are staying home with Ajax. Brad, Ray-Ray, and I are going to the candlelight service, same as every year."

"Why are you dropping off Sam, then?"

"We're going to pick Sam up from her friends' later, and she's coming with us to the service, like she has the past few years. She shouldn't drive after drinking, and besides, finding parking on Christmas Eve is impossible. Any other details I can clarify?"

"Lighten up. I just didn't realize there was a whole tradition without me."

"You are welcome to come."

"To church? No thanks."

"Well, maybe you can meet up with your own friends, then."

"No one is around or answering. I guess they're all too busy with their stupid families and kids and stuff."

"Yes, it is wild how some people actually enjoy being with their family. Sam, let's go."

Sam walked toward the door without looking at her sister. "FINE!" Kimmy barked after them. "I guess I'll be the only one who stays here to help Mom!" Sam felt sorry for Beverly, but not enough to stay behind.

As they got in the car, Stacey remarked, "How I love having our very own Grinch. Makes Christmas so much more authentic." Sam couldn't help chuckling.

Pulling up to the front of the restaurant, Stacey reminded Sam to be outside and ready to go when they came to pick her. Sam promised, and Stacey told her to have fun.

Inside, Sam found the table already partially filled with the group, and was amazed by how at ease she was. She immediately fell back into conversation with them, picking up like no time had passed since Black Friday. Sam drank mulled wine, feeling the warmth rise up inside her, matching the general mood.

As more people arrived, the group grew louder and conversation picked up. A few people asked after

Ajax, which made Sam glad. Then, on the topic of dating, Courtney started to tease Sam. "It seems like you've been having some fun lately. I've seen you tagged in lots of posts with lots of random ladies."

Sam hadn't realized how much of her dating life was public. It always surprised her when people noticed or cared. She tried to play it off, but Allison, another of Kimmy's friends, pressed her. "Wait! I thought that's what was happening, but I wasn't sure, because then it was all Ajax, all the time. So you're dating, like, a lot?"

Courtney affirmed, "Yeah it looks like she's out with a new woman, like, every day."

"I know how it looks, but it's hard to know what people are really like from apps. So you have to meet them in person. A lot of them, in person."

"As long as you're having fun."

"I'm not looking for a serious relationship. I'm just seeing who is out there."

There were cheers of encouragement around the table. Sam redirected the conversation to Steve, asking how his startup was going. He was in the middle of a detailed explanation on his approach to Software as a Service when a woman who looked familiar walked in.

"Oh my God, SAM?!" The woman ran toward the table, lunging to hug her. Recognition clicked. It was Allison's older sister, Mari.

"I thought it'd be a fun surprise if neither of you knew!" Allison clapped her hands, clearly delighted with herself.

Sam stood up to give Mari a proper hug. They slid back into the booth next to each other, and from across the table, Kendra asked "What am I missing?"

Allison explained, "Sam was Mari's first girl kiss!"

Sam and Mari both stared at her in shock.

"You remember that?!" Mari looked as bewildered as Sam felt.

"Duh! I saw the whole thing, how could I forget?!"

Allison turned to the rest of the table. "Ok, so one night, Sam was babysitting us at my house. It was me, Kimmy, Courtney, Bridget, a few other girls. Sam was having an awful night; we were really being brats. Now, Mari had been out drinking and smoking—obviously under age—with some of her friends. She and Sam were in the same grade, and you could tell Sam didn't want to be caught dead hanging out with a bunch of little kids. Remember Sam? You were so embarrassed."

Sam was currently embarrassed, but wanting to be a good sport, nodded.

"Anyway, Sam pretended she urgently needed something from the laundry room just to get out of there. We had one of those big basement laundry rooms, you know? Everyone else went back to playing

Mall Madness, but Mari followed Sam, and I followed Mari. I saw Mari go into the room, and then I saw you two kiss."

Courtney cut in. "No way! You didn't tell me that! I was right there."

"Wait, did Kimmy know?" Sam felt delirious.

"Of course not. You both looked so happy, and I knew she'd be mean. I didn't want her going after my sister like that. After you left, I asked Mari about it. She said you were such a nice person, she was glad you were her first girl kiss. I mean, by that time she'd kissed a LOT of guys."

"Aaaand, that's enough." Mari took control of the conversation. "Yes, Samantha here was my bisexual awakening. I suppose I have you to thank for at least one of my marriages."

"You mean divorces." Allison corrected her.

"One of?" Ventured Sam.

"Oh yes. I married Derek right out of college, but we got divorced pretty quickly. Next I married Tanya, and that lasted for a few years. Then I went back to Derek. Then I divorced Derek. Again. But! If it wasn't for your kiss, I wouldn't have known I wanted to be with a Tanya some day. Even if it didn't last."

Sam smiled, gulped down the rest of her mulled wine and ordered two more, one each for herself and Mari. Everyone around them turned back to other conversations, while the two caught up more. Sam had shelved that memory, and had nearly convinced herself it was something she'd imagined.

Seeing Mari in person again brought so much back to the surface Sam wasn't ready to think about, so she drank even more. Mari kept pace with Sam. They took a selfie together on Sam's phone, and agreed they needed to stay in touch.

A text from Brad interrupted the reunion. "On our way!"

Sam exchanged goodbye hugs with everyone. As she wrapped her scarf she realized that Mari's arm was on her elbow, escorting her to the exit. She looked up at Sam. "I'll wait with you, make sure you don't get kidnapped or anything."

Standing in the parking lot, Sam's head was spinning, and all the heated wine combined with her emotions, making her feel even more dizzy. She and Mari made small talk, when suddenly they were kissing, for all the world to see. "Woooo!" They heard from the restaurant door, breaking the trance. Their friends had followed them and seen the whole thing.

"Yeah Samson!" This was punctuated with a beep of a car horn administered by Brad, who leaned over Stacey from his passenger seat.

Sam had no idea she'd been observed on two fronts, but didn't really care. She was glad she got to see Mari again. She gave her one last parting embrace, and lifted herself into the back seat next to Ray-Ray, unable to hide her mirth.

"Who was that, Aunt Sam?"

"An old friend."

"She's pretty."

"She's also thrice-divorced, little man, so don't get any ideas." This was met with laughter from Stacey, in the driver's seat.

Looking in the mirror, Stacey noticed Sam on her phone, staring at the picture she'd taken with Mari. "Sam, I hope you're not planning to be on that thing all night."

"I won't. I don't want to ruin the candlelight," Sam promised, not looking up from her phone for even half a second.

"Here's an idea. You can give your phone to Brad so it doesn't tempt you, and he'll hold on to it until after church."

Sam knew how important this service was to Stacey. It was the solemn evening gathering where they sang all of the melancholy and somber Christmas songs, which were Stacey's favorites.

"I'll do you one better, Stace. I'll put it in airplane mode, too!" She did, and handed the phone to Brad, happy to stop thinking about Mari for a minute.

Sam never really enjoyed going to church, but she liked being there on Christmas Eve with Stacey, who hadn't grown up doing things like that with her family. Before marrying Brad, Stacey didn't celebrate holidays, and sometimes got overwhelmed by spending Christmas with Sam's family. Sam understood that Stacey treasured the peace and calm of that evening ritual, and was flattered she got to be part of it.

As usual, the nave was decked with poinsettias and candelabras. They sang all the usuals: "God Rest Ye Merry, Gentlemen," "O Little Town of Bethlehem," "Oh Come, Oh Come, Emmanuel," "Let All Mortal Flesh," any song written in a minor chord. It always ended with the lights turned down and each attendee holding a candle during "Silent Night," which was the closest Sam ever came to experiencing sacredness or magic.

On the way home in the car, Ray-Ray fell asleep on Sam's shoulder. Sam felt herself grow drowsy, too. When they pulled up on their street, she saw her father standing with Ajax, a few houses down from theirs. Before she finished stepping out of the car he was in her face, demanding, "Why haven't you answered your phone?!"

"I don't have it, I gave it to Brad."

"Why would you do a thing like that? Never mind."

"What's wrong, is Ajax ok?" He looked fine to her.

"No, it's Kimmy. Come with me." Looking at Brad, he nodded toward the house and said "See if you can calm them down."

Handing Sam her phone, Brad asked, "Wait, Dad, what happened?" Understandably, he wanted to know exactly what he was getting himself into.

"Kimmy saw some pictures online and started screaming, totally out of control, about how she wants to physically harm your sister. Said she's going to murder Sam as soon as she gets back, calling her a lying bitch, all sorts of things, I don't know. All I know is, Sam can't go in while her sister is still raging like that."

He took Sam by the arm, gesturing at Brad with the leash. "We're going to walk the dog. You go sort things out so everyone can all be relaxed when we get back." With that, Ray marched her away from the house.

"What picture, Dad?"

"I don't know, you know I don't pay attention to those online things. Kimberly-Anne saw something one of her friends posted and lost her damn mind. She's been yelling non-stop since. Said she was going to kill you, and frankly I don't put it past her."

Sam pulled out her phone, and turned off airplane mode. Instantly, notifications flooded the screen. As they walked she sorted through them—texts and calls from her parents, a text from Mari asking for the selfie, a stream of texts from a number that must have been Kimmy's given that they were all threats, and then notifications from social media. She opened one of them up.

"Oh shit." Sam came to a halt. Her dad looked at her silently.

It wasn't a picture. It was a video. Sam was in a fog as she processed what she saw.

Allison had made the brilliant decision to post a video of Sam and Mari kissing, with everyone cheering for them. Behind Sam, Stacey and Brad could be seen driving up, Brad's voice clearly ringing through the parking lot. At the end, the camera swiveled around to capture everyone gathered out front, clapping, settling on Allison's own face, with an exaggerated look of surprise, placing her hand over her mouth.

In posting the video, she tagged Sam, Mari, and all of their friends who were present, and included the helpful caption: "First kiss reunited! Sam and Mari feeling the #mistletoe and the #mulledwine, and we're all living for it! #ChristmasKissmas"

Panic took over as Sam tried to grasp the full weight of what had happened, the betrayal her sister must be feeling.

Not only did Kimmy find out Sam was with *her* friends, the same friends who had dodged Kimmy's communications. No, on top of that, this was how she found out Sam was gay. And that all of Kimmy's friends already knew, and in some cases had always known. Also, Brad and Stacey, and presumably even Ray-Ray, knew. The whole world knew, except Kimmy.

Sam felt ill. "I'm sorry Dad, but I messed up big time. We need to go home."

"I'm not kidding, Samantha. Your sister is unhinged, and I am genuinely concerned she might hurt you. She was smashing things."

"She was breaking things and you left Mom alone with her?!"

"I thought Ajax shouldn't be around that."

"How convenient for you. Stacey just took Ray-Ray into that mess, and that's completely unfair to them. Let's go."

Determined, Sam double-timed back to the house, only to see police cars with red and blue hood lights flashing. One of the officers posted out front tried to wave them along "Nothing to see here folks, family matter, move along."

"This is our house, what's going on?" Sam was terrified.

"One of your neighbors called to report what sounded like a violent domestic dispute, and said they were afraid for the safety of the whole street."

"Can we go in?"

The officer moved out of their way. When Sam got inside, she had an out-of-body experience. She watched herself taking in the police interviewing her family members, Brad and Kimmy separated into corners, Beverly trying to appear calm, and Ray-Ray, wailing, clinging to Stacey.

Sam knew it was all her fault, and didn't know where to begin.

Kimmy saw her first, charging, snarling. "Well if it isn't the lying lesbian! Your asshole accomplices," gesturing at Brad and Stacey, "tried to cover for you, but I know. I fucking know EVERYTHING!"

Her contorted face hardly looked human. An officer stepped in front of Kimmy, reminding her she needed to calm down. After some time passed, the police seemed satisfied no one was going to be hurt. They walked Beverly and Kimmy to the door.

"Where you going?" Sam asked after them.

"Your sister would like to go to a hotel until she can get a flight home. She's called a car. I'm going to wait with her outside until it picks her up."

Stacey took Ray-Ray to Brad's room as the police finished up and filed out, turning off their lights and driving away. Sam wondered which of her neighbors had called them, then realized it didn't matter. Even if people hadn't heard the fight, they now knew something had happened at Sam's house. Her mother was going to be humiliated.

Beverly came back in the house just as Stacey reappeared in the living room, suitcases in hand. Bev looked like she might cry. "You're leaving?"

"As soon as possible. I'll be right back down. I'm getting my son, and we're going." Looking to Brad, "You need to decide if you're coming with us."

Bev urged her, "Honey, don't go. Please."

"No. This family is a mess and I'm not putting my son through any more of it tonight. Shame on you. On all of you."

She looked directly at each member of the family. "Kimmy clearly needs serious help. She shouldn't have melted down like that, and she certainly shouldn't have destroyed things and threatened Sam. But let's not act like she got here all on her own." She jabbed her finger in the air at each of them, one by one. "Indulging her, ignoring her, lying to her, running away!"

Her last finger-jab was aimed squarely at Ray, who proved Stacey's point, huffing as he left the room, "I don't have to listen to this."

Stacey was undaunted, sweeping her accusatory hand at Brad, at Bev, at Sam. "You all don't even behave as if you're related. It's nothing but silent contempt and avoidance. You act like it's such a burden to be together, but you people have no idea how easy you've got it. Grow up. All of you! The time is long past due for his family to get its act together, and until you do, I'm out."

"Will you at least come back in the morning?" Beverly was crushed, her voice cracking. "It's Christmas Day, you can't let Ray-Ray miss Christmas."

"Can't I?" Stacey was furious. "You seem to be forgetting, I know what it's like to grow up in an unstable family. I know what it does to a child, and I'll be damned if I'm going to let my son be exposed to your dysfunction for one minute longer. Brad, if you're coming with us, load the car. Now." She ran up the stairs to retrieve Ray-Ray.

Brad immediately grabbed the bags and obeyed Stacey's order without even saying goodbye to his mom or sister. Stacey followed him, Ray-Ray asleep in her arms. She sped outside, looking at neither Sam nor Beverly again, leaving the front door open behind her.

Sam stared in disbelief and moved to shut the door. Behind her, Beverly, in a small voice, excused herself. Left alone with poor, confused little Ajax looking up at her, Sam surveyed the wreckage. The house was in shambles. She reassured Ajax, then set to straightening up, imagining how it all must have happened as she did.

She swept up shattered glass in the dining room and retrieved thrown objects from around the living room. She covered and put away the food in the kitchen, which Beverly had clearly been baking when the whole situation erupted.

Sam started the dishwasher and put away what she washed by hand. She lost track of time, and was shocked to see how late it had gotten. As tired as she felt, didn't know how she was going to calm down enough to sleep, and considered driving to her apartment.

When she finished cleaning, Sam noticed a creaking sound coming from the backyard. She picked up Ajax and followed the noise to find her mother sitting on the swing set, bundled in a camping blanket from the garage. Bev held a bottle of beer in her hand, staring up at the stars. Realizing she was intruding on a private moment, Sam turned to go, but paused as her mother timidly whispered, "This isn't what I wanted."

Sam walked gently toward her. Beverly gestured with a nod of her head at the empty swing next to her. Sam took her seat, delicately beginning to rock her toes against the ground. They sat in awkward silence for a moment, staring at their breath making condensation clouds against the frigid air with each exhale. Sam wasn't sure where her mother was going with her statement, and felt great apprehension. She couldn't recall many helpful conversations they'd had over the years.

Her mom took a sophisticated sip from the bottle and continued. "I know you've never liked me. Don't look at me like that. You are a daddy's girl, and always have been. Not that I blame you. I'd probably choose him, too. He is the calm one, the one who gets to be above the fray. Not a nag like me. He doesn't get bogged down by the drama, he brushes off the arguments.

"I wish I could do that, too. But one of us had to be a parent. Your brother and sister would have destroyed each other if left to their own devices. You think I wanted to be a lifelong referee? That my dream in having children was to spend every day walking on eggshells, trying not to set off any conversational land mines?

"They were so high-maintenance, Samantha. So demanding of my time, my focus. But not you. You were my predictable, well-behaved, reliable child. My set-it-and-forget-it girl."

"You did forget me, Mom. A lot."

"I know, sweetie. And I'm not making excuses, but I am trying to help you understand. I had so much on my plate, I was always one moment away from everything falling apart. I was the breadwinner. I was the one running the household. I was the chef, the chauffeur. I was juggling so much in my mind at any given moment, and then your siblings would explode.

They sucked up all of my attention, and there was nothing left for you.

"I know it wasn't fair. It wasn't fair to any of us. I thought I was marrying a partner, someone who would be in this with me fifty-fifty. But he disappeared. Sure, he was physically here, but mentally, emotionally, he completely abdicated his responsibilities as a husband and a father. And the more I failed, the more you loved him.

"I used to see the way you'd look at him. The way you'd talk about books you'd read together. You think I didn't want to read books, too? I didn't have the time. I didn't have the energy. And of course he chose you to focus on, you were the easy one. But maybe if he'd focused a little on your siblings, too, they'd have turned out happier or more well-adjusted. And maybe if you'd been more like them, he wouldn't have focused on you, either."

Sam didn't know what to say. She'd never heard her mother this unguarded. Sam couldn't reconcile being simultaneously touched by her mother's sincerity and disappointed in her insistence on justifying parental neglect. She took in a deep breath.

"I forgive you," she exhaled, staring at her mother from under the hoods of her eyes. She wasn't sure she wanted to make direct eye contact or talk more with her yet. All she knew was she was finally ready for bed. "Good night, Mom." Too tired to drive home, Sam and Ajax curled up in her childhood bed, and slept in late the next morning.

"We're not coming. Sorry. Talk soon." Brad's text was brief, but final.

"Understood." Sam typed back.

Ajax at her side, she walked into the living room, surveying the damage caused by the events of the night before: Brad and Stacey were gone, Kimmy was at her hotel awaiting her flight home, Ray was hiding away somewhere, and Bev was in the dining room, slowly putting away the china and crystal. Christmas was cancelled.

Sam let Ajax outside, and when he came back in she joined her mother, silently helping to wrap and store each place setting and serving dish. Sam had always loved the cheery Spode pattern, but something about it this morning made her incredibly sad. It was as if the plates and glasses taunted her with an idyllic Christmas that was now beyond her family's reach. When they were done, Bev patted Sam on the forearm.

"Thank you, Samantha. Maybe we'll try again next year." She then clutched Sam closely to her, holding her for a moment, before walking out of the room.

Sam packed the car and returned to her apartment, with the whole holiday now left for her to spend alone. Sam harnessed Ajax, and together they went for a long walk to get some fresh air and clear her head. She was confused at the thoughts racing in her mind.

Since Kimmy had been born, Sam had no memory of her mom voluntarily hugging her or paying attention to her at all, really. As she replayed the conversation with Beverly in her head, though, something clicked. Brad had been right that night in the bar when he told Sam she'd been unfair. Sam had never considered if her mom was content, and realized that of course her mom was always dejected. Beverly lived her life exclusively for other people. That would make anyone woeful.

Something broke through in Sam's head and her heart. No, it did not excuse her mother's past mistreatment of her. But it did explain it, and that was key to understanding. It unlocked in Sam a level of empathy for her mother, as she was also living a life she was less than happy with.

Sam decided that if it wasn't too late to start her own life over, then it wasn't too late to start over with her mom, either. She had to be realistic, of course, and know she couldn't expect Beverly to suddenly be a happier person to interact with.

However, Sam wasn't a kid anymore, she was an adult. As an adult, she could make the conscious decision to give her mother the benefit of the doubt. From that moment on, Sam would not judge her mom's actions in the context of every previous hurt or disappointment that had accumulated during Sam's life.

Sam would give her mother the grace of taking it one interaction at a time, with the new perspective that her mom was coming from a place of being a very unfulfilled person, and that her unhappiness wasn't a reflection on Sam. It was a relief to know she didn't have to take her mother's frustrations personally, that it was neither her fault, nor her obligation to fix. Sam felt free.

When their walk ended, she ordered an obscene amount of Chinese food and watched every version of *A Christmas Carol* she could find streaming or on TV. She opened all of Ajax's presents for him. He was thrilled by so many new things to sniff at and play with. He immediately pulled the filling out of a purple, plush dragon, looking quite accomplished as he displayed his conquest for Sam's approval.

As they finished their final *Christmas Carol* of the night, Sam whispered to Ajax. "See, that's why I love this story. Look how old Scrooge is, but he still changed. And look, look! All those people he was awful to for years, they're freaking happy for him!"

If Ajax was impressed, his snoring didn't convey this.

Lowering her volume to let him sleep, she added, "Any one of them would have been completely justified in telling him off, or refusing to forgive him. But they're happy that he's happy. That's enough for them."

She pulled out her phone for the first time since she got home, and scrolled through texts she'd missed from friends, including an apology from Allison. Sam texted back to reassure her that it was all going to be fine.

On social media, she saw an endless stream of photos her friends had posted, reveling with their biological and their chosen families. In the past, Sam would have been hurt or jealous. Instead, she was uplifted by the looks of love on their faces.

Opting to add a little cheer into the universe, she took a picture of Ajax, slumbering contently, surrounded by the fluff from his eviscerated toy. She posted it, captioning, "He didn't choose the fluff life, the fluff life chose him. Wishing you and yours a merry little Christ-mess. #AjaxTheGreat #ChristmasCanine"

Sam was inspired, and determined to channel Scrooge. She was captivated by the possibility that she could take control in her life. As she entered the new year, she was ready for all that life held, determined that 2020 was going to be the "Year of Sam."

Chapter 19: Silence in the time of COVID

JANUARY 2020

The "Year of Sam" was off to a solid start, beginning with a New Year's Eve party at Johanna and Eddie's. She was still bothered by how Christmas had fallen apart, so she channeled her energy into making plans, filling every weekend with brunches, puppy play dates, bike rides, hikes, and plenty of happy hours and parties. Her social life was so full that for the first time, she didn't even mind being single on Valentine's Day. It helped that Johanna and Eddie hosted a Presidents Day costume party. Sam went as Ulysses S. Grant, and the hosts dressed as Millard Fillmore and Chester A. Arthur. Em shook everyone's hand aggressively and introduced herself as "JQA," in a cantankerous voice, while Tali's Martin van Buren costume stole the show. Sam felt more integrated in her friends' lives than ever.

One Sunday in early March, Sam hosted brunch for Brad, Stacey, and Ray-Ray. While she hadn't seen her family in person since the Christmas melee, she had started texting with Brad and Stacey more regularly, and their exchanges were getting back to normal. Sam missed them, and decided that getting together at her place—without Ray, Bev, or Kimmy—would be a lowkey way to ease back into each other's lives. Seeing them again was greatly reassuring for Sam, and seemed to be equally fulfilling for her guests.

"You know Sam," Stacey offered. "I think this is just what we needed. Maybe we could make this a regular thing for the four of us. A monthly brunch, and we can take turns hosting."

"I'd love that! Yes, let's do it!"

"All right, it's on. Our place in April!"

But April brunch didn't happen. Nothing happened, because the world stopped. At least it did for Sam.

The pandemic was devastating for Sam. Not that it wasn't hard for everyone, but she'd just gotten used to a more vibrant social life, and suddenly she was alone. She missed Brad, Stacey, and Ray-Ray. She missed brunch and happy hours and holiday parties.

She missed her friends, she missed Emil, Dave, Sarita, and all of her other friends from Japanese class and cooking lessons. She missed being swept up in Tali's enthusiasm, and calmed down by Em's assured demeanor.

Just when Sam finally felt like she was deepening her connections with people and getting her life on track to where she wanted it, progress came to a halt, leaving her isolated. She tried to remain social through video calls with her family, friends, and colleagues, but they only heightened her sense of solitude. As much as it might have felt intimate to see people "face-to-face," she grew resentful of being the only solo face on the grid during any given call. Other people crowded around their screens as couples or in family groups.

Even when she had a good conversation, Sam couldn't help begrudging the knowledge that when they finished their hang out, everyone else would continue their lives together, while she was all on her own.

To her surprise, she found she really missed being at work. Her job had never been her life, but it wasn't until she couldn't see her colleagues every day that she appreciated what a large proportion of human interactions they provided her, especially since she'd opened herself up to being friendly with them. Seeing coworkers through a screen didn't replicate the sensation of being together.

During the day, Sam couldn't concentrate. She was unable to stop consuming pandemic and political news from TV or from her phone, and fell behind on her work, which served only to make her feel even worse. At night, she couldn't sleep, too filled with anxiety to settle her mind. She stayed up until 2:00 or 3:00 a.m., doom-scrolling through social media and news sites, waking up the next morning only to find the world was still on hold.

Tired from the lack of sleep the night before, she'd have even more trouble getting work done. Sam developed a bad habit of falling asleep randomly during the work day and missing emails, leading to a vicious cycle of anxiety that disrupted her nightly sleep and exhaustion that ruined her waking hours.

Everything felt futile in her disconnected state. She couldn't bring herself to care about how she looked or felt, going days at a time between showers or performing the most basic hygiene of brushing her teeth. She lived in the same pair of shorts and hoodie until they were nearly a second skin.

As time blurred together, she also stopped keeping her apartment clean. Trash and laundry piled up, and nothing made her care. Nutrition seemed equally pointless, as she subsisted on canned foods she'd stocked up on. After a few weeks, she stopped even heating the soup or ravioli, spooning the cold, congealed food directly from the can into her mouth.

By late May her apartment was a mess. She was a mess. She saw no light at the end of the tunnel. Everything seemed meaningless. Sam was in danger of fully descending into a period of darkness, save for one silver lining.

Sam was more grateful than ever that Tali had convinced her to adopt Ajax. He became her lifeline. He was all she had. He gave her a reason to wake up, to go outside and spend time in nature, especially when she took him on quiet, wooded paths to avoid potentially-contagious people as much as possible. Having to meet his basic daily needs provided Sam the only structure in her life.

She'd always chatted with Ajax, but that was previously balanced by interactions with humans. As she increasingly avoided video calls, she depended even more on him for conversation. After realizing she'd gone days speaking only to Ajax, Sam started keeping a voice diary so she had someone to talk to. Sadly, she realized that she had nothing to record, and felt like she'd taken a huge step backwards in her life.

Once again, Sam found herself consumed with her memories. She couldn't stop dwelling on certain events over and over in her head. All of her progress she'd made in managing her memories had ebbed away. During a text exchange with Stacey, Sam explained she felt like the memories were stuck in a loop and she didn't know how to shut it off, but that she was so very tired of seeing the same ones endlessly. Stacey suggested Sam try a different approach.

"Ignoring them isn't working," she pointed out to Sam. "So, embrace them. Choose one memory and meditate on it. When one pops up, don't run away; write it down, get it out of your head and on to a page. Clearly these are coming to you for a reason, and you need to work through them. Trust me, writing things out always helps me feel better." Sam promised to try.

Two days later, a package arrived for Sam containing a journal and matching ball point pen. There was no note included, but Sam knew who it was from, and sent Stacey a text to thank her. Sam, with an abundance of free time on her hands, started to write her memories down. At first, the act of writing them down caused her trepidation, fearing it would make them more real or force her to confront how damaging the experiences had been to her.

As she wrote, she recognized that many of her memories centered on how she got to where she was today, living in isolation with no roommate and no romantic partner. She saw the pattern she fell into repeatedly in past relationships. Desperate each time for a clean start, Sam was drawn into toxic friendships, in which various girls dominated her with their outsized personalities until they effectively ruled her life.

Rapidly scratching her pen across the pages of her journal, Sam described how invariably, no matter how the friendships started, before long, Sam was overwhelmed at how quickly the intensity of the relationship turned up, and how quickly they ended. Suddenly these instant best friends wanted to influence how she dressed, what music she listened to, how she spent her time, and who else she could talk to. Every aspect of her life was either criticized or controlled.

Writing without judging herself, she continued to exorcize the ghosts of her past. Sam wrote honestly about fearing close relationships with women, especially after the difficulty she endured in elementary school. Throughout these formative relationships, anytime Sam tried to exert her own personality, it was met with resistance from the narcissists in her life. It was as if these people sized her up immediately, understanding she was so hungry for connection she'd let them use her as a door mat. That was the only role they were willing to allow her, and if she tried to be herself, they exited her life.

She'd relived these memories so many times, but always as a forced participant. This time, Sam was writing about them as an observer, and was able to write the conclusions of what she'd learned. It was all obvious, of course, but seeing her words on the paper brought clarity. Sam understood these experiences were why, even now after successfully expanding her social circle and deepening her friendships, she still couldn't allow herself to believe that people could ever love her for who she was.

The fear remained that people simply wanted to absorb her into their own life stories, in which they were the main characters and she was there only to support. Sam lost track of time, her hand cramped, and she realized hours had passed while she'd written out so many of the toxic memories from her life. As she finished, she realized how unfounded her fears were. She now had proof from her own lived experience as an adult that she could form relationships without hiding who she was or changing herself to match someone's expectations.

The journaling session wore her out, but it did help her identify negative patterns, and ideas for how to avoid them in the future. Now that she felt more prepared to navigate relationships, she wondered when she'd ever be in a position to make new friends, or to meet a potential romantic partner.

When would life start again? How could she date when she couldn't go out? She was becoming more outwardly despondent, and people noticed. Some of her college friends grew particularly worried. In June, Tali suggested they could safely get together to walk the dogs, just to get out of their homes for a while. Sam agreed, but didn't believe they'd follow through.

Chapter 20: The Dog Days of Summer

JUNE 2020

"Come outside, bring your boy!" The text was from Em. Sam grabbed a mask, harnessed Ajax, and ran downstairs. The urge to hug her friends was difficult to override. They settled instead for awkward little waves from a distance, and a curtsy from Tali. The dogs, however, observed no such protocol, thrilled at being reunited.

The group went for a walk, maintaining space between them as best they could with the dogs rambunctiously tackling each other. As Sam complained that she felt like life was on pause and that she was treading water, Em offered a different perspective. "Time is passing whether we want it to or not, so why not control what we do during it as much as we can?"

Of course Em was unfazed by a global pandemic, Sam thought. Nothing ever gets the best of her. Sam commented that they both seemed to be doing well, unlike so many people.

Em shrugged her shoulders. "We're coping and surviving, which is the most that anyone can really hope for in a time like this. For me, it's all a matter of routine: getting up every day, showering, eating well, and making the most of my time. To be totally honest, I actually find the current pause in social obligations a relief. I've reveled in the extra time to catch up on books I've wanted to read or playing my guitar."

Tali shook her head in disagreement. "I *desperately* miss people! I don't know what to do with all my energy. I've been trying to be productive, though. I've completely gutted our house, sorting through all of our possessions to keep, sell, donate, or trash. I've reorganized and redecorated the whole place, and I can't wait to show it off once we're able to have people over again!"

Returning to Sam's apartment, they all agreed to make dog walks a recurring date as long as no one got sick. Sam hadn't smiled that much in a long time, and her face physically hurt afterward. She watched them walk away, hand in hand, and noticed how put together they looked. Was that just because they were a couple and had support, or could single people thrive in this time, too?

The visit snapped Sam out of her funk. Something in her turned over, and she decided that Em, as usual, knew what she was talking about. No one expected Sam to live her best life, but she could at least try not to give up. She suddenly felt self-conscious about the state in which she'd presented herself to them. After feeding Ajax dinner, she took a thorough shower and brushed her teeth. Having neglected her hygiene over the previous weeks, gargling mouthwash was a jolt of refreshment.

She threw on a fresh set of clothes, stepped out of her bathroom, and seeing her apartment through rejuvenated eyes, she was appalled at how much she'd let it become dirty and disheveled. It was almost unrecognizable. Pulling out her favorite graph paper pad, she started a list of cleaning tasks. It wasn't going to be quick or easy, but she had to fill the time anyway, and now she had a plan.

Next, she looked through her food and realized it was time for some new groceries, particularly some fresh fruits and vegetables and non-canned items, if she could get them. There was a concerning amount of empty beer, wine, and liquor bottles laying around the apartment. Sam didn't realize how much she'd been drinking, and opted not to add alcohol into her virtual shipping cart. She placed the order for a delivery, which would not arrive for a few days, as her local grocery store was currently overrun with online orders.

Room by room, she methodically disposed of trash, put clutter away, and cleaned surfaces. Ajax was happy to supervise. He seemed to feed off her new found energy, thrilled she was resuming normal activities. She ran laundry and washed dishes. She dusted, vacuumed, swept, mopped, and scrubbed. Her apartment glistened and gleamed.

When she was done, Sam was exhausted and drenched in sweat. It had been ages since she'd exerted that kind of effort. She hopped in the shower again, then patted herself dry, putting on her most luxurious pajamas, a pair of fluffy socks, and her fleece robe. She was proud of her progress. It felt like a new apartment, and she felt revitalized.

She made a decaf hot tea, and fueled with post-cleaning ambition, started another list. She created a proposed routine for her days going forward. Em said routine kept her going, so Sam would try to find the right mix of activities for herself.

Each day she would:
- Walk & feed Ajax, playing with him to keep him motivated and engaged,
- Workout—walking in place, lifting with her five-pound weights, anything free she could do in her apartment,
- Meditate—her friend Jolan mentioned on a previous call it was the only thing keeping him sane through lockdown,
- Shower and brush her teeth,
- Eat a healthy breakfast, lunch, and dinner,
- Work,
- Message at least one friend or relative,
- Tidy up any daily messes or clutter,
- Journal before bed,
- Avoid screen time for at least an hour before sleep,
- Limit consumption of news,
- Not drink booze,
- Only go on social media once per day.

The to-do list was aspirational, to be sure, but she felt it was the kind of structure she needed to keep from relapsing into her malaise.

The first few days, she regretted how many goals she'd set for herself. Unenthusiastic, Sam went through the motions for many of the items. Still, she decided to stick with it, because lack of routine had not helped her to this point. Eventually, the entire list became habit. She started to feel better, and looked forward to reviewing her list each night and realizing how full her day had been, even on her own.

On the Fourth of July, Sam received a text from Johanna and Eddie. "Check your front door!" She did, and found a box with her name on it from the couple. They missed hosting holiday gatherings for friends, and decided to take their celebration on the road. They made Fourth of July party kits, which included: a container of cubed watermelon, some brownies, a to-go plate with macaroni and potato salads, barbecue chicken, baked beans and corn bread, patriotic cans of beer from a local brewery, novelty American flag sunglasses, a small box of sparklers, and a plastic lighter adorned with an eagle.

They took these and distributed them to all of their friends who lived within a 90-minute drive. Sam's box even included some red white and blue dog treats from a local pet store. Eddie and Johanna had only met Ajax a few times, but still thought of him. Sam was overwhelmed by the feeling of care and inclusion. She'd always considered herself an afterthought invite, but here they were, bringing the party to her.

After opening the box, she put the glasses on Ajax (he was confused more than annoyed) and took pictures of him, as well as of herself with the food. Em and Tali had also received a party box before they came over to walk the dogs, so she got a video of them dancing with their sparklers chanting "U-S-A, U-S-A!"

Sam sent the video and photos to their gracious host as a thanks, and for the first time in months posted something on social media. Sam was incredibly grateful to Eddie and Johanna for bringing her joy. She didn't realize how much an act of friendship could move her.

The mobile Fourth of July party inspired Sam to think about what she could do for other people. She'd spent so much time focused inwardly that she'd lost track of how other people were also struggling. When her mom called to tell her that Kimmy got COVID from taking an ill-advised trip—on which she practiced no safety measures—Sam felt compelled to reach out to her sister.

"I've tried to get her to take it more seriously, Samantha, but you know your sister. She said she wasn't about to miss out on celebrating her thirtieth birthday just because other people are scared of catching, 'a little cold.' It doesn't help that none of her friends in Florida seem to believe it's worth taking precautions, either. She's lucky she's not in a hospital, but I worry she won't give herself the full time to isolate and recover." Bev let out a long sigh, and Sam tried to reassure her mother.

She got Kimmy's home address from Bev, and assembled a get well kit. She filled it with a greeting card, cough drops, medicinal shower tabs and scented vapor rubs, soft lotion tissues, soothing teas, and cozy socks. While she got confirmation from the shipping company when it was delivered, she received no acknowledgment from Kimmy. Still, Sam was glad she'd made an effort.

As the months dragged on and the pandemic neared the one year mark, Sam decided to press forward in keeping busy, incorporating hobbies to fill even more of the time. She found online options for many of her previous activities, including remote sessions of her Japanese and cooking classes. She also tried some new hobbies, such as tai chi (which she quite liked) and painting with water colors (which she did not).

She was able to mark the passage of time and celebrate holidays thanks to packages from Johanna and Eddie; a kindness which Sam returned with thank you packages of her own, filled with batches of Sam's home-baked creations.

She even organized a few virtual group classes for her friends to make dishes or cocktails. Although this meant buying ingredients she'd likely never use again, and creating a temporary mess in her kitchen, it was worth it to feel connected.

Whenever she started to feel the nagging of comparison at how her friends had someone with whom they could share their finished recipes, she shook it off, reminding herself of all she had going for her. She even wrote a list to read in these moments:

- She was safe,
- She had her job she could do remotely, allowing her to pay her bills,
- She lived in an area where groceries and household goods could be easily be delivered,
- She had her health,
- She had Ajax,
- She had friends

During these gratitude exercises she'd realize how much she had to feel good about, which helped reset her mind.

Stacey had gotten the journal to help Sam get her bad memories out of her head, which had helped, but Sam decided to take it a step further and start filling it with positive memories. That way, if she started to feel the pull of negative nostalgia, she could read about happy times instead. Each day she tried to focus on one glad experience from her life. The recent events were easy, but to her surprise, she actually started to recall more distant memories. Even though specifics of her grandparents escaped her, she found fulfillment in seeing just how much she could remember of them. Writing about them made her feel as if they were near her again.

She also forced herself to continue her video calls, since it really was the only way to "see" anyone, but she tried to stop focusing on her own face during these. She spoke to Brad and Stacey most frequently during this time. Stacey often told Sam she was proud of her for the way she was handling the pandemic with resilience and grace. Given how much she ad Stacey, Sam couldn't think of anyone whose opinion meant more to her in this regard.

Brad had been able to continue therapy by video, and was more appreciative than ever he'd been talked into starting it. "I don't know how I'd be handling all of this right now without it, honestly." It was difficult for him, and the sessions sometimes left him drained. He had spent years trying to drown out the memories in his mind, but just as Sam realized she couldn't avoid her memories, he had to face and accept his, too.

His denial hadn't been just a deflection from the concerned women in his life, but was so deeply ingrained that he surprised himself at discovering how much pain he was carrying. Sometimes after sessions he would call Sam and tell her how tired he was, that he didn't realize how much just talking could wear a person out. Sam was honored to be a sounding board, and encouraged him to stick with it.

On one of their calls, Brad and Stacey shared that Kimmy had gotten COVID a second time. Stacey tried to be sympathetic, but Brad took no such effort. He went on a small rant about how Kimmy had never taken it seriously and only focused on herself, she had complained that as an extrovert and a single woman she needed social interaction, and how she had constantly posted pictures of herself at "socially distanced" brunches and happy hours and on weekend trips, all with different people. (She didn't seem to fully grasp the concept of a pod.)

Brad classified Kimmy as a selfish individual who put her own need to feel entertained and active above everyone else's safety and consideration. "It's because of people like her that this has gone on so long. I don't feel sorry for her, I feel sorry for the people she's probably been spreading it to while chasing her own desire for gratification. If assholes like her stayed home in the first place, this could have been over in a few weeks to a month. Now look where we are, a year later." Sam still wasn't in communication with Kimmy, so she didn't feel qualified to comment, but she made no attempt to reach out to her sister this time.

In happier news, Stacey and Brad were expecting another baby, which gave Sam a project to work on. With advice from Bev, she assembled a baby shower in a box, filled with items they needed, which inspired Bev to make one, too.

"Between the two of us, they should be set! This is such a great idea, Samantha!" Sam wasn't used to being the one who brought her mom joy or merriment, but was glad to share the experience with her.

Sam also made a big-brother-to-be gift bag for Ray-Ray, remembering the anticipation of waiting for a younger sibling. Once complete, she dropped both gift sets off to their front door. Sam and Ajax stood at the edge of their driveway while Stacey and Brad opened them, and her heart swelled at seeing how much they appreciated each item. She was particularly pleased at how much her nephew liked his presents.

Although the pregnancy was considered high-risk due to Stacey's age, she was an otherwise healthy person and didn't experience any more difficulty than she had with Ray-Ray. Eventually, Stacey had the baby; a girl named after Stacey's great aunt Dorothea. No one was allowed to be with them at the hospital. Brad confided that Stacey was actually glad not to have to deal with visitors, which Sam understood, but still regretted. She'd been there in the waiting room for

Ray-Ray, and had held him in his arms the day he was born.

They debated if her nickname would be Thea, Dori, or Dot, but figured that could wait until her personality developed a little. Sam saw the pictures they posted of Ray-Ray holding his little sister, looking at her with awe. She hoped his experience as an older sibling would be better than her own.

Chapter 21: Getting to Know You

2021
(SUMMER)

By the time Dorothea arrived, Brad had not only been going to therapy on a weekly basis, but also started to volunteer remotely with an organization where veterans could help other vets. He gave virtual talks to the other soldiers his age and younger, encouraging them to seek help and to know they weren't alone. Sam was proud of her brother, knowing this was a huge step for him.

Seeing the change that had taken place in him, Sam wanted to show her support. In summer of 2021 the world slowly started to open up again. She decided that she would join him in volunteering in-person for the organization. The goal of the non-profit was to curb the high rates of veteran homelessness, suicide, addiction, and depression by offering them a safe haven where they could find recreation and respite, and connect them with long-term resources.

The veterans they supported were from all ages, having served during conflicts from World War II to present day. The largest groups were those who had served in Vietnam, Iraq, and Afghanistan. Some had been deployed, some had remained stateside, but all had trauma from their time in service. Some stayed at the facility for long retreats, for which they could also bring their families. Others came by daily for company.

Remembering her brother at the bottom of the hill with the broken sled, Sam decided that if there was anything she could do to help others like him, she wanted to be a part of it. She went a few times a week after work, bringing Ajax with her. He became an instant celebrity, and everyone wanted a turn to cuddle him or shower him with praise and treats. He was happy to oblige, often falling asleep in the comfort of the arms or nestled on the lap of one of his new friends.

Rusty from her COVID-era solitude, Sam still wasn't very confident in small talk, so she gravitated to playing board games, especially with the veterans who were sharp and competitive. Sam had a secret mercenary streak when it came to board games. As a child, when she'd played marathon sessions with her grandparents, neither of them took it easy on her because she was a kid. While she occasionally managed to beat Grandpa Tony at Othello or backgammon, Grandma Jeannie routinely defeated her at chess.

Sam hadn't played most of the games in years, but they slowly came back to her. Her most consistent opponent was Eugene, a Vietnam veteran who sometimes walked, but more often used a wheelchair. Eugene was an elderly African-American man who was notorious for his quick wit and deadpan humor. If it wasn't for the little tells on his face, when he raised an eyebrow or allowed a hint of a smile to appear, he might have come across as mean-spirited, but Sam knew he was a well-meaning class clown who never outgrew the need to get a laugh out of people.

Eugene took to Sam and Ajax, coveting their attention and reserving a gaming table for them in anticipation of each visit. He so looked forward to their time together that he started bringing treats for Ajax, who immediately leapt up into his lap, settling in for the long chess matches. Eugene had been looking for a qualified opponent to challenge him for some time, and while Sam was out of practice, she tried her best.

He nearly always defeated her, but genuinely wanted her to improve, offering her tips. One afternoon, Eugene captured Sam's rook and she saw that she was mere moves away from losing yet again. Ajax, full of treats, was curled up on Eugene's lap, snoring loudly. As they sometimes did, to mix it up, they were playing speed chess. It was then that a woman around Sam's age, whom neither Sam nor Eugene had seen before, walked up to ask if they'd like to join her new arts and crafts program.

Having watched hundreds of movies throughout her life, Sam was familiar with the concept of love at first sight, but assumed it was a filmmaker's conceit, an exaggerated trope that only happens in movies. As Sam locked eyes with the volunteer, she realized that the movies completely undersell what it actually feels like to be stuck senseless by an intense, all-encompassing passion for someone from the moment you meet. Nothing she'd felt for Tali or Molly or Mari or anyone else came even close to the storm of emotions overwhelming her. Hypnotized, Sam was incapable of forming a reply.

Unaware that his young friend was in the throes of a life-altering emotional response, Eugene dismissed the volunteer out of hand, "Not now young lady, we've got a game to finish. Your move, Sam. Sam?" He tapped the table in front of him to break her trance, eliciting a snort from Ajax.

Shaken from her fixed state, Sam looked at Eugene, answering with a confused, "Huh?" Sam obviously wanted to divert her attention from the game to talk more to this new volunteer, which Eugene now picked up on. He clicked the clock into a paused state, telling Sam, "Take your time, I'm about to win anyway."

She turned to fully face the woman and felt her initial attraction deepen as she took in the warmth of her brown eyes and the kindness of her smile. Her palms got sweaty, her mouth went dry, and a lump formed in her throat.

She didn't care about arts or crafts, but didn't want the moment to end, and managed to say that perhaps they would join.

Eugene stood his ground that he didn't want to go, so the woman gracefully accepted his rejection and walked away to invite other participants. Over Eugene's protests, Sam tipped her king and proposed they switch to backgammon, challenging him, "If I win, we go to arts and crafts. If you win, I will sneak you some of those candies you aren't supposed to have anymore." Eugene loved a challenge almost as much as he loved ignoring guidance on nutrition, and agreed to one winner-takes-all match.

It was not even close. Sam beat him in no time. While he grumbled about how Sam must have cheated,

Sam wheeled Eugene, and the still slumbering Ajax, into the session. The new volunteer, who introduced herself as Margot, was instructing people on patriotic bead work that could be used as keychains. Sam tried to focus, but was distracted by Eugene, who insisted on making it known that he was an unwilling participant who had been tricked into attending.

Sam managed to listen and replicate the demonstration, completing the pattern. It was uninspired, but as she was always good at following instructions, it looked correct. Eugene gave up, leaving a pile of fake suede strips and plastic beads, opting instead to give Ajax belly rubs and ear scratches, and repeatedly asking Sam when it would be over.

At the end, Margot called everyone to attention and thanked them for joining her first-ever class. She asked if they enjoyed it, and made the mistake of looking in Eugene's direction. Sam braced herself as the spotlight was on him.

"Well," he started. "Like a lot of you, I served in Vietnam. Saw a lot of things in the jungle. Lotta things. Survived a lot of bad days. But nothing I saw there prepared me for surviving this class." Mortified, Sam quickly wheeled him away, not looking back at poor Margot.

"That was not very nice!" she whispered hotly as they rushed down the hall. "I don't think I should play chess with you for at least a week." Eugene began to negotiate in his defense, when they heard someone approaching. Out of breath, Margot caught up with them. Mustering a smile, she handed Sam the key chain.

"You left in such a rush, you forgot this!" Sam accepted the key chain, intimidated by the direct gaze from this woman her friend had offended.

"Thanks," was all Sam could mumble. The key chain shook in her hand betraying her nerves, so she quickly passed it off to Eugene as Margot stayed to chat.

"You did a good job."

"Oh, well, I'm good at taking instruction."

"If that was true you'd have listened to me and stop sacrificing your bishop and over-relying on your knight by now!" Eugene was not going to be ignored.

Sam tried to laugh it off. "Sorry about my friend here. I shouldn't have forced him to go." Eugene avoided looking at either of them.

"No problem. Arts and crafts aren't for everyone." She turned directly to Eugene, "Thank you for showing up, sir, and at least giving it a try. I was worried I'd be teaching an empty room. Besides, you made me laugh." Then, beaming at them both, she extended her hand to shake. "I'm Margot."

Sam took her hand, and was fairly certain she said her own name, but was too focused on trying not to be flustered. She knew she was blushing, and cursed her complexion for never allowing her to hide her embarrassment. She knew her as her skin deepened to a reddish-purple, her freckles would pop out even more. To divert attention, she gestured at her companion. "This is Eugene."

"Nice to meet you, Mr. Eugene."

"Oh, 'Mr. Eugene?' I like you, you've got good manners." He was easily won over. "Now, I have to know about your background. Where are you from?"

Sam winced at an elderly man asking a clearly Asian-American woman where she was from. Sam knew Eugene well enough to understand that his question didn't come from a bad place, but still, there were literally countless videos online about how this was a bad stereotype for a reason. The underlying implication in these queries was always that anyone of Asian descent couldn't really be American, and must actually identify with the country their ancestors hailed from.

Despite Sam's concern, Eugene's inquiry didn't seem to bother Margot. She promptly responded with another dazzling smile.

"New Hampshire, sir."

"I meant," he held up the red, white, and blue key chain, jangling it as evidence, "how did a patriotic, All-American girl wind up with such a French name, Marrrrrrr-goooooo?"

Margot laughed. "I see. Well, my mother is a relentless Francophile. I think she thought it would make us less Korean? There weren't really any other Asian families in our town, but my dad had gotten a job at the university there he couldn't pass up."

Sam watched how animated Margot's face was as she talked. "My poor grandparents really wanted me to learn Korean, because they had difficulty with English. To this day they prefer to speak in Korean, but Mom refuses. She's still obsessed. Growing up, she cooked us French food, had me take French lessons, listen to French music, sing French Christmas carols, watch French movies, vacation in Paris, the whole deal."

"And how did that work out for you?"

"Well, I don't speak Korean. But I also don't speak French!" Her nose crinkled as she laughed. "I still have a deep love for foreign films, but don't pick up so much as one word. I'm terrible with languages, I guess!"

"You should have Sam help you. 'Miss World Traveler' here knows lots of languages."

"Is that so?"

To Sam's chagrin, the attention had made its way back onto her. "Not really. I mean, I am really good at memorizing and reciting words, but I'm not so good at the accents."

"That's more than I can do. Where is your favorite place to travel?"

"He's exaggerating a little there, too. I've only been to a few countries, but I guess my favorite place was Bruges. I'd love to travel more, though."

"Me too. And who is this little guy?" She leaned over to pet Ajax, who lifted his chin to let Margot scratch underneath.

"This is Ajax the Great, like the Greek warrior, but you can just call him Ajax." Eugene explained. "He's a glutton, but he's a good boy, and I'm his favorite person here.

Margot continued petting him, accepting inquisitive sniffs and licks on her hand. "I bet you smell my dog, huh?"

"What kind of dog?" Sam inquired.

"An Alaskan Malamute, named Sunny. I adopted her to help me feel safe, being a single woman living alone and all, but to be honest she's not much of a guard dog. She's a lover, not a fighter."

"That makes two of us," Eugene chimed in.

"Are Malamutes the ones that look like even bigger huskies and shed everywhere?" Sam had researched many breeds before adopting Ajax.

"Yes indeed! Next to your little man, my Sunny girl would look like a horse. She sheds so much you could make another dog from the fur I have to sweep up everyday. I don't mind, though. She's worth it."

"Why don't you bring her in some time?" encouraged Eugene. "Maybe people will be less jealous that Ajax only wants to be with me."

Sam rolled her eyes a bit and smiled, knowing it was Eugene who wanted Ajax all to himself.

"Maybe I will. I should go clean up from class now, but I'll see you around. You know, you could always bring your chess board and set up in the room with us. That way you can be part of it, but not have to actually make anything?"

"Oh I'd love to, Miss Margot, but Sam is punishing me for what I said to you. She told me she's never playing chess with me again as long as I live."

Sam quickly rushed to correct the record. "He's being silly. Of course we're going to play chess again. Maybe we'll take you up on your offer."

"I hope you will. Nice to meet you all. Good night Mr. Eugene, Ajax," and with a broad flash of her teeth, "Sam."

As Margot walked away, Eugene summarized, "Nice young lady. Terrible taste in hobbies, though."

Sam began to look forward to volunteering even more. Remembering the lesson of getting carried away with Tali, she tried not to imagine run-ins with Margot, working to stay calm and focused on why she was volunteering, which helped her on days when Margot wasn't there.

She successfully avoided mentioning Margot to Brad at all, hoping that if she didn't say out loud how she felt, she could keep her feelings in check. Eugene clearly knew how Sam felt, though, and agreed to play chess in the arts and crafts room on days when Margot taught.

A few weeks later, the center hosted a barbecue event catered by a new local company. Sitting with Sam, Margot, and Brad, Eugene loudly criticized the quality of the meal. He wasn't wrong, nor was he alone in his evaluation. Something was off with the food, and everyone agreed it was not great.

The head of the hospitality team apologized and promised they'd make it up to everyone another time. After signing out for the day, Brad invited Sam and Margot to dinner with him since none of them had eaten much. He knew of a place nearby with outdoor seating where they could bring Ajax. Everyone agreed, and were soon enjoying a much better meal.

They were mid-meal when Stacey texted Brad asking for backup with Dora (the nickname they'd settled on). Jumping up to go home and help, he quickly handed some cash to Sam and excused himself, leaving Sam and Margot alone together for the first time. Sam tried not to panic, and was grateful that the gregarious Margot was willing to steer the conversation.

They covered the basics of their jobs (Margot was a government contractor), where they went to school, and which teams they cheered for. Margot was a die-hard college sports fan. Sam admitted that while was happy to support her professional home teams, she never paid much attention unless she was physically at a game to which she'd been invited by someone else. For her, games were more of a social activity, which Margot fully understood. They discovered they both loved concerts, as well. Although Margot liked big arena shows, and Sam preferred smaller venues, they had a shared interest in similar bands.

Sam had assumed she was bad at small-talk after her brief dating life had come to a halt, but she must have made a good impression because Margot asked her if she'd like to go out again another time.

Chapter 22: A Few of my Favorite Things

2021
(SUMMER - FALL)

Over the next few weeks, Sam and Margot went on many casual dates after they finished their volunteer shifts. She liked that Margot talked with her, instead of at her, as so many people had during her first-date frenzy. The more Sam learned about Margot, the more she liked her, and found herself cautiously hoping it might lead to a relationship.

With great effort, Sam worked up the nerve to ask Margot out for a standalone date one weekend, not tied to their volunteering. Margot hesitated, and Sam apologized for asking, sure that she'd overstepped some boundary.

Always transparent, Margot revealed she was still wary of dating after her last relationship ended very badly. "We were living together, and I was planning to propose. I even had a ring. Then I found out she'd been cheating on me."

"How did you find out?"

"She was pregnant."

Sam never had much of a poker face, and couldn't hide her reaction from Margot, who continued, "We'd been living together and were exclusive for so long, she'd gone off her birth control. She didn't need it for anything else besides contraception. I didn't know she'd even been in touch with an ex-boyfriend of hers until she told me that she was about 10 or 11 weeks along. And she wanted to keep it."

Margot was clearly distraught at the memory, so Sam stepped in. "I am so sorry. I know that's not much comfort, but I am. I understand if you don't want to be exclusive or committed right now. I will tell you that I like you, that I'm not seeing anyone else, and that I want to see where this goes. But for now, I would really like to take you on just one real date, if that's all right with you."

"It's all right with me. Let's go on a real date."

They went on more than one. During their first few dates, Margot liked to ask random questions, a sort of getting-to-know-you game. After Sam answered, Margot provided her response. Sam came to love these exchanges. Margot was so direct, Sam had never had such an easy time learning about someone. No one had ever shown such sustained interest in Sam before, either.

After each date she'd rush to write everything down, her once-sad journal now filled with new entries, things she didn't want to forget. She had pages dedicated to their answers, with a column for Margot and a column for Sam:

- **Favorite movie**

  Sam: "Singing in the Rain" | Margot: "The Diving Bell and the Butterfly"

- **Favorite ice cream flavor**

  Sam: Cookies and cream | Margot: Raspberry sorbet

- **Favorite album**

  Sam: Nirvana, "Unplugged" | Margot: Nina Simone, "I Put a Spell on You"

- **Favorite breakfast**

  Sam: Breakfast burrito | Margot: Cold leftovers, especially fried chicken or pizza

- **Favorite book**

Sam: "Ishmael" | Margot: "The Scarlet Pimpernel"
- **Favorite cocktail**
    Sam: Manhattan | Margot: Kir Royale
- **Favorite beach**
    Sam: Rehoboth | Margot: Mohegan Bluffs
- **Biggest phobia**
    Sam: Drowning | Margot: Waterborne amoebas
- **Coffee or tea**
    Sam: Hot tea, iced coffee | Margot: Iced tea, hot coffee
- **Favorite color**
    Sam: Kelly green | Margot: Silver glitter
- **Dream vacation**
    Sam: Japan | Margot: New Zealand
- **Recurring nightmare**
    Sam: Being trapped | Margot: Being chased
- **Formative celebrity crush**
    Sam: Neve Campbell in "Party of Five" | Margot: Neve Campbell in "The Craft"
- **Favorite Season**
    Sam: Summer | Margot: Spring
- **Favorite animal**
    Sam: Otter | Margot: Fennec fox
- **Favorite subject in school**
    Sam: Geography | Margot: Art

- **Super-power we wish we had**
  Sam: Teleportation | Margot: Controlling the weather
- **Bookmarks, or dog ears**
  Sam: Bookmarks | Margot: Bookmarks
- **Chicken wings**
  Sam: Drums | Margot: Flats
- **Early bird or night owl**
  Sam: Early bird | Margot: Night owl
- **Favorite field trip**
  Sam: The National Aquarium | Margot: New York City
- **Top or bottom bunk**
  Sam: Bottom | Margot: Top
- **Click or twist pen**
  Sam: Click | Margot: Twist
- **Favorite holiday**
  Sam: Guy Fawkes Day | Margot: Halloween
- **Historical figure you'd like meet**
  Sam: Galileo | Margot: Nellie Blye
- **Favorite TV Show**
  Sam: The X-Files | Margot: Twin Peaks
- **Favorite Harrison Ford**
  Sam: Indiana Jones | Margot: Jack Trainer from "Working Girl"
- **Still or sparkling**
  Sam: Sparkling | Margot: Still

- **Cherry blossoms or dogwoods**

  Sam: Dogwoods | Margot: Cherry Blossoms
- **Markers or crayons**

  Sam: Crayons | Margot: Markers
- **Favorite play**

  Sam: "Hippolytus" | Margot: "Cyrano"
- **Favorite bird**

  Sam: Cardinal | Margot: Falcon
- **Biggest pet peeve**

  Sam: Tie between people who use speaker phones or video to take calls in public and people who have their headphones turned up so loud you hear it | Margot: Tie between people who stand still on the left side of an escalator blocking commuters and people who try to board a plane before their group is called.

For someone who felt like she'd ever had much of a personality, it turned out she'd had interests and preferences all along. Not only did Margot want to genuinely know her, but when she asked questions, Sam had answers!

After a few weeks of a honeymoon period, they had their first argument, just as Sam was about to start

311

cooking dinner. Sam was sure it meant the end for them.

Long-term couples know that everyone argues from time to time, which is healthy. Sure, there are couples who fight too much, but never disagreeing doesn't mean a couple is in sync. More often than not, it indicates a lack of communication or caring. Sam, however, did not know this. She'd never been in a relationship before, and had certainly never learned how to make up and move on from an argument. Sam had spent her whole life failing to move on from anything.

Margot, who knew one fight wasn't the end of the world, couldn't understand why Sam was so bent out of shape. Sam felt the words rush out of her, knowing they were wildly out of order, but hoping Margot could sift through and understand what she meant to say. To her relief, Margot did.

"I want to make sure I'm really hearing you, Sam. It's important to me that you know that I want to understand. It sounds like you have two main concerns, which stem from your inexperience with prior relationships. The first is you think you don't know how to physically satisfy me, and I'll get impatient and leave you for that. The second is that you have never been in a fight like this before and think this means we're over and I'm going to stop seeing you. Is that right?"

"Yes," whispered Sam, afraid she'd weep if she spoke any more.

"Ok. Understood. We can talk through this. First, physical alignment is important. You can't have a couple where one person wants lots of sex and the other wants none. But that's not what we're dealing with here. You want physical intimacy, I want it too. You just want some guidance on making me feel good. Well, I'm happy to work on that with you, because while it's sweet you're only concerned with meeting my needs, it's important to me that you feel good, too. If we are very clear in communicating what we want and what we like, we can figure it out together. Are you comfortable with that?"

Sam nodded her head.

"Good. That's one problem solved. As for the other: this one fight is not a big deal. I understand it feels like it is, but compared to finding out the woman you want to marry is carrying some dude's child, this is nothing. I don't say 'nothing' because it doesn't matter, but because this kind of fight is something even the strongest couples have all the time, and that we will have again in the future if we stick with this.

"Now, to be blunt, I'm not saying we're going to be together forever, happily ever after. I feel like I've been clear with you that I don't know where this is going. I've been deeply hurt in the past, and I don't know when I'll be ready to make a commitment and say I'm in this for the long haul and will never leave you. Honestly, I don't know if I'll ever be ready for that. I know that's a risk for you, to want a relationship while not knowing if I can bring myself to agree to one. If that's something you can't live with, I understand, and we can call it now. Do you want to call this all off?"

Sam shook her head no.

"I don't want to, either. I really like you, Sam. I do want to see what happens. You're a wonderful person, and you make life more fun. But all I can promise you now is one date at a time. Can we do that? I know that sounds wishy-washy, but it's the best I can do. I want to be with you, I just don't want to mislead you. So really think about it. Can we take it one date at a time?"

Sam contemplated the question. One thing she'd learned is that nothing in life is guaranteed, and few things ever worked out the way she planned, anyway. Five years ago, Sam could never have imagined how much her life would change, what she would experience, how she'd grow. Why limit herself by over-imagining her future? So what if Margot wasn't promising forever? She was promising right now, and that was enough.

She agreed, "One date at a time."

They smiled at each other, and embraced.

"Since I've never done this fighting thing before, tell me what happens next?"

"Now we make dinner, especially with all the money we spent on these ingredients."

"*We* make dinner?" Teased Sam. Margot was not a cook.

"Well, I can help you. I'll hand you utensils and help clean up as we go."

"Alright, let's cook."

So their relationship continued, one date at a time, one week at a time, one month at a time. Margot was newer to the area, so Sam invited Margot to join her friends' activities. To her delight, they all got along well. There wasn't anyone Margot couldn't find something in common with, and she was good at reading situations to make sure everyone felt included and heard. People pulled Sam aside to say how much they liked Margot, and even more, how happy she seemed to make Sam.

At first, Sam was uncomfortable being the subject of such conversation, making her feel scrutinized. It activated her lifelong, deep-seated suspicion that if people were thinking or talking about her it was for the sole purpose of negative gossip. From her journaling exercises, she knew her fears came from years of being bullied at home and at school.

Her doubt didn't last long, though, as she understood their comments just meant her friends were paying attention to her because they cared, and they wanted the best for her. All these years she'd given the people in her life so little credit, assuming she was a fifth wheel they patronized and placated, when the simple truth was they were just good people who wanted her to be well. Instead of feeling judged, she felt grateful.

As they got to know each other, Sam learned more about Margot's upbringing and the tension between her mother and her grandparents. Margot's mother wanted her to assimilate by disconnecting her from their Korean heritage. Margot knew a few phrases and recipes from spending time with her grandparents, but recently she felt compelled to know more, especially as her grandparents were getting older. Sam bought some Korean dictionaries and cookbooks, and offered to help Margot get more in touch with the culture she'd been forbidden from learning.

In turn, Margot tried to help Sam learn to love herself a little more, which Sam warned her was not going to be easy. Margot persisted, though, and Sam understood that it was part of the way Margot was wired. Slowly, she pushed Sam out of the tight emotional boundaries she'd created for herself as preservation techniques, helping Sam learn to take a compliment and think well of herself.

She respected Sam's reason for not observing her birthday in a big way, but asked if she could do at least something for her. Sam agreed, and Margot managed to put together a quiet night for the two of them that was just right. Sam felt celebrated, but at a scale with which she was comfortable.

Margot was very big on presents, and gave Sam some of the most thoughtful and personalized gifts she'd ever received. At times, Sam didn't know what to do with all of the affection, unused to being on the receiving end of such positive attention. Margot understood this, and gave Sam the space to be awkward about accepting gifts, without taking it personally.

Everything about being in a relationship was new to Sam, and she tried to soak it all in. For their first Halloween together, Margot asked Sam if she'd like to dress in a couples' costume. Sam had historically dressed in understated costumes that wouldn't attract attention. She never really liked Halloween all that much, because she'd never been asked to go trick-or-treating with anyone. Most of her Halloweens revolved around having to accompany Kimmy, hearing people gush about how adorable she was, while Kimmy lorded over Sam that she had received more candy because she was special.

Halloween was Margot's favorite holiday, though, so when Margot suggested they coordinate for the party at Johanna and Eddie's, Sam agreed. Looking at themselves in the mirror after they dressed, Sam was blown away by how it made her feel, like she was essential, she belonged.

Sam had never been conscious of how much that was something she wanted, and the night was a continuous high. She liked people recognizing their characters, and saying how cute they were together. Sam felt like it was some rite of passage, like she was experiencing all of these moments other couples took for granted. For her these had seemed so impossible or out of reach that she hadn't even dared to hope for them.

When the winter holidays approached, Margot shared that she wasn't ready to spend Thanksgiving together yet. To her own surprise, Sam was ok with that.

Em invited Sam to her family home for the holiday. "Between us, my sisters, their partners, all the nieces and nephews and whoever else shows up at any given holiday, I promise you will be very welcome. My parents have a 'the more the merrier' mindset so they'd be happy to have you."

While grateful for the invite, Sam declined; she already had plans. Her family had still not celebrated a holiday together since the calamitous Christmas of 2019, so while Margot traveled home to be with her parents, Sam spent Thanksgiving volunteering.

"Happy Thanksgiving, Mr. Eugene."

"Happy Thanksgiving Samantha. I guess this year you've got a lot to be grateful for, huh?"

"You know, I think I do. What about you, what are you grateful for this year?"

"That Margot isn't here to make us trace our hands to draw turkeys or make construction paper pilgrim hats, or whatever nonsense she'd plan."

"Maybe I'll suggest those to her for next year!"

"Not if you want me to show up." With that, he returned his full attention to Ajax, who was exposing his stomach, apparently in need of rubbing.

When Sam got home, she texted Margot pictures from her Thanksgiving, and after writing then deleting an excessive number of draft texts, settled on, "Happy Thanksgiving from your Virginia crew! Hope you had a wonderful day." Dancing dots on the screen matched the anticipation dancing in her stomach as she awaited a reply. Finally, it appeared, a selfie of Margot with her father passed out on the couch behind her, accompanied by the caption, "I think the turkey is working, Dad is out! Miss you bunches. Happy Thanksgiving Sam…I'm grateful for you."

When Christmas came around, they followed the same plan. Margot went to be with her family, and Sam took Ajax to spend the day with the veterans and their families. Eugene's son, Irving, brought his wife and children from their home in Nevada.

They surprised Sam with an elegant, carved chess set. Eugene teased "So at least when I win you have something pretty to look at!"

"And this," continued Irving, "is for Ajax. We feel like we already know him just from Dad's stories."

"That is so thoughtful! I hope he's lived up to your expectations." Sam accepted the overstuffed basket of toys and treats.

"Well, I haven't seen him walk on water yet, but otherwise he's close to what Dad promised."

They both chuckled, as Irving pulled her aside. "He'd never say this to you, and he'd be annoyed if he knew I was saying it now, but I want to make sure you understand how much you mean to him."

"Oh, he just likes me for my dog." Sam still struggled with accepting gratitude.

"I mean it. I know it's hard for him with us living so far away. We wanted him to come with us, but he wouldn't. When we had to move he was miserable. Coming here didn't help him at first the way we hoped it would, once we finally convinced him to try. We know he can seem cranky, but he is a good man, and he's let more of that goodness show since your chess games started. Thank you, Sam."

"You're welcome, but I can assure you, he's helped me, too."

"Oh he told me all about how he set you up with your girlfriend. Said the two of you were hopeless and needed a push. He calls himself the 'millennial matchmaker' now. He's very proud that his plan of tricking you into playing chess in the arts and crafts room worked."

Only Eugene could spin the disastrous keychain lesson into a personal victory, and it amused Sam. The rest of the day was full of laughter and gaiety, and she was glad she had the opportunity to be with them. For a moment, Sam regretted how her last family Christmas had collapsed, but seeing Eugene surrounded by his relatives gave her hope that there are families out there who love each other. Maybe she and Margot could have that some day.

That evening, Margot called Sam and they caught up on how they spent their days. Sam described the sweet gift from Mr. Eugene's family, while Margot lamented, "As per usual, Mom insisted we sing carols in French. I'm not saying it gets old, but ugh! I *résonnez* your *musette* right here, *l'enfant!*" Sam let out a little cackle at Margot's attempted tough guy voice.

During their calm and relaxing chat, Margot confessed to Sam, "I really miss you. I wish you were here. I got a little moody for you yesterday so I found that Fellini film you love so much and watched it. You were right; it was really good."

"Which one?"

"Don't make me say the name, you know I mangle Italian words. The *Nights of* one."

"*Le Notte di Cabiria.*"

"Show off."

"Fine, *Nights of Cabiria*," Sam said in an exaggerated Mid-Atlantic pronunciation. "One of my favorites."

Margo laughed knowingly. "Aren't they *all* one of your favorites?"

"Yes, ok, but really, that one is. It's what *Sweet Charity* is based on."

"I know, you told me. It reminded me of you."

Sam teased, "Because I'm sweet, or because I'm a charity case?"

Margot giggled, then said seriously. "No, because of that last scene, that last frame. It made me think of how, even with everything you've been through, you still hope, you still try. I love that about you."

Sam didn't know what to say, and remained silent, as Margot continued.

"I think I love you, Sam."

Before she even processed Margot's profession, Sam replied, "I think I love you, too."

"Well, I should let you go get some sleep. I know you like volunteering, but I also know mingling with people can take a lot out of you. Make sure you get a little rest, and give Ajax some snuggles for me. I'll talk to you when I'm back."

"G'night, Mar."

"Night, Sam."

After hanging up, Sam thought back to all the times she'd formed fast friendships with girls who demanded she follow their lead or treated her as an accessory. That Margot didn't feel the need to keep Sam in her proximity at all times was refreshing. She respected Sam as an individual, and Sam trusted that Margot wouldn't stop caring about her just because they were apart on two holidays.

They did spend New Year's Eve together, at a party hosted by, of course, Eddie and Johanna. Margot was a walking disco ball in her silver glitter dress, enchanting Sam as she sparkled all night. For a moment, Sam was distracted by the thought that the last time she felt good at a New Year's party was 2019 going into 2020, and that hadn't exactly turned into a good year. She didn't want to dwell on that, though, bringing herself back to the present.

This year, she had the first experience of being kissed at midnight, made even more special that it was someone she loved, someone she allowed herself to believe loved her. Sam felt like she was living someone else's life, or like she'd stepped into a movie. She wasn't sure how she'd gotten so lucky to meet Margot, but she knew she was glad for each new experience they had together, and allowed herself the hope that the coming year would bring even more.

In the months that followed, their relationship continued to deepen. They spent time with some of Sam's family, who adored Margot. Brad was thrilled for his little sister, and Stacey recognized she and Margot were kindred spirits. The two quickly developed a repertoire of inside jokes and texted each other regularly. Ray-Ray was drawn to Margot like a magnet, and Margot was wonderful with him, getting down on the ground to help him play with his toys. Even Dora seemed to be a fan.

After the initial dating phase, Sam and Margot started to enjoy more nights in together. The two women shared a love for cinema, and took turns introducing each other to their favorite films. Sam was amused by Margot's shock at the misogyny, racism, violence, and obvious lip syncing in old musicals, a genre Margot entirely missed thanks to her mother. (Except for *The Umbrellas of Cherbourg*, that is.) In her eyes, some of the worst offenders were *The King and I*, *Carousel*, *West Side Story*, and *Seven Brides for Seven Brothers*. Still, she agreed with Sam that the music was catchy and the choreography was impressive.

When it was her turn to pick movies, Margot consoled Sam as she wept during Margot's selections from around the world, such as *Au Revoir, Les Enfants,* from France, *Cinema Paradiso*, from Italy, and *Dolor y Gloria,* from Spain. She reassured Sam that there were plenty of uplifting films she enjoyed, too, but that she appreciated the catharsis of a good cry.

One genre the women absolutely agreed on was romantic comedies, especially those with larger-than-life families who help the couple find their way to each other in the end—even if they manage to get in the way a few times while doing so. They cuddled on the couch along with Ajax and Sunny—the two dogs became fast friends—and enjoyed rewatching feel-good films like *Moonstruck*, *While You Were Sleeping*, and *My Big Fat Greek Wedding*.

Sam and Margot began staying at each other's apartments every night, and their dogs became inseparable. Somewhere along the way, Margot and

Sam stopped scheduling specific dates, and just started assuming they'd spend their evenings and weekends together. Sam tried to remain grounded and not to read too deeply into this, knowing that Margot had been clear that she wasn't ready for a serious commitment. Still, they started making more long-term plans.

They took short trips together over weekends, to cities, to beaches, to historic sites, to lake houses, taking the dogs hiking or camping out in the woods. Living on the Mid-Atlantic East Coast, they could easily enjoy quick getaways to a variety of locations. Margot was impulsive with a terrific sense of adventure, and would choose a place at random. Sam the planner would figure out the logistics to make it happen.

Margot was better at remembering to take photos and share them with friends and family. She also knew Sam liked to write, and bought her a travel journal to keep a record of all the places they explored together. Each time they went, Sam tried not to think about their future and get carried away in her imagination, which she found allowed her to actually focus more on being happy in the present moment.

Chapter 23: Something Old, Someone New

JUNE 2022

In June of 2022, Sam got dressed for yet another wedding. This time, though, it was different. She coordinated with Margot, their outfits complementing, though not matching. Sam couldn't wait to get to the venue. Here she was for the first time bringing a plus-one. She was looking forward to it. She had confided her dislike of attending weddings as a single person to Margot, who was optimistic.

"I think it will be more fun this time," encouraged Margot. "Will you dance with me?" Of course, there was nothing Sam wanted more.

At the wedding, it was the usual suspects: college friends and their spouses who had been around so long it was hard to remember that they hadn't gone to school with them, too. Sam happily caught up with friends, and was relieved to see that Margot was enjoying herself too. As usual, Margot easily made conversation and charmed everyone.

Temporarily distracted by conversation with her friend Jolan, Sam lost track of Margot. Leaving Jolan, Sam saw Em, and walked toward her.

Em wore a wry smile as she looked at the dance floor. Without taking her eyes off what held her attention, she inquired of Sam, "Missing something?" Sam followed Em's eye line to see Margot tearing up the dance floor with none other than Tali.

Sam felt her cheeks flush, unsure how to react. Em chuckled and handed Sam her flask. "Three things in life are certain: death, taxes, and Tali's gonna Tali." Sam relaxed as she accepted the flask, and together they watched their dates dance through three songs.

After the DJ did the slow dance switch, Tali and Margot walked over to Em and Sam, smiling and breathless. "Whoooo! Sam, your girl can dance!" Tali declared, to which Margot responded "Em, I think I might be in love with your wife."

Em looked at Sam, clearly hoping she wouldn't take it personally. Sam was shocked at her own lack of insecurity in that moment, and instead of being upset, confidently took Margot's hand. With a knowing laugh Sam said "Yeah, you and everyone else. Now, how about that dance you promised?"

The DJ played two slow dances in a row, and for Sam, it was like time stopped. She wasn't just glad to be dancing, but specifically to be dancing with Margot. It clicked for Sam. Margot wasn't just her wedding date, she was a truly special person. Sam didn't want the evening to stop. It wasn't that she never wanted to leave the dance floor. She never wanted to leave Margot.

As their one year dating anniversary approached, Sam grew anxious about how to observe it. In the past, Sam would have stewed in her own head and tried to figure it out. With Margot, though, she knew she could be direct and just ask. So, she broached the subject, inquiring if it felt too much like a committed relationship to do something.

To Sam's relief, Margot also wanted to celebrate their anniversary, and even had an idea for it: take their first international trip together. They got each other new luggage and accessories, and spent a week together in Iceland, where neither of them had been before. Sam couldn't keep track of all the incredible moments during their trip. When she'd traveled alone she felt like something was missing, and now, here was Margot, making the experience feel complete.

On their flight home, Margot talked excitedly about upcoming holidays and asked Sam what she wanted to do for them. She suggested they spend Thanksgiving with her family in New England. She wondered where they should spend Christmas, and if Johanna and Eddie were hosting again for New Year's.

Sam understood the significance of Margot's queries. They had been patient with each other, taken their time with no agenda. Yet somehow, without even trying, they had evolved from two women who went on one date at a time to an established couple, planning for their future together. After Margot nodded off while leaning her head on Sam's shoulder, Sam marveled at the unexpected comfort of knowing she had a partner, and that she was loved.

A new memory resurfaced, and for the first time in ages Sam was able to experience it from her first-person point of view.

[1998]

It was mid-summer, and they were all antsy for a change of scenery from the garden or the television set. Sam's grandparents decided to take the train into Chicago. The three of them sat in four seats facing each other. Sam on one side, directly across from Grandma Jeannie who sat by the window, and Grandpa Tony in the aisle seat next to his wife. They had a wonderful day browsing exhibit after exhibit, and spoiling Sam in the gift shops.

On the way home, Grandma Jeannie was tired and nodded off with her forehead pressed into the window. Just as Sam thought to herself, "That looks uncomfortable," Grandpa Tony gently placed his right arm around Jeannie, shifting her toward him and using his left hand to tilt her head onto his shoulder.

Sam saw a little smile spread on Jeannie's face, and heard her let out a contented sigh as she settled into her husband's arms. When Grandpa Tony realized Sam was staring, he nodded his head and gave Sam a wink, just as Grandma Jeannie reached out her hand to take her husband's. Sam wasn't used to seeing physical displays of affection between her parents, and was touched by that tiny moment of tenderness and intimacy.

* * *

Chapter 24: The Year of Sam

2022

With the help of Margot, her family, and her friends, Sam learned to face her memories, and no longer felt defined by them. In researching meditation during her COVID isolation, Sam had come across the concept of forgiving the past to heal the present. She had to accept that she couldn't change the memories, but she didn't have to be held hostage by them, either. When memories started to take hold, she closed her eyes and calmly repeated, "I accept that this happened, but it doesn't control me today." It took practice, and consistent effort, but Sam learned to live with her past in a less combative way.

The outcome was a more pleasant present. Sam filled her life up with so many joyous moments that the old memories had less room to take hold. When one came up, she would jot it down in her notebook, and little by little took the power out of them.

By focusing her attention on the now, Sam freed herself to enjoy all the little moments she'd longed for over the years. To her own surprise, she found she wanted Margot to know her entirely, not just the best version of herself, and so she gave the memory journal to Margot to read. She couldn't imagine sharing that most private and vulnerable part of herself with anyone else in her life.

Sam hadn't sought a grand romance. She was never optimistic enough to think she'd experience one, anyway. All Sam wanted was a partner, and she had finally found her match. Every day she woke up grateful for the woman beside her.

Brad was correct: life was more manageable now that she knew she didn't have to face it alone. Sam had someone to celebrate the good times, and help her through the bad. Sam saw the world in a new light, and, convinced by the radical changes she'd gone through, was hopeful that others could change their lives, too.

Sam was content, and having a solid foundation with Margot only enhanced the other relationships in her life. Sam and her mother continued to work at getting to know each other all over again, and had grown considerably closer. Beverly seemed to come back to life. She showed a real interest in Sam, initiating a group text between herself, Sam, and Margot, and she even joined them on some of their weekend getaways.

Inspired by Sam, Bev decided she wanted to find fulfillment, so she started volunteering and taking adult continuing education classes. Sam and Margot encouraged her in all of this. Remembering how Em and Tali's animal intervention helped her, Sam and Margot also helped Beverly adopt a massive Maine Coon, the kind of cat she'd secretly always wanted. Bev flooded their group text with pictures of Meow-chiavelli, as she'd renamed him.

Sam was even able to do what she long thought was impossible—improve her relationship with Kimmy. After all, if Sam and Bev could start over, why couldn't Sam and Kimmy, too? It took much longer, and produced more limited results, but they did begin to tolerate each other more. Sam set boundaries with her sister and enforced them. She didn't take Kimmy's abuse. She directly told Kimmy when her behavior was unacceptable, then left the conversations.

After these incidents, Sam never reached out to her sister, but would wait for the next family gathering when they'd see each other again. Each time, Sam greeted Kimmy openly, but with zero expectation that her sister would return the welcome. If the situation turned negative, Sam, having enough of Kimmy's rudeness, withdrew.

Over time, Kimmy finally learned she wasn't going to get the reaction from Sam that she wanted. Neither was she getting it from Beverly, who no longer involved herself in her adult children's fights, nor from Brad, who was too focused on his own family to get drawn into petty squabbles.

Left with no other options than to either stop showing up, or learn to engage with people like an adult, Kimmy begrudgingly grew up. She still had her mean streak, and defaulted to snark, but without the escalation from her siblings or attention from her mother, these had less of an impact. Bullying seemed to give her no satisfaction without an audience. If she acted immaturely, her family simply moved on in their conversations without her.

As if she'd suddenly gotten corrective lenses for emotional intelligence, Kimmy started to demonstrate that she understood how her behavior influenced others and how much time they were willing to spend with her. Sam became aware, for the first time, that Kimmy really was jealous of Sam, not just for her relationship with Margot, but for the closeness she had with Brad. Kimmy clearly didn't know how to establish an equally strong bond, but for the first time in her life it seemed to Sam that her little sister actually cared to be accepted by her older siblings.

Once Kimmy realized she was the outsider, Sam and Brad observed that their younger sister had trouble not resenting it, and for a brief time acted out at every family function. During their great aunt and uncle's 50th wedding anniversary party, Kimmy caught Sam and Brad sneaking out to the parking lot. Approaching them, they first acted playfully as if their cover was blown, and then waved her over to hide with them. Kimmy watched her brother and sister each pull out a matching flask from their pockets, engraved with their monograms.

"Mezcal," whispered Brad, lifting his flask.

"Bourbon," Sam replied, tilting hers.

They clinked their flasks and took a sip, before Kimmy interrupted "What is going on here?!"

Sam snickered and wiped her mouth, while Brad explained, "Any time there's an event with dancing, we bring our flasks. That way, in case the bar is just beer or wine..."

"Or there's no bar at all!" Sam chimed in.

"Exactly!" Brad continued, "Any time there's a function where we want to make sure we have our hands on top shelf booze, we bring it ourselves."

"So what, you guys have a secret liquor club with your little matching flasks?" Kimmy's tone was petulant.

Brad clarified, "Well, the matching flasks are more recent, something Stacey thought of. She got them for us last Christmas"

"She really is a keeper," Sam toasted, again hitting her flask against Brad's.

"Oh." Sam sympathized with her sister: Kimmy felt left out, a feeling with which Sam was all too familiar. And what's more, Sam knew that Kimmy wasn't used to being hurt over feeling left out.

Sam tried to put herself in her sister's point of view, wondering how she would feel if, after years of hating her siblings, it now mattered to her that they had moved on without her. Kimmy was visibly disappointed, and appeared to be thinking either of something hurtful to say, to run away, or do both, when Sam redirected her attention and asked, "So, what's your poison?"

Sam and Brad each extended their flasks to her, and at first their youngest sibling did not know how to be gracious, snapping, "I see, now that I've caught you, you want to share with me, invite me into your cool kids' secret drinking club?"

Sam raised a mischievous eyebrow. "Look, if you prefer, next time we can bring gin or vodka, whatever you want. But for now, unless you want to go back in there sober and watch Uncle Gordon dance like he's in an Austin Powers movie, I recommend you take what we've got!"

At Sam's description of their uncoordinated and out of touch uncle, Brad did a spit take, spraying his mezcal on a nearby bush.

Kimmy considered the options, and grabbing the flask from Sam said, "Next time bring rum, losers." Then she defiantly took a performative, large swig and inhaled through her teeth. "Alright, let's go see Gordo get groovy, baby!"

Brad and Sam joined her laughter, took a few more drinks each, and together, the three siblings returned to the party.

Sam had no expectation that this would be the start of a sisters-as-best-friends type relationship with Kimmy. However, the simple act of not having that unfair goal was in itself a relief to Sam. Her sister was an adult, and was who she was, so Sam made the conscious decision that if she wanted Kimmy in her life, she'd have to accept that it meant seeing her sister in small doses, with no pressure on either of them to be perfect in each other's eyes.

Kimmy would never thank Sam for the second chance. In fact, in all likelihood she didn't even realize she had been granted one, but she did learn that if she was kinder, Sam responded more positively. She also noticed that, consciously or not, others followed Sam's lead, and if Sam was on good terms with Kimmy, then Beverly, Brad, Margot, and Stacey also treated Kimmy more affectionately.

While Sam and Kimmy would never be the kind of close sisters Sam read about in books, they could be civil when they saw each other, and even have fun from time to time. They weren't going to start hanging out on their own or taking girls' trips together, but they could behave like adults, take each other as they were, and appreciate that they had a relationship at all. That was good enough for Sam.

The only relationship that didn't improve was with her father. Ever since her breakthrough with her mom, she'd been unable to see Ray in the former light. It was as if Beverly had ripped a mask off him, like at the end of a Scooby Doo episode, revealing a withered, cranky old man. Where Sam had grown up seeing him as the long-suffering pacifist who didn't deserve to be burdened with family feuds, Sam now understood him as someone who simply was not now, nor ever had been, invested in his family.

When Beverly broached the idea of leaving her husband, for the first time in their lives Sam, Brad, and Kimmy all agreed with her, and offered their support.

Thus, despite Beverly's repeated advance warnings, Ray was the only one surprised on the day all three of his adult children arrived, along with Margot and Stacey, to help his wife pack her belongings and move to a new place.

The awkward tension made the morning nearly unbearable for Sam, who was still somehow hoping against hope Ray might have something meaningful to say, to fight for his marriage, to reconnect with his family.

Instead, he opted for cruelty. Pulling Sam aside privately, he said he couldn't believe Sam would be a part of this. "I expected better of you, Sam. I never thought I'd see you aligned with Kimmy, of all people."

"You mean your youngest child, Dad? You can't believe your two daughters are in agreement on something? I would have thought this might make you happy."

"Not when the younger daughter in question is *her*. I understand she's my daughter and your sister, but you know as well as I do, she's a horrible human being, beyond improvement or forgiveness. There's something wrong with her, always was, that can't be fixed.

"I knew another kid was a bad idea, I warned your mom. But she wanted her, and now look. Kimmy's rotten to the core, and we never had a chance to get things right once she came into the picture. She's a bad influence, and for your own sake you should keep as much distance between the two of you as you can. She ruins everything she touches. She ruined this family, ruined my marriage, ruined any hope of peace we ever had... she'll ruin your life too, if you let her."

Sam was gutted. This was the longest conversation she'd had with her father in years, and it was all so he could insult her sister, who had been making a real effort to turn her life around.

It was then Sam understood that while it is possible for people to change and grow, they had to first recognize that they need to, and then have to be willing to put in the work. Sam was growing. Brad, Kimmy, and Beverly, they were all trying. They had all embraced forgiveness and new beginnings. Her father hadn't even started.

Although Sam confided in Margot and Stacey that she hoped he would evolve, and that she wouldn't give up on him, she had a sinking feeling that her relationship with her father was fundamentally fractured beyond repair.

Chapter 25: We Wish You a Messy Christmas

DECEMBER 25, 2022

That year, Brad and Stacey hosted Christmas at their home, explaining that it was easier for them not to pack up both kids. Everyone brought one or two side dishes and desserts to lighten the load of cooking for the busy parents.

Walking into the house, Sam took a deep breath and savored the smells she associated with Christmas, especially the scent of the real tree, which no one in Sam's family had gotten in years. Over the mantel hung stockings with each of their names, including, to Sam's delight, a new one for Margot.

The meal went by in a sort of blur for Sam. It was the kind of Christmas she never imagined being possible. Now that it was happening around her, she was so touched she could hardly process it. She loved to watch her family interact with Margot, and to see how easily Margot got along with everyone—even Kimmy.

Sam noticed that when her mom offered wine, Kimmy declined. Sensing Sam's attention, Kimmy mentioned that her therapist told her she should probably consider limiting substances for a while, to see how her moods were more controllable when her thoughts were unclouded. Brad praised Kimmy both on getting therapy and taking the advice. Kimmy radiated in response to her brother's positive reinforcement. A little Christmas miracle.

After the meal, everyone gathered in the living room to open stockings and presents. Ray-Ray asked if he could be the elf, and with the go-ahead from everyone, he began to pass out the boxes and bags from under the tree. There were, of course, huge piles of gifts for Ray-Ray, Dora, Ajax, and Sunny. At one point, Ray-Ray scrunched his face up at the tag on a gift he held and asked "This one says 'Ray,' not 'Ray-Ray.' Is it still for me?" The room fell silent.

Until that moment, no one had mentioned Sam's father, who had opted out of Christmas. Despite the fact that Brad and Stacey's house offered neutral ground for their parents, their father decided to take a trip to the U.S. Virgin Islands rather than see his family. Thankfully, Margot was quick to reply. "How about anything that says 'Ray,' or 'Dad,' you set back under the tree, ok?" Ray-Ray happily agreed.

With the rest of the gifts distributed, everyone tore into their presents. The room was filled with the sounds of paper being ripped, exclamations of excitement, and genuine "Thank you's" passed back and forth between recipients.

Kimmy moved around the room taking photos, prompting everyone to pose with a gift and say "cheese." She herself was surprised by a gift from Stacey—a flask of her own, to match those of her siblings.

"Sorry Kimmy, I didn't realize you were going easy on drinking." Stacey reached out to take it back, but Kimmy pulled it to herself.

She was clearly flattered to be included, and uncharacteristically sweet in her appreciation. "No, it's ok, even if I just fill it with juice or something. I can't believe I'm saying this, but it's the thought that counts. Seriously, thanks."

Once everyone was done, they started cleaning up the paper and bows, but the presence of Ray's gifts under the tree distracted Sam. Clearly, it weighed on everyone else, as well, and her family discussed what to do with them.

Should they wait until he got back? No, some of the gifts were perishable. Drop them off at the house now? No, while most of them still had a spare key to their childhood home, they hadn't been back since Bev moved out, and they weren't really ready to yet. They also took turns telling Bev they couldn't believe she'd still bought him a gift, to which she waved her hand and said "He's been in my life since I was twenty years old, and he'll always be in my life. I still care about your father, so there's no cause for excluding him."

Bev's children protested that she was too kind when Margot walked into the room with a deck of cards and an impish grin. "I've got an idea!"

She fanned out the cards and walked around the room to let people draw one each. As she did, she explained, "You can't pick the gift you brought. The person with the lowest number card picks first, and so on. Face cards get to choose if they want to keep their gift or swap for someone else's already-opened item. If you draw the joker, you get to choose your own *and* decide which present everyone else gets!"

The tension that had held the room suddenly eased as people got into the spirit of Margot's game, taking their turns to open up gifts meant for Ray. First up was Stacey, who opened a basket of fruit and nuts. "Nice! Thanks Sam, thanks Margot!"

Brad got a vinyl record cleaning kit, a set of tablet screen cleaning cloths, and a gift card for the local movie theatre. Sam unwrapped a 5000-piece puzzle labeled as "expert-level." Margot received a gift card for the grocery store and some sort of orthopedic socks.

Bev opened a flannel-lined corduroy work jacket. She'd pulled the queen of clubs, so she asked to swap the jacket for the gift card and socks, but was reminded of the rule that you can't take what you brought.

Kimmy opened a pocket knife. She asked to trade it for the puzzle, but again that broke the rule. Disappointed, she recovered quickly, beaming at her nephew. "Well, that leaves Ray-Ray."

Ray-Ray let a wicked smile fill his face as he dramatically turned around his card to reveal a joker. Sam stared at Margot, who gave her a sly wink. It was no accident that Ray-Ray got the chaos card, and Sam adored Margot for it. Running from person to person like a Tasmanian devil, he rearranged and swapped presents between everyone, even splitting up multi-part gifts. Ray-Ray also disregarded the "you can't choose what you brought" rule.

Kimmy looked relieved to have the puzzle back in her possession, and Brad teased "Wow, you're really excited about puzzles, huh? 5000 pieces, too. I've never seen you work on one in your life."

Sam verified this, adding, "Whenever I used to help Dad work on them and asked you to join, you acted like you were being tortured."

Kimmy blushed, and looked down for a moment. "I still don't care about puzzles."

"Then why did you want that so bad?" Asked Margot.

"I... I took out one of the pieces."

Stacey tilted her head at her sister-in-law. "Why did you do that?"

"Because I wanted him to get close to finishing it, then realize he never could because he didn't have all the pieces. I wanted to make him waste his time, because I knew it would drive him nuts."

"Whaaaaaat?" Brad asked with a slight chuckle, sounding more amused than anything else.

"One time when we were little he threw a fit for days looking for a piece of a puzzle, acting like a high crime had been committed against him because he couldn't get closure. Remember that, Sam? He made you look everywhere, and was convinced you must have lost it.

"So, I took a piece from this one. An inside piece too, because I didn't want him to figure it out early if he saw he didn't have all the outside pieces. That would be too obvious. I wanted to make sure he was confident he'd finish, to maximize his squandered time."

"Kimberly-Anne!" Bev admonished her in disbelief.

"I know! That's why I didn't want any of you to get the puzzle. None of you guys deserve it. But I heard what he said about me to Sam, the day we moved you out of the house, Mom. I know you'll always have a soft spot for him, but what he said was terrible and I wanted to make him feel bad, too."

"What exactly did he say? No, Samantha," pointing a finger directly at her. "I want to hear it from you."

Sam cast her glance at her hands, shrugging her shoulders in the new oversized corduroy jacket that had been meant for her father. "I don't want to say, it's Christmas," she mumbled.

Seeing that Kimmy looked like she was about to break down, Sam continued, loud and clear, "It was awful, Mom. Kimmy's right to feel hurt, and I don't even blame her for messing with his puzzle. In fact, I think it was pretty clever. In like, kind of a mean way, but still. As far as pranks go, it's harmless compared to what he said about her, so, I think we should cut her some slack."

Tears brimming along her eyelids, Kimmy mouthed "Thank you," to her sister.

"Do you still have the piece?" Margot asked.

"Yeah, in my hotel room."

"Perfect. I'll take the puzzle, and you can bring the last piece over to our place. We'll make brunch, and then you can help us complete it."

"Wait... your place? As in, together?"

Margot reached for Sam's hand and smiled at the family. "Yep, we're moving in together—we actually already started. It shouldn't take too long since neither of us has very much."

Sam added, "It's a small house with a yard, so there will be much more room for the dogs... which is obviously a top priority."

Sam and Margot's announcement completely lifted the mood, as the family exuberantly offered their congratulations to the couple. Sam admired how Margot had saved the holiday, improvising how to get the party back on a positive track. For the rest of the day, Sam's family ate desserts, watched Christmas movies, and helped Ray-Ray and Dora play with their new toys, until finally, hearts full, Sam and Margot headed home.

Chapter 26: This Will be Our Year

2023

Moving in together wasn't difficult. They were both established professionals who had been able to afford some quality furnishings, so they didn't have much they needed to buy. Although they each had lived alone for some time and had their own home goods, Sam's minimal, non-offensive style made it easy to integrate her decor with Margot's.

Sam felt a thrill at putting her books on their combined shelves. For a moment she wondered how they would ever be able to tell them apart when they broke up, but she decided that wasn't a problem to worry about. Like Margot often said, don't let the worry of forever ruin the enjoyment of now.

Ajax and Sunny quickly adjusted to the new home, as well. Margot and Sam had the house pulled together well enough to host a small brunch not long after New Year's Eve. As Sam rang in 2023 in her new home with Margot, Ajax, Sunny, and their friends and family, she wished she could hit a pause button for just a moment, to keep feeling this good. She hoped it was a sign of how the year would be.

That summer, Sam finally allowed a party to be thrown in her honor: her engagement party. Well, it was meant to be an engagement party, but Sam, so tired of waiting for life, and Margot, always up for mischief, decided to make it a surprise wedding.

Em and a very visibly-pregnant Tali were their accomplices in pulling it off. Sam had never been one of those kids who dreamed about an elaborate wedding day, and didn't care about the decorations or details. She left it in Em and Tali's capable, enthusiastic care, and they had done an incredible job transforming Brad and Stacey's back yard into a rustic festival.

The tables were adorned with vintage table cloths from a local antique shop. At each place setting was a thrift store tea cup with saucer, all in different shapes, colors and patterns, meant as a wedding favor for the guests to take home. The final detail Sam recognized as Em's touch: the centerpieces were un-lidded mason jars filled with coiled fairy lights spilling out over the top.

When it was time for the ceremony to start, Sam's father still had not shown up.

Margot offered, "Sam, we can wait a little longer to get started."

Sam was sure he wasn't coming. "I don't want to wait a minute longer to marry you. Besides, I already know who I want to walk me down the aisle, anyway."

So, with Brad as her best man standing next to a makeshift altar and Stacey escorting her down the aisle, Sam walked up first. Margot followed, arm in arm with both of her parents, one on each side.

In a move that no one would have imagined a few years before, Margot asked Kimmy to be her maid of honor. Kimmy was so overwhelmed that she practically knocked Margot over with an acceptance hug. As maid of honor, her job was to escort Sunny up the aisle.

Eugene, with Ajax on his lap, served as the officiant, and predictably kept the ceremony short. He wanted to get the celebration underway. "As the man responsible for bringing you two queens together—that's chess humor some of you might not understand

—I'm proud to pronounce you wife and wife! You may kiss the brides."

During the reception, the happy couple offered a special toast to Margot's grandparents, which they delivered in Korean. It wasn't perfect, but it was worth it to see how much it meant to Margot's entire family for her grandparents to be honored this way.

Looking around at her friends and family, Sam took in how much her life transformed over the past few years, once she stopped being held back by her past, waiting for life to happen to her. Sam had finally decided to stop dreaming that things would be perfect, and started appreciating life as it unfolded, even if it surprised her.

Sam thought back to so many of her conversations over the past few years, seeing Em's wisdom when she told Sam that life isn't about going through the motions of what other people expect of you. It's not about the perfectly planned experiences captured in photos to be shared online with family, friends, and strangers alike. It's not the bright, shiny moments that make up life, but instead it's the extraordinarily ordinary moments that can fulfill us.

Sam wished her grandparents were there to see her, standing proudly with her bride. She knew they'd be happy for her, and that they'd love Margot, too. Sam thought of all the times she'd seen Grandma Jeannie and Grandpa Tony show their affection towards each other in a million little ways. No, she didn't have photos or videos to capture those moments, but who does? People often have their cameras out for celebrations or vacations, but those big events aren't what fills a couple's life together.

It's the quiet moments that are no longer completely quiet when shared. It's sitting on the couch reading together. Watching TV. Walking the dogs. Putting away dishes. Folding laundry. Together. All of the mundane requirements of adult life made better by having someone to navigate them with. Crawling into bed at the end of a long day and finding that someone is there with you and for you, that no matter what life throws your way, you have someone to face it by your side.

Snapping out of her reverie, Sam beamed knowingly at Em, who responded with a lift of her flask. Taking Margot's hand, Sam and her wife ran out onto the dance floor, together. The upbeat rhythm started, followed by Sam Cooke's rapturous voice. As Sam dipped and swayed with Margot, she sang along to the song, "And love can come to everyone... The best things in life are free."

Discussion Questions for Reading Groups

1. What emotions did you feel during the book, and did any of them surprise you?
2. Which character did you most relate to?
3. Did you relate to any of the family dynamics Sam had to face? Which character most resembles your role in your own family?
4. Have you ever wrestled with accepting an aspect of yourself, or sharing part of yourself with others?
5. Which of Sam's changes resonated most with you? What about her false starts or missteps?
6. Have you ever had a memory hold you back or stick with you? How do you get past it?
7. Did your view of any particular characters change during the book?
8. Do you think Bev, Kimmy, or Brad would have achieved their character growth without Sam's involvement?
9. Did any aspect of Sam struggling during the pandemic reflect your own experience? If not, how was your experience different?
10. Have you ever had casual friendships become close friendships, like Sam did with Tali and Em? Could

you have been as understanding and supportive as Em?

11. Different generations are represented in the novel: Sam, Kimmy, and their friends are Millennials, Brad and Stacey are Gen-X, Bev, Ray, and Eugene are Baby Boomers, and Grandma Jeannie and Grandpa Tony are the Silent Generation. Did you identify with the characters in your generation? Did you recognize the dynamics in how the generations interacted?

Acknowledgments

Thank you to:

Dan Wueste for being my first reader, my biggest supporter, and my favorite person. I don't know how I'd do any of this without you, and frankly, I wouldn't want to.

Alissa Bourbonnais, for letting me share Sam with you back in her very first draft days, and for encouraging me to share her (and subsequently all my writing) with the world.

Liz Pipher, editor-extraordinaire. If this manuscript was Sam, you were Em, Tali, and Eugene all rolled into one, helping to Sam-i-fy the book into what it was meant to be.

My family, friends, and colleagues who have embraced my writing career, read my debut novel, showed up for author events, shared your feedback, championed me to your networks, and encouraged me during the revision and publication process for this second novel. I am so lucky to have you all in my life.

The teams at Scrawl Books in Reston VA, Reston Pride, and the Winchester Book Gallery in Winchester, VA for taking a chance on a debut author, hosting me at events, helping me bring my book to readers across Virginia, and encouraging me to keep writing!

My readers, returning and new. I hope my writing resonates with you and can bring you emotional satisfaction and provide an escape from reality for a while.

My fellow authors, who have been so kind and welcoming as I've launched my writing career, making me feel like I belong in the community.

About the Author

Beka Wueste is an author whose debut novel, "The Unsent Letters of Lucy Prior," earned praise as a "deeply introspective and emotionally resonant novel" (-*Kirkus Reviews*) and "an intricate and colorful tapestry of Lucy's life, using an unconventional narrative that invites readers to delve into her most profound feelings and emotions." (*Readers' Favorite Book Reviews*).

She is also an award-winning visual artist who exhibits her visual work frequently in regional and national shows.

Born in Texas and raised in Virginia, Beka earned a B.A. in art history from the University of Mary Washington in Fredericksburg, VA, and an M.A. in art history from George Mason University in Fairfax, VA.

An enthusiastic traveler, avid reader, nature lover, lifelong cinephile, and collector of music on vinyl, she lives with her husband and their rescue Shiba Inu in Northern Virginia.

Website: www.bekawueste.com
Email: inquiries@bekawueste.com
Instagram: @bekaw13
Profiles: Goodreads | Kirkus Pro Connect | LinkedIn

Coming Soon from Beka Wueste

My Side of the World and Other Tales of Death
A SHORT STORY COLLECTION

Death takes the lead in this collection of eight disparate tales, exploring how the loss of loved ones affects us, how surviving close calls with death shape us, how the fear of death motivates us, and how we can be either lifted up or let down by our communities in dealing with lingering grief. The genres vary between stories, including science fiction, magical realism, and suspense.

My Life with Death: A child becomes friends with Death and later serves as Death's assistant, constantly grappling with how much her relationship with Death limits her ability to enjoy her own life.

The Patron Saint of Pianos: A 1980's homicide detective, exhausted by working on too many cartel and gang-related deaths, moves from the southern border to a quiet, one-stoplight northern town for a fresh start.

My Husband's Fathers: A marriage strained by a husband habitually using the death of his mother to dismiss anyone else's pain or trauma endures a new challenge when the couple fosters two young brothers.

The Girl Who Sold the World: Humanity faces an existential threat when an alien collective arrives at Earth to judge the worthiness of all species on the planet.

My Sister Agnes: A 1990's suburb is shaken by an unexpected death, which brings neighbors together for one summer, and forever shapes one of the families.

The Shattered Glass Girl: A teenage girl in the 1920's dies due to her father's cruel discipline, leaving her spirit bonded to the house, enabling her to have a second chance at happiness when a new family moves in.

My Side of the World: A married woman in her midlife discovers evidence that a former paramour may be dead, leading her to obsess over confirming his demise in the present, while also reexamining her past and the influence he had in shaping her present life.

The Red Lights: When a young girl has a recurring nightmare of being murdered, her grandmother convinces her that it is a factual depiction of what will happen.

Also by Beka Wueste

The Unsent Letters of Lucy Prior
A NOVEL

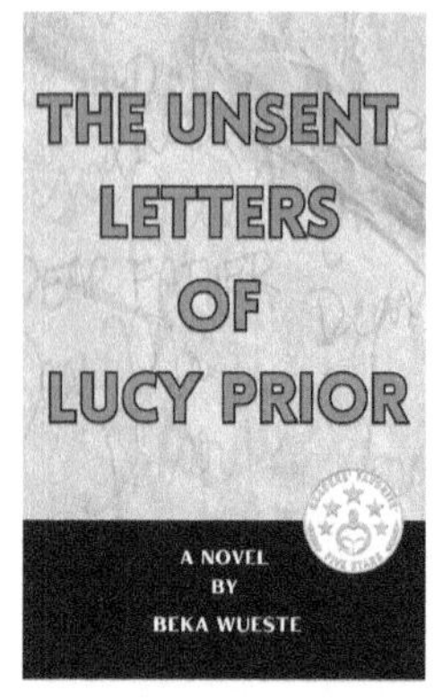

"5 Stars… Author Beka Wueste weaves an intricate and colorful tapestry of Lucy's life, using an unconventional narrative that invites readers to delve into her most profound feelings and emotions. Lucy's story feels incredibly vivid and authentic, as if it belongs to someone living in the real world." **- Readers' Favorite Book Reviews**

"Wueste's prose seamlessly balances sharp wit, aching nostalgia, and raw honesty…a deeply introspective and emotionally resonant novel." **- Kirkus Reviews**

Lucy Prior's family thought they knew her, until they discovered the stack of unsent letters...

When Lucy Prior died, she left many of the possessions you'd expect to find in an average home, with the exception of a peculiar set of letters. Written with the knowledge that her death was imminent, each chapter is a letter to an individual who played an influential role in Lucy's life, with whom she had severed connections decades before she passed away. In the letters, she revisits and confronts formative moments throughout her childhood and early adulthood, most of which she had largely repressed or intentionally hidden from even her closest relatives and friends.

Available now: eBook | Hardcover | Paperback

362

Preview Chapter from "The Unsent Letters of Lucy Prior"

To Whom it May Concern

To: The Person Responsible for Closing out my Earthly
Affairs
My House
Truckee, CA

To Whom it May Concern,

Keep, burn, send, or publish, I don't care. I'm dead! More accurately, at the time of writing this letter, I'm expecting to be dead soon. No, I'm not taking matters into my own hand. I've just seen enough death to get a sense of when it's coming, and I feel my time is running out. Yet in this state, I am full of hope. Well, several specific hopes:

I hope you, whomever you are, are well, and that sorting through my earthly possessions is not too great a task. I was married for 47 years to Timothy, my favorite person in my whole misbegotten existence. In the two years since he passed, our combined personal treasures, full of emotion and memory, have been my closest companions, so I couldn't discard them all. Think of it all as my emotional support clutter.

I like to look through our old photographs, the cards he made me, playbills and ticket stubs, all the little scraps that together still don't begin to scratch the surface of our whole wonderful, wild, unexpected story. Growing up with neither affection nor stability, my relationships before Tim always ended abruptly. Before him, I accepted that I was destined to be alone. I never dared to dream I'd find love, and yet with Tim I found love that deepened and multiplied with every adventure we enjoyed or challenge we faced. When I look at these mementos, I feel him with me again, the excitement of building a life, of growing together.

He never begrudged my nostalgia, but if the roles were reversed he'd be more successful at decluttering. I try to keep a tidy house, but Tim was always better at it than me. He never left a glass in the sink, always loaded it straight into the dishwasher. My tidy Timothy. An excellent housekeeper, except for dusting. I was better at dusting. He always forgot the tops of the ceiling fan blades. He was much better at vacuuming, though. More thorough with the furniture. He was also better than me at keeping our schedule straight. If someone asked if we were busy, I never knew, but he had it all documented. Isn't it strange, the mundane things we admire about the people we love?

I hope I died peacefully, non-violently, and non-grotesquely. I don't know how I died, so I hope it wasn't in the middle of cooking a bolognese, and you haven't had to scrape dried tomato paste or ground meat off all the surfaces of my kitchen. I hope I wasn't left for weeks, and that you all didn't have to fight off local wildlife scavenging my bones. I wouldn't begrudge any creatures if they did…everyone's got to eat, and if the coyotes don't get me, the worms will, anyway.

I hope I see Tim, my Timothy, again. He's the only person in this who truly knew me, the whole, complex ugly beautiful version of me. After he died, I just didn't see the point in most things anymore. I don't know what happens next, after this life, I only care that if there IS something beyond, I get to share it with him. Otherwise, I'm not interested. Just erase my soul, toss the scraps in a black hole in a far off galaxy.

Timothy. In all our time together as a married couple, we were never apart longer than six consecutive days, courtesy of some work trips. It got to the point that neither of us could really remember the time before we were together. I think that's how it is with most couples who had a long run like ours.

Left on my own after he died, I started thinking about the past, and the people in it. Some of these made me smile, some made my cry, and some made me rage. Without Tim to center me, I became obsessed, and with nothing better to do, I started writing. I don't know if all of the intended recipients are dead or alive. I don't know if they want to hear from me. I don't know if they remember me, but I remember them, and I want to let them know.

Maybe I'm a coward for waiting to send all of these until after I die. Maybe I should have sent these years ago, maybe I still shouldn't be sending these at all, not to people so ancient in my history. You will note a lack of letters to Timothy, as well as pretty much anyone else in my adult life from the time since we were married.

That's because I didn't need to write to those people. By that time, I was in a healthier place of telling people what I thought, of being honest and communicative. There was nothing left unsaid. No, it's only the people in my distant past that haunt me over what I should have told them. There are a few others I wish I could have written to, but I know for a fact are dead, so there's no point pretending that words scrawled on a page can reach them, no matter how sincere.

To be transparent, I have always been a poor correspondent, and consistently exasperated English teachers with my bad grammar, so please forgive the quality of the content and composition. I'm not going for a National Book Award or Pulitzer or anything. (Is there an award for best set of unsent, confessional letters? I suppose I could look that up.) In any case, these aren't polished works, they are simply things I need to get off my now-dead chest.

You have a decision to make. There are several options for how to handle each letter after reading…and to be clear, you have my full permission to read them. Not that I could stop you, what with me being a corpse and all.

- **Option A:** You can send the letter to the recipient.
- **Option B:** You can opt not to send it.
- **Option C:** You can post them, one or a few or all, online for any old person to read. Maybe it will entertain them or help them. Don't worry about editing them to make me look better, at this point I've accepted who I have been and who I am, and feel no shame about mistakes made.
- **Option D:** I suppose you could just throw the whole pile away. Even if you destroy each letter, it still won't

have been a waste of my time, as it gave me a hobby
in my dotage.

Here are the letters. You will see each has a corresponding
envelope with the best, current address I know. Additionally,
here is money for postage, should you send them. If not,
keep it for your own personal use, on the condition you buy
something fun to treat yourself. I recommend ice cream.

Well, I suppose that's all for me. Read on. Or don't.
Again, I won't know, so it doesn't matter much to me.

Yours in death,
Lucy
Lucille Françoise Martell Prior